Scanning the residue of slaughter, Volo thought he recognized one of the corpses. He was about to stoop to get a closer look when he barely saw a moving blur out of the corner of his eye, and reacted in a second, raising his dagger to a defensive posture.

He was half a second too slow.

The master traveler felt the coolness of a steel blade against his windpipe, and heard an authoritative voice say, "Drop it, or breathe blood."

Realizing he had no alternative if he wished to live long enough to get to the bottom of the bloodbath, and to eventually complete his guide to the Moonsea, Volo dropped his dagger, and prepared to do whatever the other visitor to the Retreat requested.

THE NOBLES

King Pinch
David Cook

War in Tethyr
Victor Milán

Escape from Undermountain
Mark Anthony

The Mage in the Iron Mask
Brian M. Thomsen

The Council of Blades
Paul Kidd
December 1996

FORGOTTEN REALMS®

The Mage in the Iron Mask

The Nobles
Volume 4

Brian M. Thomsen

THE MAGE IN THE IRON MASK

First Printing: August 1996
Printed in the United States of America.
Library of Congress Catalog Card Number: 95-62245

9 8 7 6 5 4 3 2 1

ISBN: 0-7869-0506-9
8563XXX1501

TSR, Inc.
201 Sheridan Springs Road
Lake Geneva, WI 53147
U.S.A.

TSR Ltd.
120 Church End, Cherry Hinton
Cambridge CB1 3LB
United Kingdom

Acknowledgments

This book could not have been written without the gracious help and input from the following: Patrick McGilligan, Jeff Grubb, Ed Greenwood, James Ward, Michele Carter, Donna Thomsen, Jon Pickens, Julia Martin, Anthony Hope and Alexander Dumas.

This book could not have been written without the musical inspiration provided by the artists who contributed to the following CDs: *If I Were a Carpenter, Stepping Out—The Very Best of Joe Jackson, Sergio Mendes & Brasil 66 Greatest Hits, Music from the Original Motion Picture Soundtrack Streets of Fire,* and *Music from the Original Motion Picture Soundtrack Clueless.*

Table of Contents

Prologue   1

PART ONE
The Prisoner, the Thespian, & the Traveler

One	*A Friend in Need*	21
Two	*Newlywed Games*	37
Three	*A Weakened Retreat*	50
Four	*Miss Alliances*	69
Five	*Under Currents*	86

PART TWO
The Swordsman, the High Blade, his Wife, & his Brother

Six	*In Morning*	97
Seven	*Past Tenses*	115
Eight	*Mates, Masks, Musk, & Meals*	139
Nine	*Dinner & Denouement*	156
Ten	*Reports, Instructions, & Revelations*	172
Eleven	*Tankards of Memories*	189
Twelve	*An Evening's Just Rewards*	204

PART THREE
The Plan, the Plot, & the Ploy

Thirteen	*Morning Maneuvers*	213
Fourteen	*Treason, and Making the Most of It*	231
Fifteen	*Guards, Guards, & Custodians*	241
Sixteen	*Fungus, Fugitives, & Fencing*	246
Seventeen	*Just Desserts*	253
Eighteen	*Covering Tracks*	266
Nineteen	*Changing Blades*	281

Epilogue   295

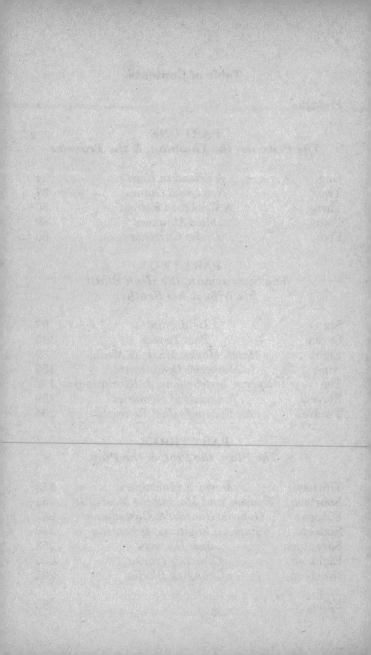

Prologue

Donal Loomis was a dwarfish gnome of a man, which is not to say that he claimed any blood lineage to either the dwarves or the gnomes but rather that his overall appearance, unfortunately, seemed to emulate the least favorable attributes of both races. With his bulbous features, stunted stature, and obese waistline, he was easily considered an unsightly wart on the face of humankind.

The jagged facial scars that decorated his hairless

head, unsightly reminders of the painful removal of tell-tale tattoos, did not help the ugliness of his physical appearance. Had he not retired to "the Retreat" he would have been a focal point for ridicule and persecution almost anywhere he went.

The Retreat, as the members called it, was originally a place of study, refuge, and retirement for those who wished to devote their lives to the study of magecraft and other magical arts. Scholarship alone, however, ceased to be enough of a reason for being or means of survival in the dour political climes of the Moonsea region, and the elder wizards who founded the Retreat many years ago decided that it had become necessary to widen their membership to certain other members of society who might help to subsidize their institution through financial endowments, political protection (whether by favors, military aid, or just good old-fashioned blackmail), or diplomatic influence. As a result, the institute of learning and refuge also became a place of sanctuary for political outcasts whose assets or knowledge could benefit their foundation, spies from the south or the west en route to the east or vice versa (Harpers were usually particularly welcome temporary guests whose incurred debts were always paid in a timely and generous manner); or just a convenient and permanent hiding place for offspring born on the wrong side of the blanket by royals or soon to be royals whose legitimate heirs had reason to worry about potential rivals.

As long as the accounts were met, no questions were asked, nor information given out. As a result, numerous members of the peculiar institution who had come to accept their lives of study had no knowledge of their parentage or lineage, and possessed memories solely of their lives within the monastic walls, nor did they desire such information nor opportunities for adventure. Loyola Ignato, one of the Retreat's founders and, according to legend, a mage of some note, had prided himself on his abilities to indoctrinate the young and inexperienced into the ways of life in the monastery. He was known to boast that if you gave him a youth between the ages of two and twenty, the Retreat would have him for life, and many nobles were more than willing to accommodate him. Without exception the Retreat had never lost an initiate to temporal temptations that lie beyond the monastic walls.

Donal, however, was not one of these members for he had actually chosen the sanctuary of the Retreat (seeing few alternatives) for himself, and, furthermore, was more than partially acquainted with his own lineage and parentage, no matter how hard he tried to forget.

The self-labeled wart of humankind rubbed the scars that adorned his bald and wrinkled pate. I wore my tattoos with pride, he thought to himself, if I regret anything it is their removal. With them, I had respect, power, and prestige despite my godsforsaken appearance.

Donal sighed.

And with them, I was soon a marked man, he continued in his reflection. Such is the case when one finds oneself on the wrong side of a revolution, and Szass Tam was one lich who definitely didn't forgive and forget.

Donal had had his telltale tattoos painfully burnt off his facial skin, and had applied for sanctuary at the Retreat, supplementing the mercy and pity that the elders felt toward him with promises of devotion and the sharing of numerous secrets of conjuration. To them, he was just another poor wizard who had fallen victim to hard times and misfortune, and so he was accepted and put to work to earn his keep.

Originally the former Red Wizard had had illusions of safety in his anonymity, and dreamt of secreting a small fortune by which he could leave the Retreat and live out his days in a secret location at a higher degree of comfort, but these hopes were soon dashed when Nathor, a fellow conspirator from that ill-fated revolution had also turned up at the steps of the Retreat.

Donal still remembered the Thayan refugee's rant to the elders trying to make them understand his dire straits.

"Have you gazed upon the Runes of Chaos, beheld the thing which sits upon Thakorsil's Seat, held the Death Moon Orb in your trembling hands, wielded Nyskar's Nightblades, entered the Devouring Portal and walked the Paths of the Doomed, or sat at the left hand of Szass Tam during the Ritual of Twin Burning?"

The others had felt pity toward him, and suggested that he be taken in until he could be handed over to the authorities as a madman in need of incarceration. Donal knew differently.

"I have done all these things," Nathor had confessed, *"and each day I pray for forgiveness, and each night at sunset I pray for deliverance from the evils that stalk me. I pray, but I fear that no gods will listen."*

Donal still remembered the chill that went through him when their eyes met. From that point on, the refugee remained silent, almost as if he had gone into a fear-induced catatonic state.

The emissaries from the asylum were due to arrive in four days.

Nathor disappeared after three days, and was never heard from again.

Since that day, Donal had been perplexed. An optimistic individual with a touch of cruelty might have chuckled over the situation. Perhaps Nathor had recognized him and leaped to the conclusion that he was a spy from Thay who had been sent after him. Little did the poor fool realize that he too was a wizard in hiding with probably an even higher price on his head.

Though Donal was cruel enough to laugh at the unfortunate and mistaken Nathor (an opportunity which the much-maligned and trod-upon self-proclaimed wart on the face of Faerûn would have been more than eager to seize upon), he was far from optimistic.

Donal was a realist and realized that his days of anonymity at the Retreat were numbered, and he quickly seized upon an opportunity to remove the danger that he knew would quickly be coming from the East, and perhaps make plans for a more comfortable future.

An opportunity soon presented itself when Donal had to take his turn as an elder of the Retreat and make the half-day journey into Mulmaster to deliver the monthly tithe. (Only elders were allowed to venture from the Retreat, as the more youthful interns were prone to distractions that might persuade them to forsake the life of scholarly pursuits, and at his eighty-plus years, Donal more than qualified as an elder).

As per usual, Donal tried to make his journey as swift and as inconspicuous as possible. His progress, however, was held up by one of the numerous connubial festivals that was celebrated by the thrice-yearly reunion of the High Blade and his bride from the Far East, and Donal's most direct path out of town was blocked by a parade in their honor.

Donal at the time did not expect to feel honored or blessed by actually seeing the city's nobility, but rather just waited impatiently to resume his journey. A chance view of the High Blade himself, however, quickly changed his mind, and from that point on devious wheels of planning and deceitfulness began to turn with a plan that would grant him safety and security for the rest of his days.

* * * * *

Donal cursed the chill of the night air, as he checked the hiding place for the pack that held all of his worldly possessions. Everything was in order, and he hoped that the escort would arrive promptly. It had not been easy to manipulate the schedule so that the young mage-in-training, Rassendyll, would follow him on watch duty, nor had he been able to make all of the necessary other preparations without alerting any of the Retreat's brethren to his machinations and preoccupations.

The drug was already in the jug of ale that the watch was allowed to partake of to ward off some of the night's chill, and Donal had made sure that Rassendyll's meal had been well salted earlier that evening. Once he had been relieved of duty, Donal would join his pack in hiding, and wait for his successor on guard duty to nod off by the sleep draught, at which point he would be free to open the gate, and meet his expected escort.

Donal had just returned to his place at the gate, when an eager young wizard crept up behind him.

"*Boo,*" the young mage said, startling the older wizard. "Hope I'm not late."

Donal closed his eyes, and bit his tongue to hold back a curse or incantation of rebuke for the young wizard. After less than a moment's hesitation, he turned around, and warmly confronted the young wizard who would prove to be the means of his deliverance unto safety and prosperity.

"My dear Rassendyll," Donal fawned, "you gave me such a fright."

"Sorry, magister," the younger wizard replied, obviously repentant for his previous action, "but I have also shown up early for my watch."

"How thoughtful of you," Donal replied, hoping that he had succeeded in removing all traces of sarcasm from his words despite the intent that existed in abundance within.

"It's all right," Rassendyll replied, "I couldn't sleep anyway. My mouth has been exceptionally dry since evening meal, and no matter how many trips I've made to the well, my throat still remains parched."

A little bit of salt and some Thayan spices usually have that effect on you, Donal replied in his thoughts, and then said out loud. "Why don't you try a sip of ale? I seem to recall a land of miners where all forms of spirited beverages were outlawed except for ale, and do you know why?"

"No, magister," the younger wizard replied, fearing that he had just re-entered some imaginary classroom in the mind of the older wizard whose kindest of nicknames was "doddering Donal."

"Because it was the only thing that would slake their thirst after a dusty day in the mines, that's why," Donal replied, then added, "so drink up."

"Care to join me?" the younger wizard offered, jug already in hand.

"I think not," Donal replied, then adding to avoid all suspicions, "I am heading to bed, and, at my age, beverages have a way of making themselves the most temporary and inconsiderate of houseguests."

"Come again magister?"

"They like to come and go as they please, and quite often at that," Donal replied with a chuckle. "Enjoy your rest."

"And you yours," Donal replied heading back to his cell. "And you yours."

* * * * *

When Donal had passed the corner of the inner hall and was thus obscured from the watchful eyes of the younger wizard, he quickly took to the shadows and secreted himself in his hiding spot, out of sight, but well within earshot. In no time at all, he heard the sound of his future salvation: Rassendyll's snoring, and the whistle of a lark.

The lark is one of Faerûn's most common birds of the morn, and since it was still well into the middle of the night, Donal quickly recognized the signal from the Thayan agents on the other side of the gate. He pursed his lips together, returned the signal, and let them in.

"He is over here," Donal instructed, not wasting time with introductions. "Quickly bind his hands behind his back with silken cords."

The shadowriders quickly complied; their telltale beards, and dirty and greasy manes quickly revealed their identities to the older wizard.

Mercenaries, he thought. Dirty hands for dirty work.

"You should also gag him," Donal instructed with great authority, now that he knew that they were merely hired help, "and perhaps put a sack over his head as well."

They once again quickly complied, and hoisted the dead weight that was Rassendyll up onto the back of a horse, and bound him to the saddle.

"Where is my mount?" Donal insisted, pausing only to pick up his pack. "We mustn't keep the Tharchioness waiting."

The tallest of the mercenaries, who had remained

mounted and in the shadows all during the abduction of the young wizard, stepped down from his steed as if to offer it to the self-described wart on the face of Faerûn.

"You are right," he replied drawing closer to Donal, "we mustn't keep the Tharchioness waiting."

As he drew closer, Donal began to make out the emblematic tattoos that adorned the tall one's cheeks, and the wig that had fallen off his pate and was now resting in the cowl that drooped behind his robe.

Donal dropped his pack, and opened his mouth as if to cry out.

"She sends her regards," the tall one said, quickly removing a crystal wand from the folds of his robe, and thrusting it into the portly wizard's abdomen, then ripping it upward until it had succeeded in splitting the lower half of the old wizard's heart, and then adding, "but she regrets that you will not be joining us. She has this thing about traitors to the cause of Szass Tam, and specifically not giving them a second chance to betray us."

The tall one regained his mount in as little time as it took for Donal to fall to the ground.

As the shadowriders disappeared into the darkness, their hoofbeats diminishing in the distance, Donal quietly died with a faint trace of a smile on his cruelly misshapen lips, his final thought acquiescing to the insight of the Tharchioness, followed by a chuckle at a secret joke, and a last groan of pain that delivered him unto his expected damnation.

* * * * *

Rassendyll came to in less than an hour, his body aching from the jostling caused by the steed he was bound to, and the awkward positioning of his bound

body upon it. He tried to cry out, but couldn't because of the horse's bit that had been fastened to his
face as if he were some uncooperative plow horse in
need of direction. Had his head not been covered
with a sack, he would have realized that it was still
the middle of the night. As it was, the only sense left
to him for observation was his hearing, and as the
shadowriders rode in silence, it too didn't seem to be
of much help . . . until, quite unexpectedly, his steed
stopped in unison with the rest of the party, and a
commotion seemed to break out.

"Who goes there? Show yourselves," the young
wizard thought he heard through the muffling effect
of the sack. This was followed by a screech of horses,
several clashes of steel, and more than a few cries of
pain, as a party of superior force soon overtook his
abductors, and mercilessly slaughtered them.

Rassendyll could barely maintain his joy. He still
had no idea why he had been abducted, nor how, nor
where he was right now. The only thing he knew was
that he was being rescued.

"Where is Donal?" he heard.

"Back at the Retreat. I killed the traitor."

"Thank you for saving me the trouble."

This was followed by one last shriek of pain, and
one last whispered order.

"Take half of the company back to the Retreat,
and kill everyone. No one must escape, and be sure
to leave this behind."

Had the young wizard not been blinded by the sack
that encompassed his head, he would have undoubtedly noticed the speaker (obviously the group's leader)
handing his lieutenant a blood-stained crystal wand
which Rassendyll, had he been conscious at the time,
would have recognized as the weapon that had been
used to kill the traitor Donal. As it was he saw noth-

ing, and, petrified with fear after hearing the plans
for slaughter, tried to maintain his wits in hopes that
an opportunity for escape might present itself.

A thundering herd of hooves galloped off into the
distance and before he knew it, Rassendyll was once
again tossed around as the party he was now an un-
willing member of raced onward into the night.

* * * * *

Rassendyll lost all track of time as the riders
raced the dawn to their destination. As the stallions
slowed down to a trot, the young wizard thought he
could distinguish from the cacophony of sounds that
included the clopping of the horses' hooves and the
verbal spurs of the riders, a change in the ground
upon which they rode, the sound of a gate being
raised, and a cock crowing in the distance. As the
gate closed behind them, he felt the horse that bore
him stop, and felt an eeriness at the peaceful silence
that pervaded the early morn.

The stillness of the air gave way to the distinct
odors of industry, smoke, sulfur, and fish.

They must have brought me to some city, the young
wizard discerned, but where? Mulmaster? Hillsfar? If
only I knew how long I had been unconscious.

A few footsteps and the sound of a blade being
withdrawn from a scabbard struck terror into his
heart.

Why did they take me all this way just to kill me?
he thought, trying to make sense of his situation.
Surely if they had intended on killing me they would
have done so before now.

Concentrating deeply, as the magisters had shown
him, he sought out with his mind the source of the
sounds. In his mind's eye he saw a one-eyed soldier

with long black hair standing right next to him, sword raised as if to strike. Fear took control of the young wizard, and as his mind's eye blinked, he felt himself try to scream, forgetting the restraining bit that was still safely lodged in his mouth.

He felt the breeze of a slash pass by his head, a moment of instability as if he had lost his balance, and then the rude concussion of meeting the cobble-stoned ground.

"Pick him up," he heard. "It wouldn't make much sense to have carried him all this way just to let him be trampled in the courtyard by the horse that bore him."

This was accompanied by a malevolent chorus of laughter, as rough hands wrangled him to his feet.

"I think he's awake," one voice said.

"Not for long," another replied.

Rassendyll tried to brace himself for the antici-pated blow, felt a sharp pain to the back of his head the likes of which he never felt before, and was con-sumed by the darkness that had already blinded his other senses.

* * * * *

A bucket of water to the face did the double duty of reviving him and drawing his attention to the fact that the sack had been removed from over his head. His entire body ached, his arms long wrenched from their sockets by the constraints of the silken bonds. He tried to move and stretch his cramped muscles, but found his freedom impaired by what seemed to be a massive wooden yoke and frame that anchored his limbs in a semi-sitting position that provided him with no room to relieve or relax his protesting limbs and also restrained his head from moving. He thought he could discern a wooden collar that was

acting as his neck yoke. The underside was torment-
ing his shoulders and collarbone with splinters,
while the topside seemed cool and smooth as if it
were lined with a metal plate. The bit had been removed from his mouth, but the tightness of the yoke
further inhibited his attempts at crying out.

Gradually his eyes became accustomed to the
light thrown by the torches that illuminated the
chamber. His captors were behind him, and cast long
and threatening shadows on the wall before him.

"Our esteemed guest is awake. Isn't the resemblance uncanny?" one of the shadows observed.

"Donal didn't lie. I guess even greedy liars and
knaves occasionally tell the truth," the other replied,
"but I guess we shouldn't ask our friends from Thay
for their opinions on this subject."

"Are you awake?" the first inquired. "I should
think that you would want to thank Sir Melker Rickman for rescuing you from those wretched mercenaries from Thay."

The source of the voice came around to Rassendyll's
left, just out of sight. "I'm sorry that you have been
treated so roughly, but one can't be too careful. You
see, there are certain laws here in Mulmaster govern-
ing the comings and goings of you mage types, so certain precautions have to be taken. I'm sure that by
now your wrists must be raw from the restraints that
have kept you from using your hands since last night,
and I must apologize. I have, however, taken steps to
alleviate the problem. Send in the smith."

The young wizard saw the back of the other pass
in front of him as he left to fetch the smith. He returned almost immediately, and this time Rassendyll
was able to discern that this one-eyed soldier with
long black hair had been the same person who had
led the party that had stolen him from his original

abductors. He was accompanied by a burly wizard who bore two large metal plates with him, as well as a hammer and a pouch that jangled as he moved. The soldier seemed to lead the burly wizard, and the reason became obvious when he stopped in front of the yoke and frame that restrained Rassendyll.

The burly wizard was as blind as a bat, his eye sockets still bearing the singe marks from where some flaming coals had been put to rest for some, what must have been interminable, period of suffering for Ao knows what reason.

"You know why you are here," the voice from behind commanded. "Begin!"

The burly wizard replied with a garbled noise of assent, for his tongue had been burnt out as well during the same period of excruciating torture, and began to place the two metal plates into slots in the yoke around the young wizard's neck, one directly behind his head, and one in front.

Once they were perfectly balanced in place, the burly wizard began to run his hands over the metal surfaces, mouthing incantations as he worked. Slowly the metal began to heat up, and soften. With hands that had forged numerous talismans and weapons of enchantment, the wizard smith began to mold the two plates to fit the contours of the young man's head.

At first, Rassendyll felt a slight sensation of warmth against his cheeks, which quickly became a torturous burn followed by a stifling oppression as the metal closed over his mouth and nose, preventing him from breathing. Before he could cry out or choke, his nostrils and mouth were assailed by the muscular fingers of the burly wizard smith as he poked holes through the metal, molding and smoothing the edges so that they just barely intruded into his breathing apertures. He followed in the same suit with the eye slits whose placement was slightly skewed by the young wizard who kept his own orbs of vision shut tight in an effort to prevent himself from suffering the same fate that had befallen the smith.

When the two halves of metal were in place around the young wizard's head, the wizard smith said aloud a new incantation, flexing his fingers in the air with various and sundry subtle motions.

Once again Rassendyll felt the metal pressing up against his cheeks and the back of his head. Then he felt his skin begin to itch around his neck and scalp as if a thousand chiggers had begun to take their bloodsucking positions along the surface of the skin. He next heard the scrape of four bolts being placed in slots that connected the front piece to the back, which was immediately followed by a cacophony of clangs as if he had been strapped to the belfry back at the Retreat during the noonday chimes.

Even after the blows of the hammer had stopped, the ringing in his head continued, only gradually dissipating over time.

"Are you sure the mask has adhered to his skull?" the soldier demanded.

The wizard smith grunted in assent, running his hand across the back of the tortured Rassendyll's head, and around his neck as if to say "here, and here."

"Good!" said the voice from behind. "Call the guards."

The soldier left once again, and returned with three of Mulmaster's most trusted and ruthless soldiers of the company known as the Hawks.

"Unbind him!" the voice ordered.

Rassendyll went limp as the Hawks began to extricate him from the yoke and frame. The itching and gnawing of the skin that had been adhered to the metal was slowly retarding to a mild annoyance that paled in comparison to the soreness that his limbs felt from being bound. As this was alleviated by the Hawks, a new annoyance came to torture him.

The voice, he thought, it sounds so familiar. Is it possible I have been tortured by someone I know?

Once removed from the frame, the young wizard straightened and flexed his appendages to return circulation to the outermost limits. Control soon returned to his hands and fingers, as he quickly formulated a plan for fighting back in the manner he had been taught by his magisters at the Retreat.

The wizard smith is blind, so if I act quickly enough, I might be able to cast a spell that will overpower my captors before they have time to react.

Almost instantaneously, Rassendyll brought his now unbound hands into action, flexing them in readiness for one of the numerous attack spells he had been taught. Clearing his now unbound throat he readied himself for the incantation that he sought from the files of his mind.

Fear seized him. He could not remember any of the spells or incantations! It was as if his entire education had been erased.

"As I mentioned before," the voice instructed with a certain degree of cruel calmness, "we have certain ways of handling mage types like yourself, here in Mulmaster. This lovely mask that conceals your oh-so-attractive features also deadens *all* of your magical abilities. You have to admit that it is slightly more comfortable than being bound and gagged all the time. Guards!"

The Hawks immediately grabbed him, one on each side. The voice came up behind him again, delicately gauntleted hands feeling the edges of the two halves of the metal mask.

"Fine craftsmanship," the voice observed. "Form-fitting, yet feature obscuring. Too bad you didn't allow much room for his beard to grow. Eventually it will probably choke him, but by that time I am sure I will have no further use for him. Guards, take him away."

Rassendyll wrenched himself away from the guards to confront his oppressor. The eye-slits in the mask necessitated that he only view objects directly in front of him. Maneuvering himself into position, he faced his antagonist dead on, and fainted dead away, for he realized that he was confronting a man whose features were identical to his own.

"Throw him into our deepest dungeon," the High Blade ordered. "The wing in which we house the other madmen, vagrants, and detritus of society."

The Hawks complied.

* * * * *

Rassendyll was tossed into a damp cell whose light was cast from a torch down the hall, its illumination barely creeping in through the guards' peep hole and the slot through which the slop that was considered food would be passed.

The weight of the mask bore heavily on his neck and shoulders, throwing him off-balance and dampening all of his perceptions. His body hurt, and he was racked with questions about his fate.

Clearing his throat, he cried out in torment and confusion, "Why? Why? *Why?*"

A lone voice answered him from one of the cells down the hall. It said gruffly, with a basso bellow reminiscent of a thespian or an opera star, "Will you keep it down? An actor needs his sleep."

PART ONE

**The Prisoner,
the Thespian,
&
the Traveler**

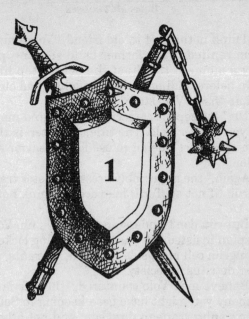

1

A Friend in Need

On a Mulmaster city street:

"Oh thank you, Mister Volo," the pudgy thespian Passepout exclaimed, his bulgy flesh bouncing beneath his tunic as he tried to put as much distance as possible between himself and his previous night's lodging, the prison known as Southroad Keep. "I don't know what I would have done if you hadn't come along to bail me out."

"Think nothing of it, old friend," Volothamp Geddarm replied to his former bond servant, pausing only a moment to adjust the beret atop his curly scalp before adding, "and I thought I had cured you of that *Mister* Volo stuff."

"No," Passepout corrected. "You cured me of calling you *Master* Volo. The title of 'mister' is the least form of respect I deign to use for my savior and salvation."

"Again," the impeccably dressed master traveler of Faerûn (if not all Toril) instructed, "think nothing of it."

"But you don't understand, Mist . . . uh, Volo," the thespian insisted. "It was horrible being locked up in a dungeon cell alongside madmen, vagrants, and the other detritus of society."

"Believe me," Volo countered, "there is far worse company you might have been keeping in Southroad Keep's subterranean dungeon, and not all of them are prisoners either."

"It was horrible, dehumanizing, and torturous."

"How long had you been incarcerated?" the master traveler inquired.

"Overnight," the pudgy thespian answered in righteous indignation, "and I didn't get a wink of sleep. An actor needs his sleep, you know."

"So I've heard."

"Of course," Passepout continued to rant. "The cell was hard and damp, the food was low-grade slop."

"How terrible for you," Volo concurred half-heartedly, occasionally fingering his well-groomed beard with the hand that he had free from tending the traveler's pack that bounced as he strode.

"It was," the actor agreed, missing the sarcasm that was conveyed by the master traveler's mischievous grin. "And if that wasn't bad enough, there was this madman bemoaning his incarceration all night, and he was accompanied by a horrible clanging as if someone were beating his cell walls with a coal bucket."

"The nerve of that poor soul."

"Indeed," the thespian continued. "I am quite sure that this incident has scarred me for life."

Volo looked around at the dark and smoke-filled streets of what had been nicknamed the City of Danger, put his arm around his boon companion, and tried to put the fellow's one-night incarceration into proper perspective.

"Surely, the legendary son of Catinflas and Idle, scourge of the Sword Coast, expert ballplayer and star goalie of Maztica, and circumnavigator of all Toril; not to mention master thespian, and sponsored actor and artist of the House of Bernd of Cormyr, will be able to put this behind him," the master traveler encouraged, trying not to be too sarcastic in his tone.

"Of course you are right," Passepout conceded. "It would take more than one torturous night's incarceration to scar me for life."

"Indeed," Volo agreed, then changed the subject, asking, "by the way, how are things with your position in the Bernd family household?"

Passepout looked sheepishly at his traveling companion, mentor of the road, and savior many times over, and confessed. "I am afraid that I am no longer in the Bernd family's employ."

"What happened?"

"I didn't do anything wrong, really."

"Well surely Master Bernd is a fair man, and his son Curtis is quite fond of you. I'm sure either of them would have stood by you."

"Curtis was away on his honeymoon with Shurleen," the thespian explained, slightly wistful about the wedding of the woman whom he had at one time thought to be the love of his life, "and my problem wasn't with Master Bernd, but rather with the authorities in Cormyr itself."

"What did you do now?"

"Well remember Sparky and Minx, the Bernd family cats?"

"Of course," Volo replied, "two nobler felines I've never met."

"Indeed," the thespian explained, "but there was a certain maid that I had taken a fancy to. Her name was Marissa, and she was quite pretty."

"Of course."

"Well," the portly thespian continued, "Marissa complained about the additional work that she had to do cleaning up after them, and mentioned her concern that the two felines might have kittens, and thus increase her workload, resulting in less time for me."

"So?"

"So I did what we always used to do back in Baldur's Gate."

"Which was?"

"I had them spayed."

Volo fingered his beard, and commented, "It is a very serious crime—in all of Cormyr—to interfere with the reproductive capabilities of a feline."

"As I soon learned," the hapless thespian replied. "The maid threatened to tell the authorities of my deed unless I vacated the premises forthwith, and so I did. It turned out that a certain young stable hand that she fancied, thought himself an actor, and it was all just an elaborate scheme to put me in the doghouse, and him in the main house. If you know what I mean."

Volo shook his head in gentle amusement, and urged his companion on. "So what then?"

"The maid was quite insistent about going to the authorities, so I figured it would probably be prudent of me not to wait for Master Bernd's return. So I left a note of apology and took to the road, to experience life in the theater known as Faerûn, once again."

"This way," Volo interrupted, indicating that it was time for them to turn the corner. "I've just checked in to the Traveler's Cloak Inn." The great traveler paused for a moment, scratched his chin, and added inquisitively, "But somehow you knew that, or else how would you have known to leave a message for me about your predicament. How *did* you know that I would be staying there?"

The thespian beamed proudly, and answered, "One thing I certainly learned from our trip was that the legendary Volothamp Geddarm always travels in style, and only favors the most noble of establishments with his presence."

The greatest traveler of Faerûn shook his head in gentle amusement, and conceded, "But of course. And the Traveler's Cloak Inn is indeed the best place in Mulmaster. At fifteen gold pieces a night, it better be. But this still doesn't explain how you knew that I would be in Mulmaster."

"Well," the portly actor explained, his voice dropping markedly as a pair of soldiers passed them going in the opposite direction along the avenue, "while I was enjoying the free and easy life on the road, I came across a leaflet that mentioned that a local bookseller was having a reception for a cookbook author who was on tour, and that the reception was being sponsored by the firm of Tyme Waterdeep, Limited, who I remembered as your publisher. Since it was a cookbook author, I naturally figured that there would be plenty of food there, so I decided to crash."

"Crash?"

"Attend without an invitation."

"Oh," Volo replied, "and they just let you in?"

"Well, not until I mentioned your name, of course."

"Of course."

"The food wasn't very good anyway, low-fat fungus flambé, and such, but I ran into a guy named Pig who claimed he knew you."

"Imagine that," Volo mused.

"Now call me suspicious, but I am not inclined to take a person at their word, particularly when they make claims of greatness."

"Like knowing Volothamp Geddarm?"

"Of course," Passepout asserted. "No telling what a rogue might claim these days."

"No one would know better than you."

"Of course," the actor conceded. "Anyway, he claimed that you and he had made a journey through the Underdark together, and that that trip had been the inspiration for the book. When I asked him where you were, he said that you were probably working on your guide to the Moonsea, and so, *voilà*, we make contact."

Volo chuckled to himself. Imagine, he thought, my two most reluctant traveling companions running into each other. I can't wait to hear Percival Woodehaus's version of the story. He then said aloud to his friend, "Well its just lucky for you that Mulmaster was my next stop. Originally it wasn't, and I wouldn't have gotten here for a month or more."

"I shudder to think of it," the portly thespian replied. "More than a night in that hellhole would surely have been the death of me."

"What did they arrest you for anyway?"

"Acting, without an official permit."

Volo nodded in agreement, and said, "And of course in order to get the official permit, you would have had to pay the theater tax, which, of course, you couldn't afford."

"Exactly."

"Sometimes I think that Mulmaster should be called the City of Taxes instead of the City of Danger," the great traveler declared, a bit too loudly for his paranoid companion who was overly conscious of the excessive number of city guards that seemed to be out on the streets. Volo, noticing the uneasiness of Passepout, quickly changed the subject.

Turning his attention back to his boon companion he said, "Enough of this idle chatter. On to the matter at hand. The Traveler's Cloak Inn is two doors away, and I have taken the liberty of changing my reservation from a single to two adjoining rooms. A few hours' rest, and you will be ripe and ready for some festing tonight. We can talk over old times, have some new times, and make plans for future times, for tomorrow I must leave."

"You think of everything Mist . . . uh, Volo. But why must you leave so soon?"

"Oh, I'll be back," the traveler answered. "I'll probably even keep the rooms on reserve until I return. You can, of course, avail yourself of their use in my absence."

"Wonderful!"

Volo smiled at once again hearing his friend's favorite expression, and ushered Passepout into the best inn in town.

* * * * *

Around Mulmaster,
the Tower of Arcane Might,
and at the Traveler's Cloak Inn:

While the master traveler made arrangements for the next few days of his research, the pudgy thespian spent most of the afternoon sleeping in the most comfortable bed that he had had the honor of lying in since he left the luxuries of the Bernd estate many months ago. Volo's research included stopping by the local taverns, inns, and festhalls to gain a few recommendations for accommodations. He was very careful not to reveal his true identity everywhere, as some of the establishments would later be graced with an incognito visitation, by him, for purposes of giving them a fair evaluation for their inclusion in his upcoming *Volo's Guide to the Moonsea.*

Volo also made it a point of checking in at the legendary Tower of Arcane Might, the guild hall for the Brotherhood of the Cloak. Volo had earlier received honorary "Cloak" status from the Senior Cloak Thurndan Tallwand in exchange for the noted author's silence concerning the source of various secret entries in his legendarily suppressed work *Volo's Guide to All Things Magical.* By checking in informally as an honorary Cloak, the master traveler hoped to avoid future problems around Mulmaster with its strict rules on magic use, while also maintaining a low profile that would enable him to come and go as inconspicuously as possible with the rigid regimens of the often-called City of Danger.

As expected, Tallwand was unavailable, at least according to his secretary.

"I am sorry," said the officious wizard who acted as Tallwand's secretary. "The Senior Cloak is very busy, and can not see you today."

"That's too bad," Volo, the ever courteous traveler, replied, "but I really did want to say hello."

"I am afraid that is not possible," the secretary replied, and returned to the work that was on his desk.

Volo stood for a moment and fingered his beard, the wheels of thought whirring in his head. He suspected that Tallwand was indeed eavesdropping on his conversation with his wizardly lackey. He just wanted to see him for a moment. He decided it was time to fight dirty.

In the few moments that Volo took for contemplation and cogitation, an older wizard had entered the Senior Cloak's antechamber. He was a sour old coot who seemed very impressed with himself. No doubt he was older and stonier than the Tower of Arcane Might itself.

"Ah, Mage McKern, you are here for your appointment," the lackey recognized. "Let me just check with the Senior Cloak. I am sure he will be with you momentarily."

Volo sighed loudly and said aloud, "I guess I will have to have the article published without giving Thurndan a chance to review it." The master traveler sighed again, and started to head to the door.

The Senior Cloak, who was indeed eavesdropping on the goings-on, immediately burst through the door. His face was a mask of enthusiasm and surprise desperately trying to hide a look of embarrassment and fear over what he had just heard.

"*Volo!*" he hailed. "What a surprise! Come right in."

The master traveler reversed his steps and said, "I didn't want to disturb you. I am sure you are very busy, and . . ."

"Not at all," Thurndan replied, putting his arm

around the shoulders of the mischievous author and
ushering him into his office, pausing quickly to turn
to his secretary and whisper, "Reschedule whatever
you have to."

As he crossed the threshold the master traveler
heard the secretary saying, "I am sorry Mage McKern,
perhaps we can reschedule for next month. . . ."

* * * * *

Volo's meeting with Tallwand was quite short. The
master traveler made up an article that he hoped the
Senior Cloak might take a look at. The Senior Cloak
quickly assented, relieved that it had nothing to do
with his earlier transgression that had made its way
into the notorious *All Things Magical,* and then set
about getting rid of the master traveler as fast as
possible.

Volo, satisfied that no one would now be able to
dispute that he had indeed checked in at the Tower
of Arcane Might and equally eager to be on his way,
verbally recognized the Senior Cloak's busy schedule
and agreed to hurry along, promising to return at
some later date when they would both have some
time to swap stories and spells.

The master traveler was quite full of himself as he
passed the secretary who had tried to bar his way.
Volo chuckled, realizing that the lackey was probably staring daggers at him. That will teach him to
try to get in the way of the master traveler of all
Toril, Volo thought proudly.

Still preoccupied with his own elan and facility,
Volo didn't even notice accidentally bumping into the
sour old mage whose appointment he had usurped.
Had he done so he probably would have apologized.
Instead he continued on his oblivious path, not even

hearing the vitriolic curses that were being spewed behind his back.

* * * * *

Upon returning to the Traveler's Cloak Inn, he was immediately greeted in the dining hall by the now refreshed Passepout, whose pleasant afternoon nap had added fuel to his already voracious appetite.

"Volo!" Passepout yelled. "Over here!"

I must remember to go alone on my visitations that require a low profile, the master traveler reminded himself, and then joined his friend at the opulently laid table.

"Dela darling," the portly thespian called to the barmaid, "Please set a place for my friend here, and bring more food. He might be hungry." Turning his attention to the recently seated Volo, he whispered, "I think she likes me. I have a way with barmaids."

"I remember," the master traveler replied. "You were always quite the ladies' man."

Dela quickly set a place for Volo, and was about to return to the bar when Passepout gave her a friendly pat on the rump, and said, "Very nice, my sweet. Play your cards right, and I'll put in a good word for you with the management."

Dela gave Volo a long-suffering look, and said, "You sure he's a friend of yours, Mr. Geddarm?"

"Afraid so," the master traveler replied.

"Well, please advise him to keep his hands to himself," she instructed, and regained her place at the bar.

Volo looked to his friend, and said admonishingly, "Well, you heard her."

Passepout was affronted. "Imagine her nerve!" the indignant thespian boomed. "I have a good mind to have a word with the owner about her."

"She is the owner," Volo instructed.

"Oh," said the chubby thespian warily. "Do you think I should leave? Or maybe apologize? A few well chosen compliments might go a long way, her being female and all."

"Just let it pass," the master traveler instructed. "Dela is a good sort, with a keen business sense, and no desire to alienate any potential paying customers. You can't ask for more in an innkeeper in these parts."

Passepout nodded, and continued the inhalation of his meal. Volo put his napkin in place, and joined in the dining experience. After a few more mouthfuls, Passepout once again struck up a conversation.

"I only arrived here yesterday," the chubby thespian confessed. "Is there anything I should know about these here parts?"

"Plenty," the master traveler replied. "But first a question: why did you come to Mulmaster to begin with?"

After a swallow and another quaff of ale, the portly thespian explained.

"Somebody around Westgate told me that there was plenty of room for my sort of trade in the Moonsea area."

"You mean acting, of course," the master traveler clarified.

"Of course," Passepout replied. "I learned my lesson after that little stay in Baldur's Gate, when you last came to my rescue."

"Go on," Volo urged, not wanting to experience another exuberant outbreak of undying gratitude from the chubby actor, nor relive his last jailbreak experience.

"So I said to myself, 'Self, where should we go?'

Zhentil Keep was obviously out of the question. I mean, who is willing to pay good money for drama when your city is in ruins."

"Agreed."

"And Hillsfar didn't exactly seem to fit the bill."

"For sure," the master traveler replied, wondering if there was still a price on their heads for impersonating Red Plumes, the city watch, the last time they were there.

"And Phlan already has a resident thespian, Ward T. James."

"Ward T. James?" Volo repeated inquisitively. "Never heard of him."

"He's a big guy, like me," Passepout explained, patting his expansive tummy in illustration. "He tours with a group called the S.S.I.—Stupendous Stagecraft Incorporated. They are most famous for their Pools series of plays that set the great classics of Faerûn in a mud pit."

"Great," the master traveler said, quickly taking out a pad and jotting down a few notes. "High drama and mud wrestling all rolled into one."

"So that ruled out Phlan," the actor finished heaping another pile of food onto his plate, to further usher it into his never-filling gullet, "which basically just left Mulmaster as the major metropolis at hand."

Volo swallowed, picked a crumb out of his neatly trimmed beard, took a napkin and wiped his mouth, refilled his mug with ale in case any parchness beset him during his lecture, and began to fill his boon companion in on Mulmaster minutiae.

"I can understand your reasons for choosing Mulmaster, now that you have explained it to me," the master traveler offered, "but I would still recommend that you pick another place to ply your trade.

As far as I'm aware no one ever tells anyone to go to these here parts unless they really never want to see them again."

"I'm sure that's not the case," Passepout protested. "Olive, who recommended this area, was quite fond of me."

"I'm sure," said the master traveler, not wanting to start an argument, "but Mulmaster is known as the City of Danger for a very good reason. If you thought the Red Plumes of Hillsfar were bad, wait 'til you get a load of the Hawks."

"Well, I did last night," the thespian countered. "They weren't too bad as far as a city watch goes."

"No, my friend," Volo corrected. "You were probably taken in by regular soldiers. The Hawks are the High Blade's own storm troopers. Rumor has it that he regularly dispatches them to do his dirty work throughout the Realms. Let me give you a little history.

"Mulmaster was founded—by various influential merchant groups—in the Year of Fell Wizardry, as a trading fortress way station between the Moonsea, the River Lis, and the Dragon Reach. It managed to not only survive, but thrive during the years of unrest, and eventually, in the Year of Thunder, made a bid for complete domination of the Moonsea, only to be put back in its place by the combined forces of Sembia, Hillsfar, Phlan, Melvaunt, and Zhentil Keep."

"Scrappy little place," the thespian commented between mouthfuls.

Volo continued in his recitation of exposition text that he no doubt had already composed for the guidebook in progress.

"There was much finger pointing after their failed attempt at expansionism, and out of the anarchy arose the formation of a single seat of power, to rule over the others. This leader was to be called the High Blade, who was to work in conjunction with the other ranking nobles who from that time on were known as the Blades. The first High Blade took power in the Year of the Wandering Wyrm, and quickly assassinated any of the Blades who didn't agree with his way of doing things. From that point on the Blades were nothing more than a puppet ruling council."

"Wonderful," the thespian observed, "so that's why he needs those shock troopers around to protect him."

"No, my friend," Volo corrected. "That's the job of the Brotherhood of the Cloak. Any mage in the city of fourth level or higher is immediately recruited to their ranks, or else."

"Or else what?"

Volo made a motion as if he was slitting his throat with the bread knife.

"Oh," said the chubby thespian, beginning to think that maybe leaving town would be a good idea.

"The current High Blade is a fellow by the name of Selfaril Voumdolphin, who succeeded his father into the job after assassinating him. That was back in the Year of the Spear."

"Did he then marry his mother? I seem to recall a play about something like that."

"I'm afraid not," the gazetteer replied. "This is one case where life does not mirror drama. He did recently marry though, to an equally powerful young lady by the name of Dmitra Flas."

"Never heard of her."

"She's also known as the First Princess of Thay, and the Tharchioness of Eltabbar, or just the Tharchioness for short. It was a major diplomatic coup for both Mulmaster and Thay."

"Wonderful."

"*She* spends most of her time back in Eltabbar, and *he's* been known to continue to play the rogue with the wandering eye despite their matrimonial vows. She visits here three times a year. I believe she just arrived yesterday for her most recent visit. Both sides claim that they were wedded due to their mutual respect and love for each other, but I wonder."

"The problem with you, Volo," Passepout said sagely, "is that you are no longer a romantic. If she just arrived back in town yesterday, I bet we won't see hide nor hair of either of them for a while. This is obviously a case of true love winning out despite personal differences in upbringing and breeding. I'll bet they can't wait to see each other."

Volo chuckled at his friend's naivete.

"If you say so, my friend," the gazetteer replied.

"True love conquers all," the thespian spouted.

The master traveler took another quaff of ale, and was instantly reminded of the message he had once read from a Kara Turan fate biscuit that was capable of more believable profundity than his corpulent companion's observation.

Volo thought aloud to himself, "I wonder how the newlyweds are getting along."

Passepout resumed eating.

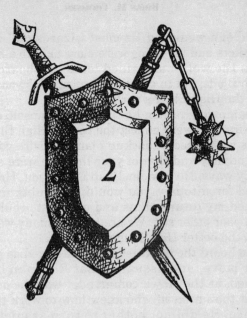

Newlywed Games

In the High Blade's Study in the Tower of the Wyvern:

He was alone in his private study, a room secret to all but his closest advisors (which did not include his wife, the Tharchioness). His robes of silk and fur already smelled of tobacco and musk.

Selfaril Voumdolphin was in deep thought.

The resemblance was striking. It was almost like looking in a mirror. True he had the bearing and build of a weakling, as most wizards did, and his whiskers and his mane were more akin to a hermit's than the well-maintained locks and beard of the High Blade, but in all other respects this young man was the High Blade's perfect twin.

Damn you, father, he thought to himself, cursing his sire. You were almost the perfect High Blade, always with a secret backup plan to assure your own ascendancy and that of your line. We were alike in many ways. No wonder I had to kill you. Had I not acted fortuitously, you would, no doubt, have discerned my future plans and plotted to replace me with your other son. We are alike in many ways, but I am the better High Blade.

He heard the bookcase that functioned as a secret door move, and assumed that Rickman had returned, as the Hawk commander was the only one other than himself who knew how to work that entrance. He did not bother to turn around. Such things as common courtesy were not required of the High Blade.

"The resemblance was uncanny," Selfaril muttered.

"Yes, your majesty," Rickman agreed. "Donal, that chancre, wasn't lying."

"Imagine his gall," Selfaril said, finally turning to face his one-eyed right-hand man. "First, he betrayed the Retreat and offered the young mage to the agents of my dear bride, and then, not satisfied with the price they offered, he came to us for a better deal."

"For which you were more than willing to comply, sire," the Hawk assented. "They offered him amnesty, we offered him wealth."

"And neither of us planned on keeping our word, anyway. Donal was a fool, and a greedy one at that."

"Agreed, your majesty, but his shortcomings were definitely our advantage."

"Indeed," the High Blade agreed, taking a seat in a chair that had been one of his father's favorites. "Have you taken care of the rest of the loose ends?"

"Yes, sire," the Hawk captain assured. "A company of my best men have just returned from the Retreat. They gained entrance under the pretence of investigating the apparent Thayan raid of the night before. The elders were ever so grateful for a prompt response to the attack, and offered my men their full cooperation. With their guard down, it was relatively easy for my Hawks to carry out your orders."

"All slaughtered, then?"

"Yes, sire."

The High Blade tapped his forefinger to his temple as if to force out a single drop of thought. "I hope that there weren't too many other secret guests like my father's other heir and rival to my sovereignty. I understand the monastery was also used as an occasional way station for Harper agents, and I have no time to deal with their peskiness at this point."

The Hawk captain quickly dispelled the High Blade's concern. "I took the liberty of instructing one of my men to leave behind the crystal wand that had been used on the Thayan turncoat Donal. It's Thayan design, and the blood of that slug will no doubt focus the possible blame for this little bloodbath on more easterly sources."

"Well done, Rickman," the High Blade complimented. "Take a seat. You have been very busy, and very productive."

The Hawk captain bowed in thanks, and took his place across from the High Blade, adding, "and of course I have seen to the unfortunate demise of our friend the blind wizard smith whose exceptional handiwork adorns the head of our secret guest."

" 'Tis a pity," Selfaril agreed, "but there is no sense in not being careful."

"Agreed," Rickman acknowledged, glad that he was not being perceived as overzealous in his performance of his duties. "So what are your plans for the dispensation of your twin brother, if I might inquire, sire?"

"My twin brother," Selfaril mused. "It's funny. Up until just this moment I never thought of him quite that way. I mean, sure, he has to be my brother, my twin, but as far as I am concerned, he is merely my father's other son, my rival, a challenger to my throne. Tell me Rickman, do you have any brothers?"

"One, your majesty, but he is dead. His name was Jeremy."

"How sad," the High Blade replied in an unsentimental monotone.

"Not really, sire," the Hawk corrected. "As he was the first born, he received all the privileges. That is why I entered the military. It was either there or a monastery."

"Your loss was Mulmaster's gain."

"In more ways than one, sire. When father died, Jeremy inherited it all. In my then capacity as sergeant of the guards, I had him thrown in irons, charged with high treason, and executed a week later. My father's estate was, of course, seized for the state, and I appointed myself as custodian. I was soon promoted, and it was turned over to me as my fiefdom."

"You're not just saying this to earn my favor, are you, Rickman?"

"I wouldn't think of it, sire," the Hawk said proudly. "All you have to do is check the civil records."

"Of course," the High Blade observed in a jesting manner, "one who has already engaged in fratricide would never stoop to falsifying civil records."

"Of course not, your majesty," the Hawk replied, jovially adding, "that would be against the law."

"But of course."

The murderers' conversation was interrupted by the quick sounding of three chimes.

The High Blade cursed.

"It's the Tharchioness, no doubt," Selfaril offered. "I left strict orders with Slater—my valet—to ring me if she inquired of my whereabouts. Word has no doubt already reached her about last night's thwarting of her plans, and she, no doubt, wants to pick my brain about what happened."

"Do you think she suspects that we are behind what happened?"

"No more than I would suspect her of wanting to depose me," the High Blade replied with a grin, coming to his feet. "Come with me. Let us seek out my still blushing bride, and let the game of cat and mouse begin!"

* * * * *

In the Tharchioness's Boudoir in the Tower of the Wyvern:

The Tharchioness was not amused.

It was bad enough that she had to endure the damp and smoky gloominess of Mulmaster for yet another one of her thrice-yearly connubial stays, but now to be surrounded by such incompetence was definitely not to her liking, and she had no intention of tolerating it.

She had purposely cut short her stay back in

Eltabbar overseeing the rebuilding of her beloved city after the devastating earthquake of a few months back because of the so-called opportunity that had been presented to her ambassador by that traitor to the Thayan cause and the sovereignty of Zulkir Szass Tam, Donal Loomis.

Her just recently executed ambassador with whom the traitor had made contact had been overly optimistic, and had presented his plan as an antidote to the oppressive yoke of matrimony that she had endured for diplomatic reasons with the slimy High Blade of the city to the west.

Szass Tam had explained the necessity of her courtship and marriage to the foul westerner as the first step toward an active Thayan presence in the Moonsea area. The powerful lich lord would then be able to extend his influence farther southward to the Dalelands, while exerting further pressures on the other tharches toward an ultimate goal of the unification of all of Thay under his eternal rule. She had been more than willing to assist him in this ultimate goal, even if it meant subjecting herself to the bondage of matrimony.

Unfortunately, both of them had underestimated the equally acquisitive ambitions of the High Blade, who saw Mulmaster's Tower of the Wyvern as the jumping-off point for his own expansion of power and authority both south and eastward, power which he had no intention of sharing with his bride, or the real power behind her throne.

The now deceased ambassador had presented such a simple plan. A double for the High Blade existed. Why not abduct him, and persuade him that it would be more advantageous for him to follow orders from them than to die an excruciatingly torturous death at their hands? They would then secretly substitute their puppet for Selfaril; placing him on the throne while the real High Blade was secretly spirited away to the east.

According to Ambassador Vitriole, the traitor who had presented this opportunity was mortally in fear of his life, and as a result, could be trusted to follow their exact orders in exchange for their lifting the sentence of death from his misshapen shoulders (which was immediately agreed to with the full knowledge that a new plan would be carried out on the spot once his usefulness had come to an end).

Donal might have been a traitorous, cowardly fool, the Tharchioness thought to herself, but Vitriole was a fool as well for underestimating his traitorous ways. They deserved each other's company in death. Had I had a competent ambassador in place, I wouldn't be in this delicate position. But no, I had to come to Mulmaster early to face my beloved husband when I displaced him as the ruling power of Mulmaster. Now what am I going to do?

The First Princess of Thay gently applied a bit of perfume behind her ears, knowing that the westerner who was her husband would find it distracting. For a similar reason, she had also chosen to wear her silken robe with the plunging neckline that flattered her ample breasts and drew further attention to her eye-catching cleavage.

I must use everything at my disposal, she thought in agitated resignation, once again cursing the incompetence of her minions that necessitated her sensual theatricality.

Her moments of silent reflection on her current predicament were interrupted by the cautious arrival of her new ambassador to Mulmaster.

"First Princess," the new and fearful ambassador said tentatively, "you requested my presence?"

"No," the Tharchioness replied acidly, "I said that I wanted you at my disposal, here and now. You *do* know what happened to your predecessor, don't you?"

"Yes, your highness," the ambassador acknowledged, trying not to show that he had just soiled himself out of sheer terror and fear.

The Tharchioness, born Dmitra Flass and now also known as the First Princess of Thay, was legendary in her cruelty, and the execution of Vitriole was only the most recent of her acts of intolerance toward what she considered to be traitorous incompetence. Anything that hindered Szass Tam's ultimate plans was considered to be treasonous within the tharch of Eltabbar, and treason was always punishable by death.

The Tharchioness gave the ambassador a quick once-over. His Mulan lineage was apparent. Rumors of non-Mulan spies in Thay were rampant, and precautions had to be taken. His hairless pate was adorned by the long-since faded tattoos of what once must have been magically-empowered images of phoenixes in flight. Now they were just inked drawings on a wrinkled and pale skull.

Great, she thought to herself, another spineless political appointee who has long since passed his age of usefulness. Why don't they ever send me someone who is young and vibrant rather than another impotent husk of a boot licker?

The Tharchioness looked him in the eyes, dead on.

He dropped to the floor, cringing in an absurd amalgam of abasement and terror.

The Tharchioness rolled her eyes, her contempt turning to cruel amusement, and said, "Well, it doesn't look like you are long for this job, and you know what that means?"

"Yes, your Tharchioness," he managed to get out through trembling lips and chattering teeth.

"Find my husband, corpse maggot, and do it fast," she ordered, revelling in the sheer terror her latest ambassador felt toward her. "I haven't laid eyes on him since I arrived yesterday."

"Perhaps he is avoiding . . ." the quivering mass offered.

"I don't recall giving you permission to speak, corpse maggot!"

"No, your Tharchioness."

"So don't just cower there, find him!" she screamed, sending him out of the room at a break-neck pace that was, no doubt, largely propelled by complete and utter terror.

The Tharchioness laughed for a moment, her thoughts temporarily diverted from the precarious situation at hand.

"And while you're at it," she said aloud with a grin, though the ambassador had long since left, "clean yourself up. You can't seek the High Blade smelling of excrement. He might mistake you for one of his subjects."

* * * * *

The Reid Room in the Tower of the Wyvern:

The two heads of state met in the receiving room, their entrances carefully orchestrated and timed by their retinues so that neither seemed to have been left waiting for the other.

"Darling," the Tharchioness cooed.

"My Thayan beauty," the High Blade countered, "I was not expecting you for another month."

"I just couldn't stand being away from you," she

replied, her cruel lips pursed in fake kisses for the husband she hated.

"That makes two of us," he agreed with just a hint of a leer that the retinues would no doubt mistake for lust, rather than contempt. "How goes the rebuilding of Eltabbar?"

"Slowly."

"Earthquake, wasn't it?"

"Right as always."

During the entire exchange neither the husband nor the wife had come any closer to each other, and still stood on opposite sides of the room. They tentatively drew closer together, still halting well before they had reached an arm's distance.

He first noticed the scent of a new perfume as they entered the room, while she recognized the foul stench of his tobacco. Their eyes never left each other, like two jungle cats each waiting for the other to be the first to blink, at which point the other would strike a lethal blow.

She's even icier than usual, the High Blade thought. She is probably already aware that her plan has gone awry.

Usually he can't remove his eyes from my breasts, the Tharchioness contemplated. Now he won't break my stare. He knows something and is trying to see if I know it, too. I mustn't give myself away.

The subtle standoff was interrupted by the arrival of some Arabellan Brandy. The High Blade seized the opportunity to seemingly relax, and poured his bride and himself a snifter each.

The Tharchioness sipped.

"Mmmmmm," she purred, licking her lips.

"I'm glad it is to your liking," he said in mock gallantry. "I always try to provide you with the best Mulmaster has to offer, but sometimes plans do go awry, as you no doubt have recently experienced."

The Tharchioness maintained her composure, and in a tone that she thought of as schoolgirlish (which, incidentally, turned her stomach every time she used it), she inquired, "What could you mean, darling?"

"Why the earthquake, of course," he replied, hesitating just a moment before adding, "dear."

"Of course," she said in agreement, realizing the subtext of taunts that he was beginning to bedevil her with.

"It's a funny thing though," he persisted, "one's misfortune is sometimes another's boon."

"To whose advantage is an earthquake?"

"Why those who are paid to make the repairs afterward, my sweet," the High Blade replied in his most subtly condescending tone.

The Tharchioness decided that she needed more time and information before further dealing with the delicate matter at hand. The High Blade obviously knew something, but of what and how much, she was not certain. She decided to change the subject.

Delicately dipping her finger into her snifter of brandy, she held it out for her husband's consideration.

"Care for a taste?" she purred.

Gently taking the proffered hand with its anointed digit in his two hands, he slowly brought it to his lips, and bestowed a kiss.

"I thought you'd never offer," he replied breathlessly, then turned to the crowds that had followed them into the receiving room and instructed the retinues, "Leave us! Matters of state and diplomacy can wait until later. Much later."

In less than the time it took for their lips to meet, they were alone and on the receiving room settee.

No further words were exchanged, and delicate situations were temporarily postponed.

* * * * *

In the Dungeon of Southroad Keep:

Rassendyll's eyes had finally grown accustomed to
the dim light of his cell, and the iron mask that en-
shrouded his head no longer shifted with every
movement he made. It was as if the metal of the
domed skullcap had taken root in the back of his
head, allowing less movement in the face of the
mask as well. The ringing had finally stopped in his
ears from the ceaseless clanging that had ensued
during his period of hysterics when he had beaten
his head against the wall in despair. The strong iron
metal of the mask had protected his head from any
major damage or concussion, and all that remained
of his temporary outbreak of insanity was a nagging
headache.

The edges around his eyes chafed his sockets,
while the slits that barely functioned as access
points to his mouth and nose pressed back against
his face providing the smallest windows of entry for
air and other sustenance. He vaguely remembered
the comment his twin had made about the lethality
of his beard's growth, and resigned himself to the
eventuality of his fast-approaching demise.

"Death," he called in a volume equal to his outbreak of the night before, and immediately regretted
it as his own words seemed to echo within the skull
that the combined mask and bone of his head had
become. He stopped, pulled himself up short, and
steeled himself for another round of beseeching the
gods.

"Death," he called in comfortable, hushed tones,
"please take me now, and spare me the suffering of
waiting."

"I'm not death," a voice interrupted from behind, "but if you don't mind, I'd like to come in and set a spell. When you get to my age, tunnel crawling is hard work."

Rassendyll quickly turned around, and saw the source of the voice.

An old dwarf, whose pure white hair and beard were as long as his entire body, was halfway through a hole in the wall that had been formed from the removal of one of the massive stone bricks that made up the foundation.

The young mage was speechless, but this didn't stop the dwarf, who quickly regained his feet, strode over to the new prisoner, and introduced himself.

"Hi," he said jovially, in a tone that was quite out of place for the dark dungeon. "I'm Hoffman, from the Seventh Dwarven Abbey. I've been a prisoner down here for I don't know how long. What's your story?"

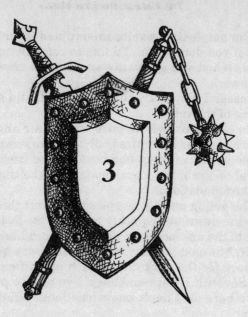

3

A Weakened Retreat

Along the Road from Mulmaster to the Retreat:

After the feasting at the Traveler's Cloak Inn was over, the festing began with a tour of some of the local hot spots such as the very popular Wave and Wink (nicknamed the W&W) and the Smashed Plate. Realizing that he had many days of work and research ahead of him, Volo took it fairly easy, managing to attract no attention to himself amidst the crowd of

Mulmaster revellers. Passepout, on the other hand, gave free reign to all of his desires with all of the *joie de vivre* of the recently released prisoner that he was. His eyes and his appetites, however, were much larger and stronger than his strength and his stamina. By midevening, the chubby thespian was quite unconscious, and the master traveler had to enlist the help of three very strong young laborers and one extremely sturdy cart to get him back to their night's lodgings.

The following morning, Volo rose before dawn, assembled his pack and scribbled down a hasty note assuring the stout thespian that he would return in a few days. He grabbed a fast breakfast, which Dela was more than willing to provide, and left the inn. The master traveler rented a horse from a nearby stable and set out for his next destination.

The sun was just inching over the horizon when the most famous gazetteer in all Faerûn passed Southroad Keep. Nodding to the city watch, who didn't pay him much attention as they were more concerned about the apparent tardiness of their relief, he passed through the city gate, and was on his way.

The absence of the city walls and buildings removed all obstructions from the force of the wind, and Volo quickly drew up a spare blanket that he had packed just for this reason, and draped it around himself as if it were a cape. Fastening it in place with a clasp, and then placing one hand on his beret and one hand on the reins, he spurred on the steed with a quick kick and "giddy-yap."

Volo looked around him as he rode, taking in the scenery, and mentally assembling descriptive passages and entries for the guide.

The mountains, he thought to himself, seem to create some sort of wind tunnel. The breezes off the

Moonsea were magnified by the funnel effect as they roared through, making everything seem colder than it should be. I must remember, he noted, to include a cold weather warning and a warm clothing advisory in the book.

With the exception of the mountains themselves, the rising sun had very little to illuminate on the landscape through which the master traveler rode. Mulmaster was surrounded by rocky, barren lands which further magnified the gloom of the smokey industrial city. The sure-footed stallion had little problem making its way over the rugged and unforgiving ground, with only a minimal amount of direction from its well-traveled rider.

Even though the smoky fog of Mulmaster was far behind and out of sight in no time at all, the gloom and bleakness of the jagged terrain remained as Volo continued on his way. The skies were almost as uninhabited as the ground, with only the occasional bird of prey or vulture breaking up the grey monotony that reached upward as far as the eye could see.

The master traveler seemed oblivious to the lifelessness around him, and contented himself with putting together new and different phrases to describe the barren landscape. Occasionally he would pass an abandoned farmhouse or inn, and would wonder what ill-fortuned farmer or hostler was foolhardy enough to try to ply his trade there. Further on in his journey, he began to pass larger abandoned structures that almost resembled Southroad Keep. From the research notes that he had prepared prior to setting out on his journey, he knew that they were monasteries and habitats for contemplative orders that had long fallen by the wayside.

There must have been something about the austerity of the landscape itself that attracted the ascetic, introspective, hermit types that had the swelled the orders that had filled these citadels in years gone by. I guess they came looking for the meaning of life, didn't find it, and left, leaving their monastic dwellings behind, he thought.

The great gazetteer smiled.

Maybe I'll include something in the guide about these places being haunted to sort of make things more exciting. Local legends have to start somewhere, he surmised.

As Volo and his steed approached what remained of a stone arch that had in some earlier era provided egress for some now long bygone structure, the great gazetteer heard a scurrying like the scrambling of rats on a cellar floor. The master traveler smiled, and reached into the inner pocket of his cloak, the tips of his fingers caressing one of the numerous blades he had secreted on various parts of his person.

Company, he thought to himself.

Guiding the horse closer to the arch rubble, Volo allowed himself to slump down in the saddle as if he had fallen asleep, while tightening his hold on the reins to keep control of his steed in as inconspicuous a manner as possible.

Easy pickings, the master traveler thought to himself, usually leads to careless thieves.

He heard the scurrying on his left and above, and readied himself for the attack.

A last scratch of a scurry from above, followed by a grunt, clued Volo in on a moment's notice that the outlaw who was stalking him was leaping down on to his not unsuspecting prey from above.

The master traveler quickly spurred his steed forward, upsetting the dim-witted brigand's planned interception, causing him instead to go crashing to the hard stone ground below.

Once again at a moment's notice, Volo reined in his steed with one hand, this time quickly turning his mount around to face the inept assailant, while flinging a throwing blade with his freed hand. The blade met its mark, passing through the shoulder fabric of the black haired brigand's cloak, lodging its tip in the seam between the stones in the road, and staking him to the ground while barely scratching the less than deserving oaf.

Dazed and bewildered, the thief looked up and began to quake in his threadbare boots, beads of sweat trickling down his face from razor cut locks of ebony as he waited for another blade to make its mortal mark.

"What is your name, O inept felon?" Volo inquired.

"James," the thief sputtered.

"Well, felonious James, or perhaps James Felonious since you do seem to be rather backward," Volo blithely explained, "I'm afraid that business demands that I go this way, and since the authorities that I would have to turn you over to lie back from whence I came, I'm afraid that I will have to leave you behind."

James the Felon tried to get up but was still held in place by the blade-staked cloak.

"I can't get up!" the bewildered and dense brigand cried, unaware that it was his own cloak that was holding him down.

"That's right," the master traveler replied. "I have cast a static cling spell that is causing the ground to grip you up against it."

Volo spurred his steed again, and began to set off at a light trot.

"Don't leave me here!" the thief cried. "I'll starve!"

"The spell will wear off soon enough," the master traveler assured, then added, "and when it does you better hightail it out of these parts. I'll be passing back this way again soon, and I'd better not find you around."

"What if someone should come upon me before it wears off? I'm helpless!" the thief cried louder.

"I wouldn't worry about that," Volo replied jovially. "From what I've seen and heard, the brigands that favor these here parts are a rather inept bunch."

After a few moments Volo looked back in the distance. From what he could make out the thief was still struggling on the ground. The master traveler allowed himself a chuckle, and continued onward.

Others might have passed through the area at a faster pace, but not Volo. This was in no way due to the potential speed of his steed, but rather by the personal choice of the rider himself. The master traveler was a stickler when it came to local flavor and color, and he had no desire to rush through it at the risk of missing something, even if the flavor of the landscape was bland and its color was gray.

I must remember to include a warning about brigands in the book, the master traveler noted. After all, not all travelers are as observant—or as adept at handling such situations—as myself.

* * * * *

Sometime past midday, the master traveler came in sight of his destination: the isolated monastery known as the Retreat. The leisurely pace with which he had traveled obviously caused him to arrive while the various hermits of the place were on their lunchtime break deep within the monastic walls, as no one was in sight in the fields around the old stronghold.

I guess I should have sent word to wait lunch on me, the master traveler reflected with a chuckle.

Maybe if I can catch the eye of one of the members on watch, a place will already be set for me by the time I arrive.

A chill unlike the one caused by the Moonsea climatic conditions passed down the spine of the master traveler.

That's odd, he thought. No one seems to be on watch. Even during meals there is always someone on watch.

Volo put his two fingers up to his mouth and let loose with a birdcall almost identical to that of the Bowl-headed Greenwood, a bird indigenous to Shadowdale. He repeated the call, listening carefully for a reply.

None came.

He immediately realized that something was not right. Where could they be? he thought to himself. The elders would always respond to a Harper signal of distress, even when it isn't given by a Harper. The network of secret agents dedicated to preserving balance in Faerûn were longtime allies of the old mages therein. Surely the Harpers could never fall out of favor with them. Where could they all have gone, and why wasn't anyone responding to his call?

Quickly reaching into his cloak to assure himself of the readiness of yet another blade, Volo urged the horse onward at a slower pace, eyes and ears wide open and ready for danger.

The gate of the Retreat had been left wide open, and though the rocky terrain obscured any tracks that might have otherwise been left, the dried spoor of numerous horses was still evident by the series of rails that were normally used for the tethering of steeds.

Volo dismounted, and, with reins still in hand in case he had to make a quick return to the saddle and an even faster egress, approached the evidential detritus, and stooped down to get a closer look at it. As I recall, the master gazetteer (who also considered himself to be a more than adequate detective) reflected, it rained just two days ago. Whatever caused the Retreat to be evacuated must have occurred since then, or else this fertilizer would have been washed away.

Righting himself and stepping carefully so as to avoid treading in the evidence at hand (or underfoot, as was the case), Volo approached the gate.

Before he had even gained entrance, he realized that he had been mistaken about the Retreat's evacuation, for there, just inside the gate, was the not quite two-day-old corpse of the Thayan exile who had been known as Donal Loomis. As two rats were feasting in the orifices of the elder's face, Volo saw no need to bend over for a closer examination. He knew the monk was dead and saw little reason to further turn his travel-worn stomach.

With a dagger in hand, the brave gazetteer stepped over the body, and ventured further into the stronghold that had been known as the Retreat. The further he went the more bodies he found, each gutted like a pig for a Mayday feast. The master traveler used his free hand to bring a neckerchief up to his nose and mouth to help fight back the gall that was rebelling in his stomach. Maintaining his composure, he tried to piece together what must have happened.

I would immediately jump to the conclusion that the Retreat had been attacked by some foreign force, he thought, but there seems to be no sign of a struggle. My second theory, he went on, would have been that they were the victims of a surprise attack, perhaps in the middle of the night, but all of the bodies are attired in their day wear, and the gate and stronghold walls show no signs of being breached, jimmied,

or assailed. Whoever engineered this horrible bloodbath must have been granted entrance by the elders
in broad daylight, and therefore were assumed by the
elder on watch to have been either allies, or harmless.
I guess the elder on watch was mistaken.

Scanning the residue of slaughter, Volo thought
he recognized one of the corpses. He was about to
stoop to get a closer look when he barely saw a moving blur out of the corner of his eye, and reacted in a
second, raising his dagger to a defensive posture.

He was half a second too slow.

The master traveler felt the coolness of a steel
blade against his windpipe, and heard an authoritative voice say, "Drop it, or breathe blood."

Realizing he had no alternative if he wished to live
long enough to get to the bottom of the bloodbath, and
to eventually complete his guide to the Moonsea, Volo
dropped his dagger, and prepared to do whatever the
other visitor to the Retreat requested.

He felt the blade pressing harder against his
throat.

* * * * *

In the High Blade's study in the Tower of the Wyvern:

The High Blade rose late that morning, having
spent a strenuous night with the Thayan serpent
that months ago he had accepted as his wife. He
sought out the privacy of his study as he wished to
avoid all of the court, social, and political commitments that occurred whenever he and his consort
were reunited. Though he was more than aware of
the necessity of such obligations and functions, he
nonetheless desired time to more adequately formulate his plans against his she-devil wife who had

sought to neutralize him. Wishing a report on his most important prisoner, Selfaril sent for Rickman.

The captain of the Hawks responded immediately.

"You summoned, sire," said the one-eyed Hawk.

"How is my brother?" the High Blade inquired, not making eye contact with his second in command.

"As you left him, my lord," Rickman responded, surprised at Selfaril's use of the moniker. "My man in the Cloaks informs me that, given normal circumstances, the mask should have dampened all of his magical abilities to non-existence by now. He is now no more of a mage than either you or I."

"What a pity for him after all of those years of study," Selfaril observed in an emotionless monotone.

"Of course, the mask also serves the other purpose of obscuring his identity from prying eyes, as you yourself planned, sire," added Rickman.

"So that no one will ever know that I have a brother," the High Blade interrupted, completing the thought of his right-hand man, and once again surprising the Hawk with his use of the fraternal label. Changing the subject, Selfaril said, "You know Rickman, for most people, family is their main source of comfort and survival. I, on the other hand, never knew my mother, killed my father, have imprisoned my brother, and am plotted against by my wife."

"Most people are inferior pawns whose very existence is only validated for as long as they are useful to superior men such as yourself, High Blade," Rickman asserted.

"Indeed," Selfaril agreed absently.

Rickman remained in place, waiting for the High Blade to issue new orders, but Selfaril remained silent, as if preoccupied with other matters. Growing uncomfortable with his master's prolonged silence, the captain of the Hawks hazarded a question.

"Your majesty," Rickman inquired cautiously, "have you confronted the Tharchioness with your discovery of her conspiracy yet?"

"No," Selfaril answered quickly, snapping out of his preoccupied malaise. "I haven't finished planning how to turn it to my greatest advantage yet. Ideally I would like to use it to rid the city of all of those diplomatically immune wizards she has seen fit to bring here, exempting them from my control, while sending an occupational force to Eltabbar to exert our own battery of diplomatic influence. As you no doubt realize, this is more than just a wife wishing to kill her husband. This is war."

Rickman was surprised at the recent amount of anger and emotion the High Blade had made evident. What had started out as a political chess game with what was initially considered to be a worthy opponent had quickly escalated into a ruthless shadow war. Rickman was in a quandary as to what he should offer to do next.

"Should I have some of my men arrange for the removal—permanent or locational—of the Tharchioness?" he inquired.

"Not just yet," the High Blade answered. "We must play this situation very delicately."

"What if I were to send two of my men back to the Retreat to investigate the unfortunate slaughter of that order of contemplative mages. They could discover the Thayan wand that was left behind, and report it to their immediate superiors who would then pass this discovery up through the chain of command. . . ."

"And with gossip being what it is in the lower ranks, passing out into the unwashed masses as well."

"Indeed, sire," Rickman agreed. "Maiden rumor will spread, fermenting public outrage against the Thayan murderers. I will have Wattrous and Jembahb dispatched immediately. Neither of them are known for their discretion."

"Indeed."

"In regards to rumor, sire," Rickman continued. "Wouldn't it be wise to remove any threat of it interfering with our plans?"

"To what do you refer?"

"The prisoner, sire," the Hawk captain explained cautiously. "Though his appearance is obscured, he can still talk. Perhaps he should be further isolated from the other prisoners in the dungeon."

Selfaril shook his head and chuckled.

"I really don't think that is necessary. A trip to the dungeon is a one-way journey for the hopeless, penniless, and terminally unfortunate. What are the odds of someone getting out, and even at that, what of it?"

Rickman became quite serious.

"Through my sources, I have learned that the prisoner in the cell next to your brother was released yesterday. An unemployed actor I believe."

"What of it? If he heard anything at all it was the ravings of a madman. I find very little reason to fear an unemployed actor who probably knows nothing, nor anyone, of importance."

"Just the same, your majesty, I would like to assign one of my spies to keep an eye on him, at least until your plan has come to fruition."

"Fine, fine," Selfaril responded. "Spy on him, kill him, whatever you desire. Just don't waste my time with it."

"Yes, your majesty," the captain of the Hawks answered dutifully. "And the Tharchioness? Does the same hold true for her?"

"No, Rickman," the High Blade responded with a lascivious grin as he recalled the night before. "I'm not quite finished playing with her just yet."

* * * * *

*In the chambers of the First Princess of Thay
in the Tower of the Wyvern:*

"Your majesty," the fearful ambassador hesitantly interrupted the Tharchioness's late morning meal. She had awakened to find her husband already departed from their bed, and was not in a very good mood at all.

"What is it, worm?" she spat back with the venom of a recently disturbed cobra.

"You requested an update, your majesty . . . from our spies?"

The beautifully evil Tharchioness stood up, towering over the gelatinous bulge of her obsequious ambassador, spitting back: "And?"

"Well, your majesty," the ambassador replied, trying to maintain some composure while averting his eyes from hers, only to find them now locked on the satin V of her gown, and the ample breast that rested behind it. "Rumor has it that a group of riders were seen outside Southroad Keep on the early morning after the night of the abduction. Other sources indicate that there is a new prisoner in the keep's dungeon."

"Has anyone been dispatched to verify the identity of this prisoner?"

"Yes, y-y-y-your majesty," the ambassador stuttered, "but according to an easily bribed guard named Smagler, he is just a madman."

"And you trusted an easily bribed guard named *Smagler* to know the truth about an exceptionally sensitive matter like the imprisonment of the High Blade's own twin brother?" she barked, ready to arrange for the cowering diplomat to join his predecessor in the job.

"No your majesty," the ambassador quickly replied, a tone of pleading in his voice. "I then sent another of our spies to verify the identity of this madman, and see for himself. So he gained access to the dungeon, and snuck a peek into the new prisoner's cell."

"And. . . . ? You try my patience! What did he look like? Was he the High Blade's twin?"

"We do not know, your majesty," the ambassador said meekly.

"What do you mean we do not know? Was our spy captured?"

"No, your majesty. I just finished debriefing him."

"Well, what then?"

"It was the prisoner, your majesty."

"What about him? What did he look like?" she interrogated, losing her temper, and pummelling the pudgy ambassador with closed fists about his bald head and stooped shoulders. "I don't see what could have been so hard. The High Blade is the most recognizable of all this city's wretches!"

"He wore a mask, your majesty. A magically resistant, iron mask," the ambassador cried between sobs and moans of pain. "No matter how hard my spy tried, he just couldn't penetrate its ensorcellments."

The Tharchioness instantaneously regained her composure.

"He *must* be our prisoner, or else there can be no reason why my loving husband would be obscuring his identity."

"My spy also observed that the mask seemed to have a magical dampening effect within, as well as without."

The Tharchioness chuckled sinisterly.

"My husband has always been uneasy around magic. It is only to be expected that he would hobble the abilities of the mage-in-training."

With her fingertips, the First Princess gently massaged the tattoos that adorned the left side of her completely bald pate.

"The fact that his identity is concealed from the outside world is a point in our favor. It indicates that my dear husband is uneasy about his presence, and has no desire for his lovely citizens of Mulmaster to be made aware of it. We too must keep the existence of his brother secret." The Tharchioness turned and faced her ambassador who was regaining his composure after the physical interrogation that he had just been put through. "What of your spy?" she inquired calmly.

"I killed him," the ambassador replied, adding, "You stressed that absolute secrecy must be maintained, your majesty."

"Good," the Tharchioness agreed. "For the time being, secrecy must be maintained at all costs. Leave, worm. Your presence nauseates me."

"Yes, your majesty," the ambassador replied obsequiously, as he backed out of her ladyship's private chambers, dreading the day when his own usefulness would no longer outweigh the Tharchioness's desire for secrecy.

* * * * *

In the Dungeon of Southroad Keep:

Rassendyll looked at his strange visitor.

The dwarf seemed inordinately cheerful for a prisoner in a dungeon, or at least so thought the imprisoned young mage. Perhaps he was a spy.

The dwarf spoke again.

"I can't see your eyes with that funny coal bucket on your head, but I still think I can tell what you're thinking. You're probably saying to yourself, 'Self, who is this crazy old coot?' Well, I already answered that question, but I don't mind repeating myself. My name is Hoffman, and I am formerly of the Seventh Dwarven Abbey—of which I was senior abbot and protector of the legendary Seal of Robert, I might add—and I have been a prisoner down here for quite a long time, since before something that someone told me happened, the Time of Tremors, or something."

"You mean the Time of Troubles," the masked prisoner corrected.

"I might do, I might do," the dwarf assented. "You're probably also asking yourself, 'Self, can I trust this crazy old coot? Is he a spy? Is he a madman?' Well the answers to those questions in order are : yes, no, and maybe. The Seventh Dwarven Abbey was attacked by Zhent agents, and I alone survived. Once I had ascertained the safety of the Seal, I came to Mulmaster in search of help. The powers that be claimed I was a spy, threw me in the dungeon, and forgot about me. It is a fate worthy of a sole survivor . . . in a cosmic sense. Don't you agree?"

"I'm not sure," Rassendyll responded, not realizing the apparent similarity of their situations.

"Now what did a fine young fellow like yourself do to wind up in a place like this?" Hoffman quickly inquired.

"I don't know," Rassendyll replied, "and how do you know if I'm young or not?"

The dwarf started to laugh.

"Heckuba," Hoffman swore between guffaws, "just about everyone around here is young compared to me."

Unexpectedly, the dwarf's laughter was quickly halted and replaced by a racking cough that seemed to shake the former abbot's entire body. Rassendyll immediately came over to him in hopes of casting a spell to help him, but quickly realized he was unable to, and instead settled on putting his arm around the dwarf and helping him into a recline on the floor of the cell.

As soon as the coughing fit seemed to subside, Hoffman cocked his head to the side as if to listen for something, and said in an urgent whisper, "Quickly, the guards are coming, and they mustn't discover me here or it will go badly for both of us. I must return to my cell. Help me over to the tunnel, and return the stone to its place blocking it. I promise to return shortly, once the coast is clear."

Rassendyll helped the old and now obviously infirm dwarf over to the tunnel, through which the visitor quickly scurried. The masked prisoner had no sooner replaced the stone to its proper location, when a light was flashed through the small window in the cell's door.

"You there," a stern voice bellowed, "take your plate or go hungry, madman. Whatever you choose doesn't matter to me."

The light remained in the window, while Rassendyll crawled on hands and knees to the door. A plate had been placed at its base, and the young mage was barely able to reach it through a narrow slot in the door. The guard moved on as he began to eat. The food was rancid, and probably the most inedible sustenance that he ever encountered in his entire cloistered life, but as it had been over two days since he had last eaten, he managed to choke it all down.

Once his meal was over he replaced the plate through the slot at the base of the door and looked back at the stone that he had just recently put in place in hopes that the jolly gentleman with the long white beard would return as he had promised.

* * * * *

In the Captain's Quarters in Southroad Keep:

Rickman was not amused.

"Blough, what do you mean that itinerant thespian has disappeared?" he shouted.

The fearful Hawk maintained his composure, even though he knew that he had just told his commanding officer information contradictory to what he wanted to hear, and repeated his report.

"The thespian, a certain Passepout, son of Idle and Catinflas, was bailed out yesterday by person or persons unknown. After leaving the custody of the keep, he apparently disappeared. The city watch at the gate has no record of his having left Mulmaster in the past twenty-four hours, and he is not on the registry of any of the local inns. A drunkard matching his description may or may not have been at the Wave and Wink last night, but other than that we have no leads."

"Did you check the most recent roundup of vagrants that were picked up after tavern closing last night?"

"Yes, sir," the efficient Hawk replied. "I even checked with the officer on duty for last night's round up. According to him, Lieutenant Boston, the streets were free of human debris before sunrise. If he had passed out, he would have been found, sir."

Rickman made a minor adjustment of his eyepatch as he was wont to do while thinking. The thespian was obviously in hiding, but why? Surely he didn't have an inkling that his presence among the living was no longer desired by the Mulmaster powers that be. Where could he be?

"When he arrived in Mulmaster was he alone, or with someone?" the one-eyed Hawk captain inquired.

"According to the city watch officer who was on duty at the gate at that time," Blough answered, "he was alone."

Rickman readjusted his eye-patch once again. Tension usually brought on a certain degree of discomfort in his now vacant eye socket, as if the missing eye had somehow returned with an exceptionally annoying feeling of irritation and itchiness.

No stone must go unturned, the captain of the Hawks thought to himself, or the High Blade will have my head.

"Are there any other aliens who have arrived in Mulmaster within the last three days?" he demanded.

"I assume you mean above and beyond the normal merchants who travel in and out of the city like clockwork, paying the necessary duties as they sign in and out on schedule."

The captain of the Hawks answered with a quick nod.

"Well, there is the entire entourage of the First Princess of Thay," Blough answered, adding, "and because of their diplomatic immunity, none of them had to register . . ."

Great, Rickman thought to himself, the High Blade will have my head for sure.

". . . and there is one other," the efficient Hawk added, "a travel writer by the name of Volothamp Geddarm. According to the city watch on duty at the gate, he left Mulmaster early this morning, but has maintained his accommodations of two adjoining rooms at the Traveler's Cloak Inn for at least an additional week, paid in advance."

Volothamp Geddarm, the captain of the Hawks repeated to himself. Why does that name sound familiar?

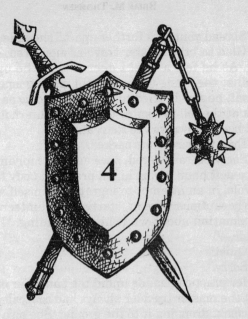

Miss Alliances

At the Retreat:

Volo did exactly as the voice he now recognized as female instructed, dropping the blade from his hand, and moving his arms away from his sides, palms out and empty. All of this was done slowly and carefully, without any sudden movements.

The master traveler of all Faerûn (if not all Toril) had no desire to drown in his own blood.

"Spread your legs further apart," she ordered.

"Glad to," the master traveler answered, complying. As he felt a slight decrease in the pressure against the blade that was still resting against his throat, he slowly tried to turn his head so as to get a look at the fellow visitor to the slaughterhouse that had been known as the Retreat.

"Eyes forward!" she barked.

"Sorry," he answered, once again complying, as he felt a deft hand giving him a practiced body frisk.

Volo, in an attempt to ingratiate himself with the overly cautious woman, started to volunteer certain information about what he was holding. "I have a bando—"

"Quiet!"

"Sorry."

Her practiced hands undid the bandolier of blades that the master traveler always had concealed under his cloak, dropping it to the ground. She also quickly removed several of his other concealed surprises (though missing a few that the master traveler thought better of volunteering).

The frisking done, the mystery woman made a strange request.

"Remove your hat," she ordered, "and do it slowly."

Volo slowly followed her instructions, eyes still forward, and legs still spread apart. With beret in hand, he felt her hand gently tug at his beard, and run through the flowing locks that covered the top of what he thought to be considered as one of the more handsome heads of Faerûn.

"Well, at least I don't have to worry about you being one of those murderous wizards from Thay," she said. "You can turn around, but very slowly, hands still away from the sides of your body, and no funny stuff."

"Gladly, my dear," Volo answered in his most charming tone, as he slowly turned around to face the woman who had come very close to slitting his throat. "Your wish is my command."

She was slightly taller than the master traveler himself, and was attired in a garb more suited to a ranger than the ravishing beauty that she was. Her tight leathers enveloped an obviously well endowed and maintained figure, and her flowing brown hair seemed to reach the base of her back, barely obscuring the long sword that was sheathed behind her.

Drawing on his extensive knowledge of all things public, and most things private and secret in Faerûn, Volo hazarded a jibe.

"Is that a long sword," he asked with a light gesture from his left hand, then added jovially, "or are you just happy to see me?"

The female ranger ignored the double entendre, and answered simply, "What if it is?"

"Then Storm Silverhand sends her regards," the master traveler responded, "as I assume that I am addressing Chesslyn Onaubra."

"How do you know the legendary bard of Shadowdale?" she interrogated.

"Know her," Volo quickly answered, trying appear more at ease than he really was. "I've stayed at her farm on numerous occasions." He then quickly changed the subject, shifting focus back to the armed and deadly woman who was standing in front of him. "Rumor has it that you can hurl that long sword for a distance of up to fifty feet. How much of an exaggeration is that?"

"It isn't an exaggeration," she replied, letting her guard drop ever so slightly. "And what is the name of this loquacious friend of Storm Silverhand's who seems to know so much about me?"

Volo quickly replaced his beret, which sat atop his head just long enough so that he could once again remove it with a flourish and a bow saying, "Volothamp Geddarm, master traveler of all Faerûn, at your service."

The Harper secret agent known as Chesslyn Onaubra shook her brown locks with a guarded laugh and an amused chuckle and said, "I should have known." Extending a hand of friendship to the master traveler, she added, "And what brings the master traveler and scourge of the dopplegangers to the Moonsea?"

"A new book," he answered, jovially accepting the Harper's proffered hand, "what else? Though it would appear that more is going on here than would usually be included in one of my travel guides."

"Agreed," Chesslyn assented seriously, withdrawing a blood-stained crystal wand from her pack and holding it up for the master gazetteer to examine.

* * * * *

The Office of the High Blade
in the Tower of the Blades:

"Sire," Rickman cautiously interrupted, "a word with you if I may?"

"What is it Rickman?" the High Blade answered impatiently. The rigors and demands of dealing with the lesser nobles who, in the eyes of the people, really ruled the city, always left him in a bad mood, and he always saw interruptions to his business affairs as merely means to prolong his own bureaucratic misery.

"In private, sire?" the captain of the Hawks whispered with a degree of urgency.

"As you will," the High Blade assented, and quickly dispersed the nonessential politicians with whom he had been dealing with quick directions. "Leave me now," he ordered brusquely, "and don't return until you have a concrete plan for restoring our navy in half the time you are currently projecting."

"Yes, sire," the nobles all said in unison, though the looks on their faces indicated that such a task was almost impossible, and that they would be spending the next few weeks avoiding the High Blade in order to dodge his wrath when he discovered their gross failings. They quickly fled the office of their supreme commander.

"Well, that should keep them out of my hair for a while," the High Blade said with a fiendish chuckle. "Now what did you deem to be so important that it was worth incurring my ire by interrupting the second most unpleasant part of my day?"

"The second, sire?"

"The first being waking up to discover myself next to the Tharchioness, who still happens to be breathing."

"Yes, sire," Rickman acknowledged, quickly returning to the matter at hand. "In an effort to, how shall I say, tie up all of the loose ends, I am afraid that I have discovered one that is not all that easy to tie up."

"How so?"

"That thespian who was released yesterday."

"Yes?" demanded the High Blade, beginning to loose patience.

"We can't locate him."

The High Blade could barely contain the rage that had been building within him since he had first discovered his wife's plot against him. The captain of the Hawks hastened to continue his debriefing.

"My spies have narrowed down the source of his sanctuary to two possible allies in the city."

"So he is still in Mulmaster?" Selfaril asked. "Are you sure of this?"

"The city watch at the gate is quite confident he has not left the city walls since his release from Southroad Keep."

"Well that is a small consolation," the High Blade acknowledged. "Who are these possible allies? Spies and agents within the city perhaps? Maybe a Harper agent?"

"No, your majesty," Rickman replied with great confidence and surety. "My sources are quite confident that organizations such as the Harpers and their ilk have no presence within the city walls of Mulmaster. The Cloaks constantly scan the area with their psionic surveillance, and have always come up empty. Harper interference is the least of our problems."

"Go on," the High Blade instructed, relieved that one of his fears was unfounded, though still perturbed by the amount of dancing around the truth that Rickman seemed to be doing. "So who are these potential allies of this common itinerant thespian whom your men saw fit to release?"

Rickman tried to skip over the reference to the incompetence of his men and continued. "Since we have safely ruled out all normal residential city inhabitants, this reduces our suspects to recent arrivals to the city."

"Agreed."

"Unfortunately, your majesty, our most likely candidate is one of your wife's people, or more specifically someone in her entourage."

Selfaril's composure began to slip again.

"You mean this so-called harmless itinerant thespian was a Thayan spy!" he shouted, confident that the soundproof walls of his office prevented anyone from eavesdropping. "Your men released from their custody a Thayan spy!"

"No, your majesty," Rickman quickly tried to explain. "What I meant to say was that your wife's people, for some reason presently unknown to us, might be offering him refuge."

Selfaril winced at Rickman's repeated use of the phrase "your wife's," but continued his interrogation nonetheless.

"You said there were two possible allies for the thespian within the city. Who is the other one?"

"A writer of some renown who arrived at the city the day after the thespian. One Volothamp Geddarm, guide book author and world traveler," the captain of the Hawks explained. "Curiously enough, he seems to have secured himself accommodations for two, though the city watch reported that he entered the city alone."

"Well, have him arrested," Selfaril ordered matter-of-factly. "If he knows the location of your harmless thespian, we'll no doubt get it out of him with torture. If not, we will at least have succeeded in ridding Faerûn of one more annoyance. If there is one thing worse than an itinerant actor, it's an itinerant writer. Believe me, he won't be missed."

"Unfortunately, at least according to the city watch, it would appear that he has already left the city, though there is every indication that he plans on returning as he has maintained his lodgings at the Traveler's Cloak Inn, paid in advance."

Selfaril fingered his carefully coifed beard with a neatly manicured fingernail that he kept sharp enough to draw blood.

"Issue a warrant for his arrest and for the thespian

as well," the High Blade ordered. "Search his lodgings immediately and confiscate his belongings. If anyone asks what he is suspected of, be vague, but leave the implication that they are both involved with a plot to kill my dear sweet wife, just to make it interesting."

"Yes, your majesty," Rickman replied, admiring the deceitful mastery that the High Blade choreographed as he tightened the noose around the Thayan bitch's neck. "And are there any new instructions concerning your brother, sire?"

The High Blade gave his second a glare that could only be described as a death look.

"Rickman," Selfaril said in an ominously controlled voice, "you are quite valuable to me, but not so valuable that I would hesitate having you permanently removed in a millisecond should the mood strike me. It would be in your best interest to refrain in the future from the use of any familial terms in my presence. Do you understand?"

"Yes, your majesty," Rickman replied, his lone eye averted and downcast.

"As for the prisoner," Selfaril concluded, "there are no new orders. I can't imagine that we will have to keep him alive much longer. Soon he will be used to embarrass the Tharchioness by exposing her seditious plot, and after that, he will be disposed of. For the time being, he's harmless, and he's not going anywhere."

* * * * *

At the Traveler's Cloak Inn:

Passepout, though he had slept well past the midday point, was still quite groggy, and slightly queasy from the previous night's merriment.

A sensible individual would probably have taken things easy, until his hangover had passed. Unfortunately the chubby thespian's mammoth appetite had no desire to be ruled by common sense, and as a result Passepout soon found himself in the dining room placing a food order that at once combined the sustenance and bulk of a midnight snack, breakfast, brunch, and lunch.

"You'll be sorry," the usually understanding and accommodating Dela advised.

The chubby thespian just harumphed back at her, trying to clear his head of the miasma of Morpheus, and paying no mind to the worldly wisdom offered by the best hostler in all Mulmaster.

When the plate was placed in front of him, he immediately dug in without so much as a thank you or other acknowledgement for the efforts of the hard working innkeeper.

True to the advisement of Dela, he was midway through his second plateful when his stomach revolted, and his faced turned a sickly color of pea green.

Dela, who had been keeping a close eye on her least favorite guest of the moment, decided that she had taken quite enough abuse up to this point. She strode over to the chair that was straining under the weight of the heavy thespian and, taking him by the collar, none too gently escorted him to the door.

"There will be no getting sick in the Traveler's Cloak Inn for as long as I'm still the proprietor," she sternly instructed. "I don't care if you are a friend of Volothamp Geddarm's, or not. You are an embarrassment to all of the well-mannered gentlemen who have passed through these doors before you. I don't care where you go, just don't come back here until you have learned yourself some manners."

The portly thespian tried to protest but found himself unable to hold back the upcoming deluge from his stomach and formulate words at the same time. Passepout instead concentrated on just keeping from passing out.

Releasing the actor's collar, and with a little bit of encouragement from the sole of her shoe, Dela propelled the green-faced thespian out into the Mulmaster city streets, where the human projectile quickly wandered off, and passed out.

Moments later, Dela's afternoon tea was interrupted by a contingent of Hawks with a warrant for the arrest and confiscation of goods for both Volothamp Geddarm and Passepout, son of Idle and Catinflas.

Dela, the perfect innkeeper, informed the guards that both guests were no longer on the premises, and that if either of them returned, she would immediately inform the local authorities.

Mentally she added in her own mind, once I've warned them and sent them on their way, of course.

Dela had no desire to alienate either the local authorities or her guests, which is probably why she was considered to be a model innkeeper for all Faerûn.

* * * * *

In the dungeon of Southroad Keep:

A light was flashed once again through the window in Rassendyll's cell, when the guard retrieved the plate that had previously borne the slop that had been dinner. As the footsteps of the guards retreated off into the distance, Rassendyll waited for the return of his visitor.

Seconds stretched into moments, moments into hours, hours into immeasurable blocks of time that felt like years, yet the abbé Hoffman did not return.

Rassendyll reflected as he waited. Before the arrival of the dwarf, he had despaired and welcomed death, accepting it and his own continued captivity as inevitable and beyond his own ken.

The appearance of the cheerful dwarf had changed all of that. Maybe his inevitable fate was not all that cut and dried after all. True, his magical abilities and secrets had left him, and he was imprisoned in a hideous mask of iron in the bowels of a Mulmaster dungeon, but no matter what he had thought before, he was far from helpless and the time for action had arrived.

Rassendyll decided that it was time to take control of his destiny for the first time in his cloistered life. If an old dwarf has the spark of life within him, why not a mage-in-training?

Checking the small window in the door for a guard who might overhear his actions, and finding the coast to be clear, he moved away the blocking stone from the tunnel entrance, and with great care to avoid the telltale sounds of metal on rock caused by the hitting of the mask against the dungeon wall, Rassendyll shimmied through the entrance and crawled through the dwarf's tunnel.

The girth of the dwarf's torso necessitated a wide tunnel so the masked prisoner had little trouble moving through it. Within seconds, he arrived at its apparent end, and carefully pushed a stone not unlike the one on his end of the tunnel away, and hauled himself up into the dwarf's cell.

Hoffman was resting with his back against the cell wall. His eyes were closed and his breathing was unduly labored.

Rassendyll's heart sank. It appeared that his newly found reason for living was in his final hours.

As the masked mage moved the stone in place, he accidentally hit his head. The clang, soft as it was, announced his presence, and the dwarf opened his eyes.

"I have company, I see," Hoffman said with a weak grin.

"Good manners required that I return the neighborly visit," Rassendyll replied, approaching the infirm dwarf. He was shocked by how sickly the dwarf now appeared, when he had seemed so robust, not counting the coughing fit, when he had visited Rassendyll's cell earlier.

Hoffman instinctively read the look of surprise that existed beneath the mask on his fellow prisoner's face. "I hope you don't mind me not going to the effort of casting a keeping up appearances spell. It would take a bit too much out of me at the present moment."

"Not at all," Rassendyll replied, his grin obscured by the iron mask.

"You were going to tell me how you wound up with that coal bucket on your head," the dwarf reminded him.

"A blind wizard smith put it on me at the direction of a cruel but handsome looking man who resembled myself."

"Tell me a little more about this good looking fellow, the bad guy. You can fill me in about yourself a little later."

"He was dressed in silken robes with fur trim, and around his neck was a pendant of a blood-encrusted dagger. The blood was made up of red gemstones. Rubies, maybe," Rassendyll tried to recall.

"That pendant represents the office of the High

Blade of Mulmaster. I believe that the tormentor who looks just like you is the tyrant Selfaril himself. Rumors pass occasionally through these dungeon walls, and I recall that he ascended to the throne after killing his own father," the dwarf explained. "Are you sure that you resemble him?"

"Indeed," Rassendyll replied. "If I could remove this mask, I would show you."

"Don't even try," Hoffman advised with a cough. "It is clearly ensorcelled. I'm afraid that not even during my younger years would I have been able to defeat a spell as strong as this one."

"It also seems to have removed all of my own spellcasting abilities."

"You were a spellcaster?" the enfeebled dwarf inquired.

"A mage-in-training," Rassendyll explained. "I had been in training for my entire life. Now, all those years have been wasted."

"Maybe not," Hoffman asserted. "Though the ability to do is desirable, the ability to wield and recognize is also of great benefit."

"I don't understand."

"The enchanted metal of the mask acts as both an insulator and a leeching conductor of your magical abilities and spells. It prevents any spells formed within from being cast out, while conducting the knowledge and innate powers from within, onto its metallic surface, and eventually causing them to dissipate in the air around you. What it doesn't do is prevent you from using the general knowledge you obtained in your studies, such things as recognizing spells that are cast by others or using magically powered artifacts and objects."

Rassendyll chuckled at the dwarf's optimistic observations. "Little good those vestiges of my training will do me here," he said, trying not to sound too despairing in the presence of the obviously dying dwarf.

"Don't be too sure," Hoffman replied, his voice weakening rapidly. "My years of tunneling around here are coming to an end. Originally I had an agreement with the former resident of your cell, that when my time had come I would aid him in his escape from this hateful place."

"What happened to the former resident?" Rassendyll asked.

"He died at the hands of an overly playful guard, whose solution to the boredom of his regular duties was torturing the prisoners. In Kupfer's case, he went a little too far."

"Oh."

"When a person dies in the keep, their body is placed in a sack with a weight and dropped down the same drain that the garbage goes. It leads to an underground canal that eventually empties out into the Moonsea. The dead are bagged and weighted before the dinner service, and then collected on the same trip they retrieve the plates. I've seen it happen many times over, and it runs like clockwork. You can tell when it happens. The guards ring a bell to signal that someone has to bring down a sack and a weight."

"Kupfer and I," Hoffman continued, "hatched a plan that when one of us died, the other would sneak into the cell, and trade places with him in the sack, on the off chance that there was a chance of surviving the underground trip out to sea."

"Was Kupfer a dwarf too?" Rassendyll asked, intrigued by the plan.

"No," Hoffman answered, his voice hardly a whisper, "he was a firbolg."

"Don't you think they would have noticed the difference in the size and weight?"

"Not with this, they wouldn't," the dwarf explained holding out a charm. "Don't touch it. I'm not too sure how long it will last in close contact with that mask of yours. It transmits an aura of disguise so that, for a limited amount of time, the guards will believe that the burden they are carrying is actually the mass of the previous bearer of the charm."

The dwarf carefully placed it back in the pouch beneath his beard, making sure that the young used-to-be mage-in-training saw exactly where he kept it.

"Now quickly return from whence you came," Hoffman instructed, "and just let old abbé Hoffman die in peace. I am old and it is about time. When you hear the bell, wait for the dinner service to begin, and then hightail it on over here. Drag my body back to your cell, being sure to place it in the darkest corner possible. We only have to be able to trick the watch once. Then take my place in the sack, and go with Dumathoin, my son. Perhaps you will be able to find someone who can remove that coal bucket from your head."

Rassendyll was saddened by the weakening condition of his newfound friend.

"Maybe you're being a bit premature about this whole thing," he offered.

The dwarf shook his head slightly.

"Nope," Hoffman replied, starting another frightful coughing fit. "Afraid not. I'll be gone by dinner, and with any luck you'll be gone not too much later."

"Why should I benefit from your death?" a tearful Rassendyll asked.

"Because it would be a darn no good waste of a near perfect escape plan, that's why," Hoffman replied. "Now back to your cell, and let me die in peace."

Rassendyll returned to his cell to meditate on the

opportunity that had been presented to him. His thoughts were soon interrupted by the clear tolling of a bell.

It tolls for he, Rassendyll thought to himself, and he steeled himself for the hours ahead.

As Hoffman had indicated, the evening meal came like clockwork, and as soon as he heard the guards move on, he set his plate to the side, and shimmied back down the tunnel.

Hoffman's body had already been placed in the sack, a weight carefully attached to its end.

Carefully, the masked prisoner removed the body of the dwarf from its low-budget shroud, being sure to remove the charm from around its neck. He then pushed the corpse of his recently acquired friend back through the tunnel and up into his cell where he placed it, as instructed, in the shadow-most corner. He then placed his plate back outside of the door, and raced back down the tunnel, pulling the blocking rock back into place behind him, and rushed at breakneck speed back to Hoffman's cell hoping that he would be able to beat the guards there, be disguised by the powers of the old dwarf's charm, deceive the guards, and survive the trip downstream and out to sea.

He realized that all of the odds were long, but knew that the gamble would be worth it because it was the only game in town and he was no longer content to just wait for death.

No sooner did he cinch the sack shut from the inside, than Rassendyll heard the lock to the door of the cell being opened, and two guards coming inside. Rassendyll clutched Hoffman's charm to his bosom, desperately trying to keep it from making contact with the magic-leeching iron mask. Please work long enough to get me out of here, he prayed.

With a heave-ho one of the guards hoisted the burial sack over his shoulder, magically unaware of its newly added bulk.

"Good riddance," said the guard who opened the doors for his corpse-laden associate. "That's one less prisoner to keep an eye on."

"And one less dwarf to blight Mulmaster," the other added, as they ventured further into the keep's bowels, toward the entrance to the sewer.

Rassendyll could smell the stench of sewage getting closer when he heard the guard who was carrying him complain: "Gee, I must be out of shape. This dwarf is getting awfully heavy."

Rassendyll prayed that the spell would last just a little while longer.

The guard stopped for a moment, and the masked prisoner expected to have his presence revealed at any moment.

One guard opened a trap, releasing an aromatic draught of sewage stench. The other guard shifted the weight of his burden and carefully, so as not to entangle himself in the shroud's downward descent, dropped what he thought to be the corpse-filled sack down into the sewer below.

Before the sack made its splash in the water below, Rassendyll thought he heard an alarm sound in the chambers above. His disappearance had been discovered, but he was already on his way down the drain and out to sea.

5

Under Currents

In the Tharchioness's Boudoir
in the Tower of the Wyvern:

"Your majesty," the ambassador said in urgent
hushed tones, momentarily forgetting the breaches
of protocol that he had just committed.

"Silence, worm!" the First Princess of Thay ordered. "My husband is on his way. My spy in the
Tower of the Blades believes that he intends on con-

fronting me with evidence of our conspiracy."

"But your majesty—"

"Silence! Do you wish to join the ranks of your predecessors? Don't try my patience! I must concentrate before he gets here. It will require all of my feminine wiles to distract him."

"The prisoner escaped!" the ambassador blurted out, just as the Tharchioness's backhand made contact with his doughy cheek.

"What did you say?" she asked, her hand poised to strike again.

"My spy in Southroad Keep just informed me that all havoc has broken out due to the escape of a certain prisoner. Two guards have already been executed for gross incompetence."

"Have they recovered the prisoner yet?"

"Not according to my sources, your highness," the ambassador answered, his head still ringing from the last blow.

"Is there anything else I should know, worm?"

"Only that the last words of the executed guards were that they were sure he was dead—drowned, or something."

"Did they find the body?"

"No," the ambassador answered cautiously. "They believe it was washed out to sea."

The Tharchioness stroked her own brow seductively.

Well, this does change things, she thought. No body, no evidence. No evidence, no conspiracy. It would appear that my dear husband has snatched a stalemate out of the jaws of victory. I will have to comfort the dear lad.

The Tharchioness let loose a fiendish laugh, and continued to apply her makeup. The ambassador took the opportunity of his mistress's distraction to escape from her boudoir with his life in hope that she had already forgotten his several infractions of protocol.

Once in the safety of the public hallway, the ambassador breathed a sigh of relief at having cheated death yet again.

* * * * *

In the Courtyard Between
the Towers of the Blade and the Wyvern:

"What do you mean he's *gone?*" the High Blade demanded.

"We believe him to be dead, sire," Rickman explained. "My experts believe that the sheer weight of the iron mask would have made it quite impossible for him to swim, and that he would undoubtedly have drowned before he even reached the open sea."

"How can we be sure?" Selfaril demanded.

"We can't, sire," the Hawk captain conceded. "The men responsible for this severe foul-up have already been executed."

"That is not good enough," the High Blade blustered. "Your Hawks have been slipping. First, they could not hold onto a possible witness to our plans, even though you yourself thought him to be nothing but an itinerant thespian. Now, they have allowed the prisoner to escape."

"There was no way he could have survived, your highness. It is obvious that we underestimated the suicidal lengths a desperate man would stoop to."

"Indeed," the High Blade answered. "Rickman, I am holding you personally responsible for cleaning up after this mess. There must be no evidence left that the prisoner ever existed."

"At least he is not in Thayan hands, sire."

"That is small consolation. Evidence of their seditious plan was all I needed to castrate my bitch of a wife. Now things are just back to status quo."

A Thayan courtier appeared out of nowhere.

"Your majesty," the courtier said, "the First Princess is waiting for you in her boudoir. She saw you coming across the courtyard from her window, and was troubled by what was possibly detaining you. Is everything all right?"

"Everything is fine," the High Blade announced with a roll of his eyes that only Rickman noticed. "Tell my dearest bride that I will be there directly."

The courtier gave one final message.

"Sire, the First Princess said to tell you that she would be counting the minutes," the Thayan said, and returned to his post.

As am I, the High Blade thought, to your death!

Selfaril turned back to Rickman, delaying his trip back to his wife even further. A thought had just crossed his mind, and he was grinning in fiendish glee.

"Have your men returned from the Retreat with the bloodstained wand yet?" he inquired.

"No, your majesty," Rickman replied.

"Notify me immediately when they do," Selfaril instructed. "The Retreat was under Mulmaster's protection, and I would hate to see the unfortunate slaughter of those wizards turn into a diplomatic hot potato, if you know what I mean."

"Yes, your majesty," Rickman replied, understanding what the High Blade was planning. "It wouldn't be the same as a plot against the throne."

"No," Selfaril agreed, "but sometimes we have to settle for the next best thing."

* * * * *

At the Retreat:

"Where did you find that?" Volo asked the lovely Chesslyn.

"Over by the ugly monk's body, out by the gate," she replied. "It's obviously Thayan in origin. That's why I checked your head for tattoos. I thought you might be one of those Red Wizard murderers."

"So you believe that this mass slaughter was the product of a Thayan invasion?"

"That's what it looks like to me," she replied.

Volo fingered his beard and thought for a moment. The master traveler was no stranger to matters of bloodshed and the like, having survived numerous deadly altercations on his journeys around Toril. Pteramen, murderous Mazticans, and deadly dopplegangers—he had survived them all.

"That still doesn't explain why there was no sign of a struggle," he asserted, suspicious of the circumstances at hand. "Though the elders of the Retreat welcomed all refugees, I see little reason that they would open their gates to an armed contingent of Red Wizards. I—"

"Quiet!" she hushed with great urgency. "I hear horses. We'd better hide."

Volo looked from side to side, and then at his trusty steed.

"What should I do with him?" he inquired in a whisper.

"In here," she instructed, quickly leading him to a shed, then explaining, "It's where I put my horse when I heard you coming."

"If you heard me coming, why didn't you respond to my whistle?"

"Later," she answered.

When they had stowed the master traveler's horse

next to that of the secret Harper agent, they closed the doors, and took a ladder up to the shed's roof.

"This gives us a perfect vantage point to see and hear our new arrivals without being seen or heard ourselves," Chesslyn explained.

"Are you sure?" the master traveler asked.

"Well, it worked when I was watching you," she replied.

They had no sooner reached their vantage point when the Hawks named Wattrous and Jembahb entered the courtyard.

"Look at this mess!" Wattrous said. The older weasel-like Hawk was barely able to control the gorge that was working its way up his throat.

"What are we supposed to be looking for?" the younger and taller Hawk inquired, apparently oblivious to the stench of the rapidly rotting bodies.

"Captain Rickman said there should be something by the body of the bald guy at the gate," the shorter and senior Hawk instructed, "but there doesn't seem to be anything there."

"How did he . . ." Chesslyn said a little louder than Volo felt comfortable with.

"Quiet!" the master traveler hushed, then added in a whisper, "Later."

"Well, if it's not here, let's leave," Jembahb said. "This place gives me the creeps."

Volo cupped his hands together, and blowing through them, carefully made the sound of an undead specter advancing into the daylight. He could tell that Wattrous recognized the sound; the Hawk instantly became wide-eyed and frantically looked from side to side.

"Good idea," he quickly replied to his junior Hawk, valiantly trying not to show his fear, but then adding, "but you have to be the one to tell Rickman."

"No problem," Jembahb replied as they remounted their horses. "But where will you be?"

"I have business in Hillsfar," the weasel-like Wattrous quickly replied, saying the first thing that came to mind. He thought to himself, knowing how Rickman dealt with an undesirable report, maybe Hillsfar wasn't such a bad idea. Perhaps he could join the Plumes. Jembahb was a nice enough guy, trusting and naive, and would, therefore, be the perfect scapegoat for their failure to complete their mission as directed. Yes. Hillsfar would be just far enough to save his own skin.

As the two Hawks set off back for Mulmaster, the Harper secret agent and the master traveler lowered themselves from their hiding place.

* * * * *

The Sewers Beneath Mulmaster:

Rassendyll felt a sensation of falling rapidly through midair, which was quickly followed by the slap and splash of the weighted burial sack's contact with the rapidly moving river of sewage-spoiled waters.

The thick viscosity of the underground fluid coated the burial shroud amniotically, without managing to permeate the sack itself. As a result, as long as the masked prisoner was able to hold the top cinch of the sack tightly closed, no air was able to escape, and for at least a few brief moments Rassendyll was able to breathe within the linen-lined bubble that was cascading through the underwater tunnels of Mulmaster.

The masked prisoner realized that he had to time his escape from the sack very carefully: too soon and he would be wasting precious drops of air that he might need before finishing his journey out to sea; too late and he would find himself too far below the depths of the icy Moonsea, and long drowned before reaching the surface.

The sheer power of the sewer stream propelled the bag and its contents forward, the leaded weight that was attached to it occasionally dragging against the bottom of the downward tunnel. Battered, bruised, and bounced around, Rassendyll struggled to listen to the tell-tale tones of the burial rock that would eventually drag the sack to the sea bottom. He knew that when the sound stopped and the ride smoothed out, that the course would have changed from forward to downward, and that only seconds would remain for him to escape and head to the surface.

It was only when he turned his head to the side and felt the drag of the iron mask against the linen lining did he remember that he too would be weighted down even after he left the sack. As this moment of realization hit him, he realized that the change of course had begun.

Seeing no rational alternative, he braced himself for the liquid onslaught, opened the sack, and valiantly kicked toward the surface, the weight of the mask resting heavily upon his shoulders.

* * * * *

On the Shore of the Moonsea:

Passepout's head hurt.

The last thing he remembered clearly was staggering out of the Traveler's Cloak Inn, and walking down an alleyway. From there, things seemed to blur. Pressmen hitting him over the head. Passing out. Waking up on a boat. Getting sick to his stomach. Being thrown overboard.

It had not been a good day.

Somehow aided by the buoyancy of his bulk, he had managed to float ashore. The hefty thespian groaned as he rolled his bulk on to his side for a cursory survey of the area. He opened his eyes for a quick look, and closed them even more quickly than he had intended due to the glare of the sun off the surf. He felt like a beached whale after the tide had gone out.

What could go wrong now? he thought to himself.

Carefully opening his eyes again, and shielding them from the setting sun, he surveyed his surroundings, and discovered that somehow his foot had gotten entangled in a pile of rags and a metal bucket.

Shaking his foot to get it loose, he was met with a surprise: the pile of rags and the coal bucket had started to move.

The stout and brave thespian quickly returned to unconsciousness as he fainted.

PART TWO

**The Swordsman,
the High Blade,
his Wife,
&
his Brother**

6

In Morning

*The High Blade's Study
in the Tower of the Wyvern:*

A new day had just dawned and once again the High Blade had stolen from the connubial chamber that housed his cursed marriage bed and loathsome spouse prior to first light—in order to avoid any possibility of having to converse with his despicable bride—and proceeded to his morning meal. Slater,

his valet, whose sleeping accommodations varied
from night to night so as to be available at his master's first stirring, had anticipated the High Blade's
impulse and had risen from the folded-down pallet
outside the door of the couple's chamber prior to his
master's stirring. The faithful servant held his master's silk and fur morning robe in readiness for a
quick escape to the secret study where Selfaril could
enjoy the early morning serenity.

Once his master was safely ensconced in his
study, Slater was free to fetch the High Blade's
breakfast without fear of his master being disturbed
by anyone but his closest confidantes, which, of
course, did not include the Tharchioness.

The sun had just peeked over the horizon, thus
signaling the next change of the city watch, when
Selfaril's breakfast arrived, not borne by Slater as he
had expected, but by Rickman.

Selfaril immediately realized that the captain of
the Hawks must have been bearing important information or he wouldn't have risked the High Blade's
ire at having his breakfast interrupted. He also realized that the information at hand would probably
not be to his liking.

"Ah, Rickman," the High Blade said, addressing
his right-hand man with deprecating sarcasm, "perhaps, you are auditioning for a new position that is
more in line with the limited abilities of you and
your men."

The captain of the Hawks held his tongue for a
moment to allow the invective that was almost on
his lips to pass into silence to be replaced by a
simple, "If that is what you wish, sire."

"I wish for many things," the High Blade responded, beginning to dine off the tray that the captain was carrying. Rickman's inner instinct for

survival prevented him from interrupting the High Blade by placing the tray on its usual place on the table.

"I wish that I had never married that traitorous she-devil," the High Blade continued. "I wish that I had acquired Thay as my domain rather than the Tharchioness as my bride. I wish that the ineptitude of your men had not bungled away the means by which my wishes might have been fulfilled."

Rickman stood stone-still, despite the tongue-lashing that coupled the strain that the heavily laden tray was bringing to bear on his awkwardly poised forearms. He knew that the High Blade already acknowledged his own disgust with the stupidity, ignorance, and ill-luck of a few of his men who had already borne the lethal brunt of his own anger.

Having finished two eggs from which he had taken his time delicately removing the shells, Selfaril drank a draught of juice, and, with a swipe of a napkin, wiped the breakfast residue from his mouth.

"Don't just stand there holding that tray," the High Blade ordered. "Put it down and pour me a cup of coffee."

Rickman did as instructed and turned around to pour the pot.

"You may as well pour yourself a cup as well," Selfaril added, the sharpness of his tongue slowly disappearing.

"As you wish, sire," the captain of the Hawks answered, adding, "I don't mind if I do."

When he turned back to face Selfaril, and placed his cup in front of him, he noticed that the High Blade's robe had loosened when he had used the napkin, and that three apparently fresh parallel lacerations of no less than three inches each were visible on his master's bare chest. The High Blade

was scratching them absently, not even realizing
what he was doing until he noticed Rickman's stare.

Rickman quickly averted his eyes, and returned
his attention to the placement of the coffee cup.

"Oh, sit," Selfaril instructed with a dismissive gesture.

Rickman sat, his body still at attention. Inwardly
he was bemoaning his momentary lapses in deco-
rum: his overly familiar acceptance of the High
Blade's offer to join him in coffee, and his conspicu-
ous staring at the scratches.

Selfaril discerned the uneasiness of his very necessary right-hand man, and immediately tried to set
him at ease. He had punished him enough for the
moment, and further castigation could wait 'til later.

The High Blade took a drink of his coffee, then set
it down on the desk before him. Once again he began
to scratch at the scabbed lacerations on his chest.
Rickman's eyes involuntarily followed the path of
Selfaril's hand, then quickly darted back to the High
Blade's eyes which met his own dead on.

The High Blade maintained his locked-on stare
for a moment, blinked, then cast his own eyes down
on the source of his epidermal irritation, and with a
chuckle slightly tinged with exasperation, resumed
scratching.

"The First Princess was a little ferocious in her
friskiness last night," the High Blade explained with
a grin. "Blast, if only she didn't have a brain she
would be a perfect wife."

"Sire?" Rickman responded, not quite sure of how
he was supposed to react.

"I mean it," Selfaril continued, trying to put the
captain at ease. "It's a pity that she wants to depose
me as much as I want to depose her." The High Blade
swallowed another mouthful of coffee, and feeling al-

most fully awake, readied himself for the first disappointment of the day. He asked, "Well Rickman, breakfast is finished. You may ruin my day now. What is the latest on the situation at hand?"

Rickman drained his own cup, and began his report.

"My information is mixed at best, sire," the captain of the Hawks explained.

"Has anyone discovered my brother's body yet?"

"No, sire, and I am confident that no one will. The harbor has been filled with ships as of late. Several of them are from our allies who have agreed to assist us in the rebuilding of our navy, while others are from certain other interests whose press gangs we have allowed to harvest our detritus in exchange for certain considerations. My spies in the ranks of both have indicated no sightings of bodies in the harbor or beyond. I believe it is safe to assume that his drowned corpse is either hung up in a subterranean sewer alcove, or safely resting at the bottom of the Moonsea itself."

"You must be right," Selfaril agreed, scratching his chest. "I realized that the mask would be the death of him, just not quite that way."

"According to my experts in the Cloaks," Rickman expounded, "the mask itself is only adhered to the flesh that surrounds the back of the skull. Once the flesh has decayed, the mask will separate and fall off. At that point, the features of your brother's face will have already fallen prey to the appetites of the scavengers that crawl along the bottom of the Moonsea. It will have ceased to be recognizable and, therefore, no longer of any use to anyone."

"Well, that is one small consolation," Selfaril acknowledged. "What about that missing actor?"

"Still unaccounted for, the same for the writer, I'm

afraid," Rickman replied. "Though without the prisoner, any claims by them would be unsubstantiated. They cease to be a major threat, particularly with foreigners."

"Agreed," the High Blade assented, "but I still want them dead. One can't be too careful."

"Agreed, sire," the captain repeated, adding. "I assure you that they will soon be joining the ranks of those men who have failed to perform up to your expectations."

"Good."

"If I might also mention, your majesty, those ranks have just swelled with another addition."

"Who have we executed for their incompetence this time?"

"A Hawk by the name of Jembahb, sire," Rickman explained. "He was one of the two men I sent to retrieve the Thayan crystal wand as evidence of the Tharchioness's people's involvement in the slaughter at the Retreat."

"What did he do?"

"He returned without the wand. He claimed that he couldn't find it, even though they were clearly told where it had been left. The other Hawk, a weasel named Wattrous, appears to have deserted. No doubt he realized the penalty for failure. A price has been put on his head, and I expect to have it on my mantle shortly."

"Good."

"Before his sentence was meted out, Jembahb did mention running into a thief on the way back to Mulmaster who claimed to have been paralyzed by a great and powerful wizard whose appearance matches the description of that writer Geddarm. Unfortunately the incompetent failed to bring him in. I have men patrolling the area with orders to retrieve him."

"That will have to do," the High Blade acknowledged, not happy with many of the implications.

"As to the incriminating evidence of Thayan involvement in the slaughter at the Retreat, I have dispatched another assignment of Hawks to scour the place, and then burn it to the ground. If we are unable to find that which we seek, we will at least remove any evidence that might incriminate us in the unpleasant matters that have taken place there."

"Indeed," Selfaril acknowledged, "it would appear that at the present time we will have to settle for a return to the status quo as a temporary victory."

"Unfortunately," the captain said, his eyes downcast in shame, "I am afraid that I will have to agree with you."

"It amounts to a stalemate with my mate, and I hate stalemates almost as much as I hate her."

* * * * *

Off the Road
Twixt Mulmaster and the Retreat:

Honor Fullstaff arose from his slumbers, and stretched, noticing the warming rays of the already risen sun. He hadn't intended on sleeping so long (despite the fact that he always did), and, blaming it on his sumptuous meal of the night before (which was no more sumptuous than his normal dinner fare) resolved to make better use of his early morning hours on the morrow (a daily resolution), and perhaps partake of an predawn walk that might help to reduce his physical bulk that he feared was rapidly going to flab.

Fullstaff rubbed his eyes, stretched again, and scratched his still solid chest, his finger combing the wooly vest of his chest hair

"Hal! Poins!" he summoned his servants. "Fetch my robe, my jug, and my sword!"

A twin chorus of "Yes, milord!" was heard in the antechamber followed by the scurrying of slippered feet, scampering in pursuit of their master's wishes.

Hal arrived first and helped the six-foot-six former gladiator into his robe, then quickly exited to fetch his master's sword. Poins immediately took his place, and handed over the jug of ale to the former captain of the Hawks so that he could slake his thirst after his long night's respite.

Fullstaff drained the jug in four gulps, and held it out to be received by Poins, whose unburdened hands had tied his master's robe so that it would no longer flap open and possibly impede his swordsmanship.

After a hearty belch, the master tutor of all things swordsmanlike reached out and grasped the broadsword that Hal held out to him, and quickly began to twirl it as if it were no larger than a throwing dagger. The two servants, following their strict routine for this time of day, quickly took four steps back to allow their master room to move and maneuver.

Once Fullstaff had achieved a certain centrifugal force with the massive broadsword swirling in one hand, he reached out with the other and quickly flipped the sword from his right hand to his left, without interrupting the baton-like swirling of the massive broadsword.

"Now!" he instructed, and the two servants jointly hurled a second broadsword at the master, which he quickly caught with his right hand, and immediately started to twirl in the opposite direction.

The muscles on the arms of the over sixty-year-old veteran of many a battle, stretched and firmed at the joyous exertion and strain, as Fullstaff's jaw became set and tightened into a grin that emphasized both the physical trial, and the adrenal ecstasy that the master swordsman was feeling. Faster and faster the blades flew through the air, twirling and twirling with their orbits intersecting like the gears of a gnomish machine as Fullstaff swapped them from hand to hand, their twirling never stopping, their blades never making contact with each other.

Faster and faster the master swordsman drilled, until a single bead of sweat began to make its appearance on his forehead.

"Halt!" he ordered, as he brought both blades to a simultaneous standstill, his shoulder muscles almost spasming at the added exertion that was required to stop their rapid motion.

As was typical of this daily ritual, Fullstaff had stopped their movement in mid-twirl, and had finished with the two broadswords crossed, barely one inch apart, elbows at his sides, arms crossed back at the wrists, and the blades resting a fraction of inch from the master swordsman's vein-mottled nose.

Without a word from their master, the two well-trained servants quickly stepped forward, and each accepted a broadsword. They then reverentially placed them in their scabbards, and fetched the next two weapons the master needed.

Poins handed Fullstaff a saber, as Hal placed a dagger in his master's palm.

Brandishing the saber he made a series of practice slashes from side to side as he tossed the dagger hilt-over-blade several times, his head never moving from its eyes-forward placement as the blades flew through the air like well-practiced falcons.

"Now!" he instructed, and the two servants threw a melon and an apple at the master.

The melon was slashed in two, while the dagger claimed the apple, catching it fast to the point. Full-

staff paused for a fraction of a second while the two
servants once again stepped forward, this time to retrieve the two melon halves.

They were no sooner back in their place than the
master swordsman tossed the dagger-bisected apple
into the air and quickly slashed it in mid-flight,
chopping the apple in two, and freeing the dagger
blade from its fructose prison. As the two halves of
the apple fell to the ground, he plucked the simultaneously falling dagger out of the air, catching it twixt
two fingers on its blade point.

This was followed by similar drills with rapiers,
epees, axes, and scimitars. As the pile of sliced fruit
grew, so did the beads of sweat on the master swordsman's brow.

The final drill involved a complicated sword maneuver where Fullstaff caught ten daggers thrown
one at a time by the two servants twixt the blades of
two sabers, being careful to nick nary a blade, nor allowing any of them to make contact with the ground.

When the drill was over, Fullstaff had five daggers in each hand, as well as the saber securely
brandished therein.

"Enough!" the master swordsman announced, and
Hal and Poins quickly accepted the many bladed
weapons from their master. As Poins gathered up
the lethal practice weapons, Hal fetched a towel, and
wiped his master's brow.

"That felt wonderful!" the former gladiator exclaimed. He loved the feeling of sweat on his brow
and his chest, and revelled in the scent of his own
manly perspiration. "Well done fellows! Well done!"

The two servants bowed as was their routine.
They were as practiced at Fullstaff's mid-morning
workout as the master swordsman was himself. Neither said a word throughout all the maneuvers, real-

izing that a single distraction, mistake or slip could cause either their own injury or death or that of the master they loved dearly.

Fullstaff slipped out of his robe, and toweled off his bare and glistening chest. Poins was in place with a heavier robe, while Hal set a pair of sandals at his feet.

Robe-clad and belted, feet shod in sandals, the master swordsman stretched again.

"I think I'll sit outside while Hotspur finishes his breakfast preparations," he bellowed in a friendly tone.

"As you wish, milord," they said in unison.

Poins quickly made his escape to aid Hotspur in the kitchen, while Hal led their blind master to his favorite seat, out by the villa's gate.

The sun's rays were warm and glorious as it neared its peak above the horizon. The master swordsman took his place as if on guard duty for his morning vigil of solar absorption, the warm rays reflecting on his still glistening body.

* * * * *

The Tharchioness's Boudoir
in the Tower of the Wyvern:

The First Princess had risen in solitude hours after the First Blade had stolen from their chambers like a thief in the night. She was glad that he was gone, and hoped that her labors of the previous evening had not been for naught.

The High Blade was always under the mistaken impression that she never rose before the noon hour, and she had no intention of disabusing him of this notion. She had always asked not to be disturbed

until then, and he had naturally assumed that it was
the sanctity of her slumbers that she wished to pre-
serve.

Such was not the case.

Her mornings in Mulmaster betwixt the hour of
her husband's departure and her own appearance at
the midday meal were important, as they were the
hours that she set aside for planning and consulta-
tion with her own advisors.

The High Blade's courtiers gossiped among themselves about the many frequent visitors to the First
Princess's boudoir, and she did little to discourage
them. Their assumptions of promiscuity shielded her
from their possible detection of her seditious plans,
and did little to elevate their opinions of the High
Blade who they now saw as just another simple
cuckold toyed with by his opportunistic wife.

A cautious series of knocks at the door indicated
that her advisors had arrived. Slipping into her
sheer silk robe, she went to the door and bade them
enter.

The ambassador that she referred to as a corpse
worm (and who she assumed would be executed at
her whim sometime prior to her return to Eltabbar)
led the group of three into her boudoir.

The three males did their best to avert their eyes
from the partially open silken robe that did little to
hide the beauty of the form that resided beneath it.
Mischa Tam, the only female among the advisors,
noticed their discomfort and made subtle eye contact
with her superior and shared a silent laugh with the
Tharchioness who considered such silly prudishness
to be hypocritical at best.

The First Princess rearranged her silken wrap
cinching it at her waste. She had no desire to provide
any of her advisors with an excuse for not devoting

their full attention to the matters at hand, even when such things did provide the Tharchioness and her female companion with much amusement.

"Reports," she commanded.

"Perhaps you would prefer to wait for the arrival of breakfast . . ." the wormlike ambassador began to suggest, but quickly changed gears in response to the Tharchioness's withering stare. "As you wish, your majesty. It would appear that the High Blade's men have been unsuccessful on three charged accounts and men have been executed as a result."

The Tharchioness licked her lips as if savoring some rare delicacy. "I can always count on my husband being just as demanding as I am," she replied to no one in particular.

"Yes, your majesty," the ambassador continued. "Their continued search for the body of the prisoner has turned up naught, and they have accepted that it will never be recovered."

"Thus we are back to square one."

"Yes, your majesty," the worm continued quickly, "though the High Blade has also ordered a search for a certain thespian named Passepout and a travel writer named Volothamp Geddarm. There have been vague suspicions that these two might be related to the prisoner in some way."

"Hmmmn," the Tharchioness muse. "Find out more. I want them located and apprehended before my husband gets his sweaty hands on them."

"Wh . . ." the ambassador began to question, then thought better of it. "Yes, your majesty."

"You may leave," the Tharchioness instructed.

The ambassador became flustered, and said, "But there is more to report."

"The others will see to it."

The ambassador understood now that he was the

only one being sent away, and almost asked for permission to stay for breakfast, but thought better of it.

"Yes, your majesty," the worm acknowledged, backing out of the boudoir in an almost ludicrous series of bows and abasements.

When he had left, the Tharchioness broke into peals of derisive laughter that was soon augmented by that of her advisors. The sheer grossness of the overt cowardice of the ambassador had set the rest of the group at ease, and they were now prepared to get down to work.

"Now that we're alone, we can proceed," the Tharchioness announced.

"What about our new ambassador?" Minister Konoch inquired. "I fear that he is no more capable than his predecessors."

"Exactly," the Tharchioness replied, "and he will therefore be the perfect scapegoat, should my beloved husband become suspicious."

"Or if we fail," added Mischa Tam, with a grin that suggested the cat who had just swallowed the canary. "Szass Tam is even more an enemy of failure and incompetence than you are, First Princess."

"Indeed," the Tharchioness replied, now slightly ill-at-ease.

* * * * *

On the Road Back to Mulmaster
from the Retreat:

Upon completing a thorough examination of the Retreat's grounds, Volo and Chesslyn had decided to pass the night together before heading back to Mulmaster in order to allow the Hawks Jembahb and

Wattrous a wide berth on the road, thus assuring their own safety and anonymity. Both the master traveler and the Harper agent had ample experience doing things that would hedge their bets in order to maintain their secrets. In their respective lines of work their continued survival often depended on it.

With the first rays of dawn, the two packed their kits and prepared to set off for Mulmaster. As Chesslyn swung herself into her saddle she asked her new found riding partner, "Did you encounter anyone on the way here?"

"Just a felon named James who thought me an easy mark," the master traveler replied.

"Well, we can't be too careful," the Harper agent instructed. "We'd better not retrace your steps. Let's take the long way back. I know a place just outside the city where we can hole up for the night."

"Sounds good to me," the wily gazetteer agreed, relishing the continued company of the attractive woman.

"I'm due back at the temple by tomorrow midday," Chesslyn continued as they rode out of the Retreat's gate, "so it would probably be better if we left separately tomorrow."

"Why?" Volo asked, trying not to sound too disappointed.

"It wouldn't look right for a guard at the Gate of Good Fortune, in service of Tymora, to be seen traveling in close company with an outsider, particularly given the circumstances at hand."

The master traveler, realizing that she was right, nevertheless countered with an argument.

"But surely being seen with the legendary travel writer Volothamp Geddarm is not that out of character for one of Tymora's minions."

Chesslyn abruptly stopped her steed, and turned

to face Volo, her look and bearing betraying her seriousness.

"I have survived as a Harper agent in Mulmaster for quite a while, and I have no desire to risk betraying my true identity. To do so would invite the placing of a price on my head. My presence in Mulmaster as a set of ears, and an occasional helping hand, is invaluable to many, and not just the Harpers, given the current political situation."

"But surely . . ." Volo started to argue, then abruptly changed gears. "How have you managed to escape detection? I mean, if things are that dicey, why haven't the Cloaks picked up on your presence before now?"

Chesslyn reached inside her blouse, and removed an amulet that was nestled inconspicuously between her breasts and held it out for him to see.

"Because of this," she explained, continuing in her tone of grave seriousness, "my amulet of non-detection. It's probably my most important possession. If Storm hadn't mentioned you to me the last time we met, I probably wouldn't have acknowledged you at all. I don't make friends easily, and am exceedingly careful about who knows I'm a Harper and who doesn't."

The master traveler fingered his beard for a moment. He realized that it was futile to argue, particularly since she was entirely right, and he was just being lasciviously selfish.

"An amulet of non-detection, eh?" he asked. She replaced it back into its safe hiding place, as the master traveler followed its journey with his eyes. "Always wanted to get my hands on one," the master traveler continued, adding, "the amulet, I mean. That accounts for why you were able to get the drop on me so easily back at the Retreat yesterday."

Chesslyn chuckled.

"And I thought it was because of my superior skills as a ranger," she countered with a smile.

He replied only with a grin, glad that there were no hard feelings.

They once again continued on their way, Volo urging his steed forward so that they could ride side by side for as long as the narrow road would allow it. After all, they didn't have to part until the next sunrise, and much mutual enjoyment of each other's company could take place until then.

Volo struck up a new topic for discussion.

"So," he asked, "what do you think those two buffoons were looking for yesterday?"

"Probably the crystal wand," she replied. "Rickman is Selfaril's right-hand man, and the head of the Hawks. He probably sent them to investigate the slaughter. Kind of funny, though. My confidential sources are the best in Mulmaster, and I didn't know that anything had happened there. I was there just on the merest of coincidences. I had promised one of the elders that I would deliver his winnings to him, once they exceeded a certain amount."

"Come again?"

"Only the elders of the Retreat were allowed to come to Mulmaster, and then only on a rotating basis as the need arose. One of the elders, Damon of Runyon, would stop by the temple on his visit and leave a series of bets with very specific instructions. When his winnings reached a certain point, it was my place to bring a portion of the kitty to him, and, for a tidy fee, to bring out new betting instructions. He was pretty lucky, at least up until now."

"Obviously."

"So, anyway. He must have been surprised at the attack."

"At least."

"As surprised as we were to discover it."

"Right."

"So how did Rickman know to send some men to investigate it?"

"And how," Volo added, "would they know to look for something as specific as the bloodstained Thayan crystal wand?"

"Unless," Chesslyn continued, "he knew what they would find, and how would he know . . ."

". . . unless he himself was involved."

"Agreed," the Harper agent concurred. "Curiouser and curiouser. The sole piece of evidence, the bloodstained wand, may not point to Thayan perpetrators since it might have been placed there by allies of Rickman."

"Which still doesn't explain the reason for the attack on the Retreat and merciless slaughter within," Volo added.

"Or why, beyond the obvious, Rickman would want to pin it on the Thayans."

Volo fingered his beard once again, this time in confusion. "What's the obvious?" he asked, unashamed of his ignorance.

"Rickman is Selfaril's right-hand man, and Selfaril hates Thayans," Chesslyn answered.

"But he's married to one," Volo countered.

"That's right," she replied with a grin. "Sometimes life's a bitch, ain't it?"

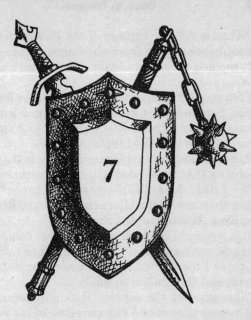

7

Past Tenses

*In the Office
of the Captain of the Hawks
in Southroad Keep:*

"Captain Rickman?" inquired an out-of-breath Hawk by the name of Danovich who hoped that the news he bore was sufficiently urgent to warrant disturbing the second most feared man in all of Mulmaster.

"What is it?" the captain of the Hawks demanded without looking up from the surveillance reports that seemed to form a blotter of paperwork upon his desk.

"You requested updates on the searches for the escaped prisoner, the released prisoner known as Passepout, and the travel writer Volothamp Geddarm?" Danovich asked tentatively.

Rickman looked up, his stern visage betraying the throbbing that resounded within his tortured brow.

"So I did," he said in a sarcastic tone. "Let me guess, they are all now in custody, along with Elminster, King Azoun, and the Simbul."

"Uh, no sir," Danovich answered, not comprehending Rickman's sarcasm, "and I only have updates on the three I mentioned. Should I add Elminster, King Azoun, and the Simbul to the list?"

"Just give me the report," Rickman demanded, a touch of weakness and exasperation in his voice. He couldn't help but be reminded of the inferior quality of men under his command since the Year of the Bow, when their fleet was destroyed by forces from Zhentil Keep. Back then men didn't just obey orders, they understood them as well.

"On the status of the escaped prisoner and the travel writer," Danovich reported officially, his mustached upper lip trembling, "there is no change. The escaped prisoner is still presumed dead, and the travel writer has not returned to Mulmaster since his observed exodus early yesterday morn."

"As I expected," Rickman observed, "but what of the itinerant?"

"According to one of our spies upon a Sembian merchant vessel of the name *Tanyaherst,* the former prisoner Passepout was shanghaied by a press gang, pressed into service, and subsequently thrown overboard when it was determined that he would be more of a hindrance than an asset on their journey eastward."

"Go on," Rickman urged in stern seriousness.

"He was thrown overboard, evidently still groggy from the physical persuasion that was inflicted on his cranium during his recruitment. Given his condition, and the deadly Moonsea tides, he is presumed dead. Officially, unless we want to challenge it upon the ship's return to Mulmaster, he will be listed as missing after an unfortunate shipboard accident."

"Any other interesting tidbits?"

"Well," Danovich answered tentatively, "the itinerant named Passepout was actually an actor by trade."

"What does that have to do with anything?" Rickman demanded.

"Nothing," Danovich replied sheepishly, "just that I, too, was trained in the theater."

Rickman rolled his eyes to try to suppress his rage at the incompetence and feeblemindedness that seemed to abound within the ranks of his men.

"Anything else?" he said, half under his breath.

"No sir," Danovich reported.

"Then back to work!"

"Yes sir," the Hawk replied doing a quick about-face, a smile crossing his lips as he left his superior's office, thankful that he, unlike previous men in his position, had not incurred the captain's wrath.

Rickman stood up and, hands clasped behind his back, strode to the lone window of his office, stopping only briefly to summon his batsman by means of the signal cord.

The batsman, Roché, arrived in a flash, finding his captain contemplating the sky over Mulmaster.

"My instinct tells me that a storm seems to be

moving in," Rickman asserted.

"The weather scryer in the Cloaks has predicted as such, sir," Roché said officiously.

"Any word on the condition of the sea?"

"According to the last report from the Lighthouse, high tide is just now coming in. The seas are choppy, and a mariner's advisory has been issued. The Moonsea is quite unforgiving of those who challenge her, even under the best of conditions," Roché responded, confident in the degree of detail expected by his captain. He had been in service to Rickman for close to eight years.

"What odds for survival would you give someone thrown overboard during such seas?" he asked, still staring out the window.

"Slim to none, sir," the batsman retorted.

"Just as I thought," Rickman replied, turning to face Roché. "Nothing is ever certain. You may go, Roché, but please put in a change of orders for the soldier who was just in here."

"Lieutenant Danovich, sir?" the batsman confirmed.

"Yes."

"Where will his new posting be, sir?" Roché inquired, a pad instantly in hand to take notes.

"Use your own judgment, Roché," Rickman answered, once again taking his place at his desk, and starting once again to go through the surveillance reports. "Just make sure it's an assignment far from Mulmaster, with a very small survival quotient."

"Yet another one-way assignment, sir," Roché confirmed.

"You draw up the papers and I'll sign them," Rickman said with a sense of finality. "It is the only way to weed out the incompetents from *this* man's army."

Roché returned his note pad to its proper place in

his uniform pocket, executed a perfect heel-toe pivot about-face, and silently left the office of the captain of the Hawks to carry out his master's will.

* * * * *

On the Moonsea Shore:

For Rassendyll it had all seemed like a dream.

The viscous membrane that had held out the poisonous onslaught of liquid sewage during his flush-propelled journey under Mulmaster was quickly washed away by the strong Moonsea currents. Once his exodus from the sea-bound burial shroud had been successful, the sack began its weighted, one-way journey downward.

The cold sea water instantaneously inspired an adrenalin surge in the iron-helmeted prisoner, and his body began to shiver violently.

Rassendyll realized that he had no leisure moments to allow himself the luxury of the anaesthetic effects of aquatic thermal shock, and with every ounce of strength that existed in his being, he frantically kicked toward the surface. He knew he had to maintain control, for to panic was to die.

It was just as important for him to maintain a vertical position as it was to continue to scissor-kick his way surfaceward. The least deviation out of a vertical position would result in the sheer weight of the iron mask dragging his body downward head first. With the weight centered on his shoulders, his neck muscles taut to keep his iron-encased head in place and erect, his lungs exploding from lack of air, and his arms and legs valiantly pumping him upward, the young mage concentrated his efforts on maintaining the energy upward.

The mask prevented him from feeling the air of the surface when he managed to break the Moonsea surf, and his lungs had refilled themselves with air before he consciously realized that he had made it.

The flash of recognition interrupted his stroke and at the precise moment of victory, he immediately re-submerged, the weight of the mask fighting the natural buoyancy of his body to meet a deadly equilibrium beneath the water's surface.

Rassendyll remembered the surge of strength, a last jolt of adrenalin fueled by the two lungfuls of oxygen before he re-submerged. He remembered struggling back to the surface, frantically looking for something to hold onto, something to add to his own buoyancy to compensate for the added mass of the mask that, despite his escape from the dungeon, still threatened to be the instrument of his death sentence.

Vaguely he remembered seeing the shore in the distance, and hearing the faint sound of breakers on the shore. He remembered the despair of thinking that it was too far, his strength quickly waning, his body trembling.

He felt himself slipping into unconsciousness when a great sea mammal seemed to pass by, riding the surf shoreward.

With his last focus of energy he reached for a fin, hoping that the whale would drag him to safety like so many other sailors of Faerûn's nautical lore.

Then he blacked out.

His ragged breathing, occasionally interrupted by coughing and the spewing of salt water, awakened him to the knowledge that somehow he had survived the trip to shore. He tried to move, and quickly regretted it, for every muscle in his body was cramped and contorted from its quest for survival, and further agitated by the awkward posture it had wedged itself into once it had reached shore.

The iron mask had become entangled in seaweed, and had wedged itself into the sea-softened sand of the shore at an extreme angle to the rest of his body.

His entire being yearned for more time to replenish itself, and Rassendyll would probably have remained unconscious longer, had the surf not returned to reclaim its rightful place at the high tide line.

Have I been lying here for a full day? he thought, realizing that it must have been the previous day's high tide that had delivered him to safety.

The high tide and the noble sea mammal, he recalled, trying to get his bearings, working out the kinks in his neck, and clearing away the seaweed and sand from the openings of the second shell of facial skin that the mask had become.

Rinsing his head in the shallows that would have previously brought his death, he carefully cleaned the mask and bathed as much of his face as he was able to, given the limited access afforded by the mask's apertures.

Reluctantly his vision began to clear, and he was able to look around. He first looked to the sea, and to his relief saw only the waves, and two seagulls diving for prey.

Had I not made it, he reflected, they would probably be perched on me, their beaks searching for the tender filling that lies within the iron shell of the mask. It is better that they content themselves with their regular diet.

His thoughts suddenly turned to images of his savior, the noble whale that must have beached itself to assure him of his salvation.

If it is still alive, he thought, I must return it to the surf or it will die.

Energized with what he thought to be his debt-required duty, he looked away from the waves, toward the shore, to find the beached leviathan. Out of the corner of his eye-slit he saw a large white mass that seemed to be smaller than he remembered his albino mammalian savior to be.

Staggering to his feet, his body protesting every effort, he dragged himself toward the white blob, blinking to clear his vision.

He looked down and laughed. It was his savior, he realized, but it was no whale.

It was a man.

Rassendyll continued to laugh out loud at his own misconception, a laugh that was uncontrolled and free, the first that he had allowed himself since the moment of his abduction.

The roar of his humor, coupled with the roar of the surf, and the moist lapping of its eddies, awoke the fainted-unto-sleep Passepout, who opened his eyes and, seeing Rassendyll standing above him, quickly took on a look of abject panic and fear.

Rassendyll quickly stopped laughing, and, realizing the panic that was evident in his savior's face, quickly said, "I mean you no harm."

The near valiant thespian swiftly replied, "Well, that's good. What are you doing with a coal bucket on your head?"

Rassendyll took another step closer to the still prone Passepout to assist the actor in coming to his feet. The thespian immediately misinterpreted this as a threatening act and, perhaps, a response to what the iron masked fellow inferred as an insult.

Thinking on his feet (or on his back, as it happened), the thespian quickly added, "Not that it's unattractive, I mean to say. Of course, not everyone could carry off this look, but on you it's quite impressive; one might almost say 'singular.' "

Rassendyll was amused by the verbal antics of the fellow, who undoubtedly had no idea that his natural buoyancy had not only saved his own life but Rassendyll's as well, and he was certain that his face would have conveyed this grateful amusement to the dripping and corpulent gent had it not been obscured by the infernal mask.

The mask, however, did not muffle the laughter that was once again escaping his lips.

Passepout smiled, taking the masked fellow's amusement as a good sign, and accepting his proffered hand and assistance at getting to his feet.

"*Oooofff!*" he exhaled as he got to his feet. "Why thank you, kind sir, for your gracious assistance!"

"Think nothing of it, my mutually waterlogged colleague," Rassendyll replied, noticing some threatening clouds that seemed to be approaching from the sea horizon. "It looks like a storm is brewing. We probably should try to find some shelter."

Passepout remembered the warm and comfortable bed back at the Traveler's Cloak, and the unceremonious exit from the inn at the urging of Dela's boot sole.

"Good idea," the soggy thespian agreed. "Any ideas where?"

Rassendyll quickly looked around, noticing a few buildings and ships in the far distance. One of the buildings was a lighthouse, and, if memory served the former Retreat student, nearby was a small barracks housing no less than thirty-six soldiers.

"That-a-way," the masked mage instructed, pointing in the opposite direction along the shore.

"Fine," Passepout agreed, following the iron-masked man. "I hope we are not too far from Mulmaster," he added, not realizing that they were headed in the opposite direction from the city.

Not far enough for my tastes, Rassendyll thought to himself as he set off down the shoreline.

* * * * *

*The Tharchioness's Apartment
in the Tower of the Wyvern:*

Once Ministers Konoch and Molloch had finished their reports, the Tharchioness dismissed them so that they could attend to the inane duties of state that passed as the excuse for their presence in Mulmaster. The First Princess was always concerned with the pretense of diplomacy which had succeeded in obscuring the presence of her spies and conspirators in the court despite the equally thorough spy network of Hawks and Cloaks that was available to the High Blade.

Mischa Tam remained behind to assist the First Princess in the preparation of her appearance for her obligatory court appearances, aiding in the application of cosmetics, and the choosing of the proper gown for the ceremonies of the day.

"What to wear, what to wear," the First Princess murmured absently, as Mischa held one gown after another up against herself, thus serving as a live mannequin. "The citizens of this abysmal hamlet have certain expectations that I must live up to. I am the great beauty who seduced their High Blade, the eastern, exotic witch whose mystical powers hold him in her thrall. I am both their queen and their enemy. Their nationalism demands that they both love me and hate me."

"So many demands on a single woman," Mischa commented in a neutral tone that succeeded in masking any implication of either sarcasm or sympathy.

"On a married woman, sister," the Tharchioness corrected. "Remember it was the will of Szass Tam that bound me to the infernal bonds of matrimony."

"Of course, dear sister," Mischa acquiesced. "The battles for the expansion of Thayan interests are sometimes fought in the bedroom, as well as on the battlefield."

"With the High Blade, there is very little difference."

Both sisters laughed at the Tharchioness's humorously apt remark. Settling on a quilted silken gown of green, blue, and turquoise, the First Princess sat at her vanity seat so that Mischa could paint her face in the appropriate cosmetic color scheme.

The First Princess closed her eyes, and pursed her lips. Mischa knew what to do, and was not to be distracted by idle conversation until she was done.

Mischa began to apply the base to the Tharchioness's cheeks and forehead. The First Princess's silence came more from a desire to enforce a certain class formality in their relationship rather than from any honest concern about Mischa's need to concentrate on her task. As the Tharchioness's half sister through an unidentified assignation on their mother's part, Mischa Tam realized that she had very little claim to actual nobility, and even less to the authority of a tharch such as her sister. She was neither as potent a magic-wielder or as popular a politician as the First Princess, and she was reminded of it every day of her life, and accepted her fate of never being more than the one who was referred to behind her back as the Second Half-Princess, and the sister of the Tharchioness.

She sighed and accepted the limitations of her

station, at least for the present time.

It was fortunate that the First Princess didn't know that her half sister secretly hated her, and was patiently awaiting the day when she would replace her in the favor of the illustrious Szass Tam.

Well, Mischa thought, at least I don't have to be an enforced concubine and brood mare for some smelly infidel like Selfaril.

The last eye line in place, Mischa announced, "Done." The Tharchioness opened her eyes, to assess her own appearance in an ornate mirror.

"So, sister," the First Princess said, "am I beautiful enough to distract my wretch of a husband?"

"Of course, sister," she answered.

"Will I bring a stirring to his loins?"

"Don't you always?" she replied.

"Not that it has done me any good," the Tharchioness observed. "Once I am with child, the High Blade will cease to be a necessary participant in my marriage bed. I will train his heir to take his place on the throne, the same way Selfaril succeeded *his* father."

"Only this time, the new High Blade will be Thayan," Mischa pointed out.

"In all eyes but those of the wretched citizens of Mulmaster. He will be one of them by birth."

"A brilliantly conceived plan," Mischa said, secretly knowing that the High Blade's heir could just as easily be raised by his beloved aunt as by his vain and pompous mother.

When the time comes, she thought to herself, Szass Tam himself will choose.

The Tharchioness rose to her feet, and once again admired her appearance in the mirror.

"You have done me well, sister," she complimented. "Now all we have to do is wait for the charms that we have ordered."

I am very good at waiting, the half sister observed silently, and my time will come.

* * * * *

At the Private and Secluded Residence
of Sir Honor Fullstaff, somewhere between
Mulmaster and the Retreat:

Fullstaff walked into the kitchen where the dwarven cook named Hotspur was busy in preparation for the evening meal.

"Something smells splendid," the blind swordsman exclaimed, as he used his keen senses of perception to home in on an open pot that had a ladle in it, and was thus easy access for sampling. Hotspur was a creature of habit, and Fullstaff knew that he always kept the ladle resting in the first pot on the left.

"I wouldn't be sampling anything in that pot, master," the dwarf replied.

"And why not Hotspur?" the master replied with a certain degree of mock haughtiness. "Is this not my kitchen?"

"Indeed it is, milord," Hotspur replied, his back to the master, his concentration focused on the chopping at hand.

"And are these not my pots?" the master inquired, slowly lifting the ladle to his lips, careful not to spill a drop or make any sudden noise.

"Indeed they are, milord," the dwarf replied, then explained, "but that one does not contain your dinner."

"Well, then, my insubordinate cook," the master interrogated, the ladle poised a fraction of an inch from his lips, "what does it contain?"

"My socks," the dwarf explained. "They got stained when I was making wine out back, and boiling them is the only way I'll ever get them clean."

Hotspur, his focus still on the vegetable-chopping at hand, smiled as he heard the ladle drop, making a subtle splash in the laundry-filled pot.

"And don't go sampling any of the other pots, master," the dwarf instructed in a similar tone to the one his master had adopted earlier. "One of them contains your old sword belt. Poins and Hal believe that they may be able to stretch it to a more suitable length for your expansive girth, once the boiled water softens it."

"Just as well," the master replied. "Without my occasional midafternoon snack, their expansive efforts on my belt's behalf might prove to be unnecessary."

"Besides that, milord," Hotspur reminded, "you have company coming to join your evening repast."

In a fraction of a second Fullstaff removed a dagger from his belted scabbard, tossed it in the air, snapped his fingers, and returned it to its place. He said, "Oh, that's right. Old McKern is stopping by for dinner on his way back to the Retreat. I hope, in addition to the sumptuous meal that you have prepared for me, you have also prepared something sensible and strained for the old wizard. When you get to his age, there is no reason to tax one's intestines."

"Indeed, milord," Hotspur replied, choosing to omit mentioning that he knew that his master and the old wizard were indeed the same age. Secretly he looked forward to overhearing the old former captain of the Hawks swapping made-up memories with the former Cloak, who had been retired to the Retreat almost as long as the master had been blind. Their both being put out to pasture at the same time had formed a bond that made them seem like friends for life, despite the fact that they had never actually served side by side during their tours of duty.

Realizing that his slight desire to nibble and sample did not warrant the risk of a sip of cleaning water or boiled leather, Fullstaff left the kitchen, and followed his long-memorized route to his practice studio.

Undoing his robe, he bellowed loud enough to be heard throughout the entire villa, "Hal! Poins! It's time for my afternoon practice session. Hurry up boys! I want to be finished with enough time left so that I can take a bath before my company arrives!"

I'm sure Master McKern will appreciate it, Hotspur thought to himself, as well as anyone else caught down wind.

The soft padding of slippered feet, followed by several huffs and puffs and the clash of steel, let the dwarf know that practice had begun, and that the ladle could be returned to its proper place, the risk of nibblers now nil, as the chronic perpetrator was otherwise engaged.

* * * * *

In the Apartment in
the Tower of the Wyvern
that the High Blade shared with his Wife:

"The First Princess of Thay approaches," a eunuch elven herald announced.

"Well, it's about bloody time," the High Blade hissed to the captain of the Hawks, who was stationed at his side. "She knows I hate to be kept waiting, particularly in my own home."

"Unfortunately, your majesty, it is her home as well," Rickman whispered in return. "The fact that it annoys you is probably why she does it."

The doors to the suite flew open with a slight push of mystical wind, and Selfaril and Rickman stood up to receive the Tharchioness, who entered flanked by her lady-in-waiting, Mischa Tam.

"Darling," the Tharchioness cooed, her arms open to receive her husband. "I am sorry to have kept you waiting."

"You, my dear," Selfaril replied with all the sincerity of a polygamist professing his chastity, "are always worth waiting for."

The two met, once again in the room's center, and exchanged their requisite kisses that never involved their lips actually touching each other.

Selfaril was the first to resume insincere spousal blandishments. "If all women looked like you after sleeping in all morning," he expounded, "all of the men of Faerûn would gladly forego having their breakfast made for them."

"A simple woman such as myself," the Tharchioness replied, "has few duties more important than maintaining her desirability in the eyes of her husband. I only regret that it denies me the pleasure of your company when I awake. An empty bed is a poor follow-up to a sleep of dreams."

"I am sorry, dear, but you know that duty demands that I attend to affairs of state even before the cock crows."

"And after, and during," the Tharchioness replied, adding, "With all of your duties, one might think you could do with a respite . . . or perhaps a retreat?"

"If only I could spare the time," Selfaril countered shrewdly, then, with an expansive gesture toward the her lovely half sister, added, "You are blessed with the lovely Mischa Tam as a sister. I, alas have no one to substitute for me. After all, it's not as if I had a brother to call my own."

"Such an idea," the Tharchioness replied. "I don't think I would be able to stand it. One of you is heaven. Two of you would be . . ."

"Interesting?" he interrupted.

"A challenge," she replied, her hand beginning to play with a Thayan pendant that hung around her neck, thus drawing her husband's attention yet again to her desirably ample cleavage.

"Well met," he replied.

The two spouses stared into each other's eyes, both conveying their animal attraction, and cunningly trying to read the other's mind. Their desires were so similar, and they both knew it. It was a pity that their ultimate goals were mutually exclusive.

A courtier approached Rickman and whispered in his ear.

"Your majesty," the captain interrupted, "various envoys await your and the princess's arrival in the antechamber. They bear gifts and petitions from far-off lands and important companies."

"Must we?" the Princess asked her husband with a pout.

"We must," he replied with a restrained leer.

"Than we shall," she answered, and arm-in-arm they entered the antechamber, doors forced open by the gentle yet powerful breezes that were conjured by the Tharchioness.

Out of routine and protocol, the captain of the Hawks and the lady-in-waiting also joined arms and followed them inside, neither realizing that they were sharing similar impressed thoughts about the exceptional acting ability of their respective lord and lady.

* * * * *

Along the Back Roads Twixt
the Retreat and Mulmaster:

Volo and Chesslyn had been riding for hours, exchanging the idle conversation that strangers sometimes engaged in when they wanted to appear more at ease with one another than they really were. Conversation of the slaughter at the retreat, and the mysterious goings on in the Mulmaster area, soon gave way to tales of youth and adventure far from current shores.

The route that Chesslyn had chosen lengthened their journey by at least half a day, and as the sun began to make its descent towards the horizon the master traveler decided it was time to query his traveling companion about their possible accommodations for the night.

"Well, I must thank you for this marvelous impromptu tour of the Mulmaster area back roads and byways," the master traveler said. "I'd label it the scenic route, but unfortunately there's not much to look at."

"We agreed that it wasn't worth the risk being seen together, given where we were coming from, and all that has happened," the Harper agent admonished.

"Yes, yes," the master traveler agreed amiably, then added with a leer. "I'll call it the 'Lover's Route.'"

"The Lover's Route?" she asked, giggling with an air of incredulity.

"Sure," the master traveler replied, "the route one takes when wants to be alone . . . or perhaps when one wants the circumstances to dictate an unexpected extra night on the road. Which reminds me, you mentioned that you knew a place that would provide us with discreet overnight accommodations."

"Indeed, I did," she answered assuredly, "and discretion is guaranteed."

"My! A place out here in the middle of nowhere, where we don't have to worry about being seen together," Volo answered, taking his own turn at mock incredulity.

"Not by the lord of the manor, at least," she added.

"What's that?"

Chesslyn smiled, and explained. The road had leveled off slightly, and she seemed to be able to trust her steed to lead itself along the intended route.

"Have you ever heard of Blind Honor?" she asked.

"Sure," the master gazetteer replied, then paused for a moment, and ventured an explanation. "It's when something is so sacred between two people that both are bound by honor never to reveal their—"

"It's a person," she interrupted.

"Never heard of him," he conceded.

Chesslyn threw her head back and laughed.

"Imagine that," she declared. "I've stumped the master gazetteer of all Faerûn."

"Of all Toril," Volo corrected. "Here, let me get out my notebook. I can ride and write at the same time."

"I don't think so," Chesslyn ordered, reining her horse around so that she was once again confronting the master traveler with direct eye contact. "Our discretion is mandatory. If I find a listing for the home of Honor Fullstaff in your upcoming guide to Mulmaster, I'll . . ."

"Cleave me in twain," the master traveler offered, immediately replacing his notebook in his pack before he had even finished extricating it.

"Something like that," Chesslyn affirmed with a

smile that did not undercut the seriousness of her message. The Harper agent once again righted her horse, and proceeded along a parallel path to that of the master traveler.

"Well, between just you and me, and not for publication, under any circumstances, who is this Blind Honor guy?" Volo asked, a slight bit of impatience evident in his tone.

Eyes set ahead on the trail yet to be traveled, Chesslyn began her explanation. "Simply put, Honor Fullstaff is the master swordsman of all Faerûn," she asserted.

"So why have I never heard of him?"

"He's been retired since before you began your illustrious career of *belles lettres*."

The master gazetteer made a mental note to try to remember as many specific details about the sword wielder as possible. With any luck, he imagined, he would be able to gather corroborating information from other sources. After all, a tale told a second time nullifies a promise of silence to a former source.

"He began his illustrious career in the gladiatorial arenas of Hillsfar where coming in second leaves one with a very short career."

"And life," Volo added.

"I forgot that the master traveler has already been there, as well as everywhere else," she acknowledged.

"With no clue to his true parentage," she continued, "who probably either died in the arena before he came of age, or on some oppressive slave plantation, Honor realized at an early age that he had a natural propensity toward the mastery of all things bladed. He was on his way to an undefeated career in the arena when he led a slave revolt, thus instigating the escape of over half of Hillsfar's gladiators."

"I bet the Red Plumes were none too happy."

"Not at all," she conceded, "but the powers that be realized that a band of gladiators who could engineer their own escape from the arena were probably of more value to Hillsfar as allies than as outlaws. They offered Honor and his comrades a contract as a mercenary force, and they accepted."

"Not a bad move for the former lead act for the afternoon bloodbath," Volo conceded, making a mental note to have someone check on the gladiatorial victory records for the pertinent years for the book currently underway.

"As with most mercenary bands, attrition, opportunism, and disparate goals eventually caused them to break up, and Honor accepted a position in Mulmaster, with the Hawks, where he quickly rose through the ranks, and became the right-hand man of the High Blade himself."

"Selfaril?"

"No," Chesslyn corrected, "his father."

"Whom Selfaril killed to take the throne himself," Volo interrupted, trying to show that he wasn't a complete dullard about all things Mulman.

"Right," the Harper conceded, "but you're getting ahead of the story."

"Sorry."

"Legend has it that Merch, that's what Selfaril's father's name was . . ."

"I'm aware of that," Volo replied in slight indignation.

"Sorry. As I was saying, Merch and Honor were said to be closer than brothers. In addition to handling the day-to-day operations of the Hawks, he also supervised the City Watch, and was responsible for the security of both the City and the High Blade himself, a turn of events that did not necessarily please the then-head of the Cloaks, an aristocratic mage by the name of Rathbone who saw the safety and security of the High Blade to be his sole responsibility. Honor's low-born background didn't help matters in the eyes of the egotistical wizard, who set about to remove the master swordsman from his position."

"You don't want to tick off a jealous wizard who feels his position is in jeopardy," the master traveler agreed.

"So Honor found out," Chesslyn confirmed, as she continued the tale. "Honor used to always supervise the forging and tempering of his own weapons, and it was on one such occasion that there was a terrible explosion. Miraculously no one was killed, but Honor was blinded beyond the limits from which any available cleric could cure."

"Thus, his new moniker: Blind Honor."

Chesslyn continued: "Rumors ran rampant through the Mulmaster court of Rathbone's complicity in the explosion, but nothing was ever proven. The Cloaks once again became responsible for the security of the High Blade, and when Honor had recovered sufficiently to get by on his own, he resigned his commission and left the city, reportedly to spend the rest of his years in retirement."

"Whatever happened to Rathbone?" the master traveler inquired, recalling that his name was not among those listed in the current Cloak registry in Mulmaster.

"He committed suicide," Chesslyn explained. "He held himself responsible for Merch's assassination. His main motive for replacing Honor, at least in his own self-justifying mind, was the overall safety of the High Blade, and when he failed to prevent the High Blade's death, I suppose he asked himself the question of whether or not it could have been avoided."

"And the answer was 'yes,' " Volo offered, "if only Honor had still been by his side."

"Rathbone was found dead in the Tower of Arcane Might. He had hung himself. Soon thereafter Thurndan Tallwand was appointed Senior Cloak, and he immediately pledged his support to the new High Blade Selfaril, and thus the transition of power was complete, at least as far as the citizens of Mulmaster were concerned."

"They didn't mind that there was a murderer on the throne?" Volo asked incredulously.

"Well," Chesslyn explained, "Merch himself was far from an angel, and the fact that Selfaril was his son was looked upon as just a slight deviation from the normal rules of ascendancy."

"That slight deviation being patricide," the master traveler commented.

"Wasn't the first time, and probably won't be the last," the Harper agent conceded.

"So the old swordsman, now blind, went into retirement, living out the rest of his days in peaceful isolation and seclusion?" Volo ventured.

"Not bloody likely," Chesslyn corrected. "One might say that he set himself up as a martial alternative to the Retreat."

"Come again?" Volo queried.

"He bought himself a villa, and set himself up clandestinely as a master teacher of the bladed arts. Usually no more than one student at a time, tenure of stay to be determined solely at Honor's discretion. His students have included kings and thieves, and their tuition has varied from debts of gratitude to villas in Cormyr."

"Not bad," Volo said. "Those who can no longer do, can at least teach. Not bad for a former master swordsman."

"I never said former," Chesslyn corrected. "He still is more than a match for anyone, with choice of bladed weapons, and as a teacher he is the best."

"That's a rousing endorsement from a master of the long sword such as yourself."

"Honor taught me everything I know," Chesslyn said reverentially, "and I'm sure he will have no problem with us stopping by for the night. He has plenty of spare rooms, and is always amenable to offer hospitality to friends of friends who can be trusted."

Chesslyn delivered her last remark with such a withering degree of seriousness that the master traveler began to think better of featuring the legendary swordsman in his upcoming guide book. Perhaps confidentiality should be preserved in some cases.

Chesslyn reined in her horse, shaded her eyes from the midafternoon glare, and scanned the horizon.

"We should be there right about sundown," she said. "Knowing Honor, he'll be out front catching the last few rays of the setting sun before sitting down to a sumptuous dinner feast. We'll be just in time to join him."

"Can't wait," the master traveler said, eager to meet the teacher who had instilled such admiration in one of his students.

8

Mates, Masks, Musk, & Meals

In the High Blade's Study
in the Tower of the Wyvern:

The conspiracy of the moment over, both threat
and advantage now neutralized, Selfaril felt a palat-
able taste of normalcy as things returned to the status quo.

He still hated his wife, and she him.

Eltabbar and Thay were still distant opportunities and menaces for the glory of Mulmaster and the High Blade himself.

He had grown used to the game of cat and mouse that he and his bride played. It excited him more than he liked to admit, and he was sure that she felt the same way. Why else did he always feel an adrenal rush whenever she was around? What else could account for the mixed feelings of excitement and revulsion he experienced whenever she entered the room?

For him, love was an abstract concept, not at all alien, just different from that normally felt by others. It required respect; yet did not the best of enemies command respect? It caused a physical attraction, yet did not the flame attract the moth to its death?

Love and death: they were intricately tied in his mind.

Looking back he remembered wanting to be like his father, the great leader who taught him by example and was revered by all his subjects; Selfaril had accomplished this goal by killing his father and taking his place.

Family was the greatest threat of all, yet he felt a certain emptiness within, almost as if something was missing. Perhaps it was the fate of his brother; could this be what had left him feeling incomplete? Though he had been assured that his twin must have drowned during his futile escape attempt, how could he be sure?

There was an emptiness inside Selfaril, an incompleteness. Less than a month ago he had not even known that his twin existed, and now the stranger was forever on his mind, and all because the sheer incompetence of his men had cost him the ecstatic pleasure of seeing his brother die.

Selfaril shook his head in remorse over the experience he had been denied. Oh well, he thought, I still have my wife. . . .

* * * * *

On the Back Roads
Outside of Mulmaster:

As the clouds began to move in on them, and the sun inched closer to the horizon, Rassendyll and Passepout pressed onward.

The iron-masked escapee realized that he and his overweight traveling companion would have to avoid any of the numerous Mulmaster outposts, or he would soon find himself back in the dungeons of Southroad Keep. The combination of the sand, salt, and seaweed that had taken to roost in the collarlike ring of the mask's neck piece was rubbing raw his skin adjacent to it, causing an extremely uncomfortable mixed sensation of burning and itching. As he reached the rise of the next hill, having first scanned the area to assure it was deserted, he paused once again to rub at the chafed area.

"Is your neck bothering you?" the out-of-breath thespian asked, as he too reached the rise, adding tentatively, "Why don't you just take the helmet off? I'm sure you can't be that ugly. If you don't want to be recognized, well, don't worry about me. A famous actor such as myself knows all about traveling incognito to avoid overzealous fans. I'll keep your secret, whatever it is."

Rassendyll looked at the amusing fellow, and said, "You're a famous actor?"

"That's right," Passepout replied, with an out-of-place flourish and semi-bow. "Passepout, only son of the legendary thespians Idle and Catinflas, at your service."

"Never heard of you," Rassendyll replied, still distracted as he rubbed the raw spot in search of relief.

"You know," the thespian ventured, "if we were back in Cormyr, I'd know the perfect thing to rid you of that dry, flaking, skin problem you have. It's heartbreaking watching you suffer. A friend of mine by the name of Seau Raisis had that problem."

"What did he use?"

"Well," Passepout answered, scratching his head as if to stimulate a memory, "as I recall there was a cleric, named Oleigh if I remember correctly, who would treat Seau's problem by rubbing it with oil that he made specially for such ailments."

"Did it work?"

"I think so," Passepout replied, "but I can't really be sure. After the oil of Oleigh was applied he never complained about the problem again, but. . . ."

"So it must have worked."

"Not necessarily; that is, I mean to say the problem was taken care of, but it might not have been cured by the oil."

"What then? I mean, if the problem with his neck abrasion went away and he never complained about it again, why do you doubt the effectiveness of the cleric's treatment?"

"He was beheaded."

"The cleric?"

"No," Passepout explained. "Seau. At least his neck rash problem was taken care of."

Rassendyll looked at the pudgy thespian and laughed once again.

Passepout smiled back, almost at ease in the company of the masked stranger.

"Well I for one would rather avoid such treatments and cure-alls as the one that worked on your friend Seau."

"Indeed," the pudgy thespian agreed. "By the way, what is your name, or at least what should I call you?"

Rassendyll thought for a moment, glad that the mask obscured the thespian from seeing the wary change of expression on his face. He himself was no actor, and he was sure that his face would have conveyed the indecisiveness he felt about whether he could trust this funny fellow or not.

"You can call me Rupert," Rassendyll answered, "Rupert of Zenda."

"Well met, Rupert of Zenda," Passepout returned. "Can't say I recognize the name."

"Hope not," the masked escapee replied inadvertently.

"What was that?" Passepout inquired. "That coal bucket you're wearing gives you a bad case of the mumbles, if you know what I mean. By the way, why don't you take it off?"

"I wish I could," Rassendyll retorted, "but I'm afraid that it's stuck."

"Too bad," the thespian replied.

Rassendyll scanned the area once again. He didn't like the looks of the storm clouds that seemed to be rapidly bearing down on them. *We should be on our way and looking for shelter,* he thought.

Passepout in the meantime had concentrated his visual faculties on the ground around where they sat. Seeing exactly what he was looking for, he struggled to his feet and walked back over the ridge, picking up a sturdy branch. Rassendyll noticed his efforts once he returned. *Good thinking,* the masked escapee thought, *he found a walking stick.*

Rassendyll was about to stand up when he felt

Passepout trying to wedge one of the ends of the branch under the metal collar.

"Hey! Cut that out!" Rassendyll exclaimed, not wishing to add the discomfort of splinters to his long list of woes.

"Just hold still," Passepout assured, continuing to try and wedge the branch between the masked man's collar and his clavicle. "Once I have it wedged in place, I'm going to put my weight on the other end of the stick, using your shoulder as a fulcrum. It should force it off in no time."

"Which? The mask or my head?"

"The mask, of course. Now just sit still."

Rassendyll quickly wiggled out from under the awkward hands of the pudgy thespian, and got to his feet.

Passepout appeared bewildered at his sudden retreat. "What's the matter?" the thespian implored. "I just wanted to help."

Rassendyll shook his head, and said, "Thanks anyway, but it wouldn't have worked."

"How can you be sure?" Passepout asked.

"It's been magically bound to my skull. I fear it won't come off without separating my head from my shoulders as well."

"I'm sorry," Passepout apologized. "I didn't know."

"No reason you should have."

"I bet you got on the wrong side of a powerful wizard of some sort."

In return Rassendyll murmured something indecipherable, as he began to remove splinters from his shoulders.

"Me too," Passepout replied as if he understood what the masked man had said. "I've run afoul of a few myself. Now, of course, the likes of Elminster and Khelben are indebted to me, but even so, you can't trust a wizard."

"Oh, no?" Rassendyll responded, cocking his head at an awkward angle so that he could look the thespian straight in the eye.

Passepout paled.

"You're not one of them are you?" he asked in a panic.

Rassendyll thought for a split second about his current condition, and laughed. "I guess not," he replied with a chuckle. "At least not for the time being." He then quickly added, with a mischievous, almost conspiratorial tone, "I used to be, though."

Passepout joined in his chuckle, and said, "That's all right. I used to be a thief."

Thunder began to rumble in the distance.

"Then let us steal away," Rassendyll replied, "and find shelter."

"Good idea, Rupert," Passepout concurred, then asked, "I can call you Rupert, can't I?"

"But of course," Rassendyll answered after a moment's hesitation. He then thought, I'll have to remember that that's my new name.

The thunder rumbled again, as the two continued their trek in search of shelter.

* * * * *

*In the Tharchioness's Boudoir
in the Tower of the Wyvern:*

The Tharchioness was primping for dinner when her half sister Mischa Tam entered.

The First Princess finished buffing her scalp, and began to touch up the exotic eye liner that framed the seductive windows of her soul.

"Dear sister," Mischa said tentatively, hoping that the First Princess was not in one of her many moods that would have made this sudden, unannounced intrusion a gross act of insubordination.

"What is it, Mischa?" the First Princess asked impatiently, yet not necessarily hostilely.

"I have been giving your—I mean our—situation a great deal of thought."

"Which of *our* situations?"

"The existence of stumbling blocks that are succeeding in preventing the Thayan annexation of Mulmaster."

"You mean the High Blade."

"Yes," Mischa agreed, then added quickly, "your husband."

Mischa felt her half sister brace, her back growing erect like a viper about to strike. She realized that she would have to tread lightly if she wished to succeed in the deadly cat-and-mouse game of family and politics.

"What about him?" the First Princess demanded, turning around to face her half sister, her eyes fixed like a jungle cat contemplating its prey.

"Well," Mischa started, averting her eyes from her sister's predatory stare, "as I recall, your mission was to seduce the High Blade, and gain control of the throne of Mulmaster."

"Yes," the First Princess replied, clipped and clear.

"It was at your own suggestion that the seduction was metamorphosed into a diplomatic liaison cum marriage that would form an alliance between Eltabbar and Mulmaster."

"Correct," the First Princess acknowledged. "This is what Szass Tam and I agreed upon. It was our mutual feeling that such an official alliance would be more advantageous. I do hope you are not wasting my time with a simple regurgitation of the plans to date. My memory is quite acute and needs no prodding."

"I would never presume to doubt your cognitive processes or powers of retention, First Princess, but I am curious about one thing. . . ."

"And what is that?" the Tharchioness demanded, all matters of primping temporarily set aside.

"Why is it taking so long? It is almost as if you are enjoying this game of prey and predator at the expense of the ultimate objective. Rumor has it, I fear, that you have become fond of the High Blade, and that perhaps your focus has become distracted or, how shall I say . . . channeled into other pursuits."

The First Princess did not respond, maintaining an icy stare that seemed to lower the temperature of the room well below the freezing mark.

Mischa quickly changed her tact.

"Of course I don't believe such stories, but I fear that they may reach the ears of Szass Tam himself."

"I have never given Szass Tam any reason to doubt my loyalty!"

"Of course you haven't, dear sister," Mischa said, her tone becoming disarmingly comforting, "but you have been married for quite a while now, and still you have not yet become with child, thus securing Thay's stake in the throne of Mulmaster. I am not saying that I believe this, but some of your ministers have speculated that perhaps you are artificially postponing such a conception, as you are enjoying the prerequisite maneuvers too much."

"Who dares to sully my name and honor?" the First Princess demanded.

"*Who* is not important, dear sister," Mischa insisted. "What is important is how things might look to those back east. Though I admire your ingenuity in this plan involving the High Blade's twin—"

"It was not *my* plan!"

"Sorry, First Princess," Mischa apologized in a

conciliatory tone. "I did not wish to imply that it was. After all, if it had been, it would surely have succeeded; still, your endorsement of it might still look like an unnecessary detour from the original plan, without the necessary approval of back east. Once again, I must point out that your actions might be construed as an unnecessary and dangerous dalliance for your own amusement."

The Tharchioness stood up, and turned her back on her sister to contemplate her wardrobe for her evening meal with her husband, and the festivities that would surely follow.

"The game of diplomacy is dangerous in both the throne room and the bedroom," the First Princess said, her back still to her sister. "One must always wear the proper armor."

"Yes, dear sister."

"The High Blade is also prone to wearing armor. For some reason, even after our exchange of vows he does not trust me. Can you imagine that?"

The First Princess unhooked a gown of the sheerest Thayan silk Mischa had ever seen.

"We were supposed to be dining in private tonight," the Tharchioness instructed, "but matters of state have interfered. I guess I will have to find something more appropriate to whet my spouse's appetite, lower his guard, and raise his ardor."

"No one has ever questioned your ability to do that, dear sister," Mischa confirmed. "Yet, you still have not been able to complete the mission that you have been sent on, and I have been thinking. . . ."

"About what?" the First Princess demanded.

"If, indeed, even in times of great ardor the High Blade is on his guard. . . ."

"Yes?"

"Perhaps he needs to have that guard lowered."

"By what means?"

"An enchanted charm perhaps."

The First Princess threw her head back and gave forth a derisive laugh, the likes of which she usually reserved for the mentally defective, freaks, and idiots who were brought forth for her amusement (or for particularly wormlike ministers).

"Of course," the Tharchioness said in mock-naive revelation. "Oh, wait a minute, maybe I did. That's right, I did, and then I dismissed it because it wouldn't work, but thanks anyway dear sister. I'll remember to summon you if I have a need for someone with an acute grasp of the extremely obvious."

"But, dear sister, why do you dismiss my suggestion so lightly?"

"Because it is doomed to failure."

"How so?" Mischa asked in a sincere tone that masked the contempt that she felt for her half sister's deprecating manner.

"Because of the damned Cloaks who have sworn their allegiances to protecting the High Blade, that's why. They would detect such a charm the minute it was brought into the city. Even though our people are exempt from searches, we are nonetheless closely watched, and even our most sophisticated mages would be noticed bearing the necessary amulets when they entered the city gate."

Mischa tapped her bald temple with the lacquered fingernail of her index finger, as if pausing to think deeply. After a practiced pause, she feigned revelation, and said, "That is true, but what if nothing was brought into the city? What if the charmed object was constructed here, married with a personal piece of the High Blade himself within these walls, and cast in the privacy of your own bedroom. Surely the Cloaks are not watching you there too, and the High

Blade does not exactly strike me as the type who has spent a great deal of time being schooled in the matters of high magic."

The Tharchioness braced again, followed by a slow, ecstatic chill that went through her body as if the recognition and anticipation of the action to come was as good as the experience itself. The pink serpent of her tongue moistened her dewy lips in anticipation.

"Once charmed, he would disregard his armor," the First Princess said softly, almost as if she were voicing her thoughts to herself.

"Possibly, dear sister," Mischa said in encouragement.

"And then he will be mine!"

* * * * *

At the Villa of Honor Fullstaff,
Somewhere between the Retreat and Mulmaster:

Fullstaff was enjoying the pale warmth of the day's last rays of the sun. McKern, his guest for the evening, had arrived at the expected hour, and was now busily cleaning away the road dust in preparation for the sumptuous meal that he knew would be ready at sunset. As this was not the first time that he had joined the old swordmaster for dinner, he was more than aware that Fullstaff was a creature of habit who expected his meals on the same schedule each day. A late arrival might be welcomed to join in the feast, but usually Fullstaff would extend the invitation with a full mouth and gesture to enjoy that which remained of the leavings. Time, tide, and dinner at Fullstaff's waited for no man.

The blind swordsman stood up from his chair and approached the veranda's edge. As always, he wished to absorb every sensation possible as the day drew to a close. Behind him wafted the sweet aroma of the meal to come, and in front of him the clean scent of the deserted countryside. Behind him was the cacophony of pots and pans as Hotspur, Poins, and Hal prepared the table, and in front of him the gentle sweeping brush of the wind relocating granules of the road outside of his home.

Honor took a step farther out. An unaccustomed observer might have feared that the blind man might fall off the veranda's edge, but those who knew "old blind Honor" would entertain no such worry. Honor had long ago memorized the number of steps between his chair and the edge, and his exacting remaining senses could feel the textural difference that indicated the edge was there. As always, Honor merely wished to feel the breeze that was obscured and deflected by the villa's wall.

He felt the cool caress of the wind on his left cheek, and turned his head to face it.

"A storm's coming," he said out loud to no one in particular. "It will probably reach us by the second course."

An almost nonexistent noise was picked up by his right ear when he turned his head to catch the wind.

"Two horses are approaching," he reported, "both bearing riders. I guess that guests are like the storm. It never rains but often pours."

* * * * *

"Chesslyn, what a wonderful surprise!" Fullstaff hailed from the villa's gate. "And just in time for dinner, too!"

"Of course," Chesslyn replied good-naturedly as her steed approached the blind swordmaster. "Why else do you think I'm stopping by now? Surely it's not to renew acquaintances with an old friend."

"Of course not," Fullstaff replied. "And who's your young friend? By the click of his heels against his stirrups and the unusual flapping of his cape, I would say that he's not from around here."

Volo reined his steed closer to Chesslyn and whispered, "I thought you said he was blind."

Chesslyn went to hush her traveling companion as the blind swordmaster boomed, "Blind I am, though not deaf!"

Volo immediately went on the defensive and tried to apologize for his thoughtlessness.

"I'm sorry sir, I—"

"Didn't realize that a living legend such as yourself would have such acute senses to compensate for your blindness, nor that you would look so young and virile. That's what you were going to say, right?" Fullstaff said, finishing the gazetteer's sentence with words of his own choosing.

"Of course, sir," Volo said with a smile, now set at ease in the presence of the blind swordmaster.

"Thought so," Fullstaff replied, "and it's not 'sir', it's Honor. Now, Chesslyn, come and give a dirty old man a hug."

The Harper agent quickly dismounted with a facility that belied the fatigues of a long day in the saddle, and ran up to the broad old swordmaster, giving him a kiss full upon the lips, which he returned with great zeal and an accompanying bear hug. Their lips unlocked, she slid against him and turning around so that she comfortably rested her back against his chest, the hilt of her long sword barely missing the chin of her former teacher.

"Is that a long sword," Fullstaff asked, "or are you just happy to see me?"

"Both," Chesslyn purred.

How original, Volo thought to himself sarcastically as he dismounted, then strode over to the embracing couple.

Chesslyn disentangled herself from the arms of her former teacher.

"Honor," she said, "I'd like you to meet a new acquaintance of mine, Volothamp Geddarm."

"I knew you weren't from around here," Fullstaff asserted, vigorously clasping the master gazetteer's hand in his muscular paw and pumping it vigorously. "It's not often that we host a famous author in these parts."

"Oh, you've heard of me," Volo said in mock modesty.

"Who hasn't heard of the master traveler of all Toril, and author of Faerûn's best selling travel guide series," said the master swordsman releasing the author's hand before his writer's arm had been overtaxed too much.

"Have you read . . ." Volo started to ask, then thought better of it given the blindness of his host, and tried to change the subject, ". . . I mean . . ."

"Read any of your books?" Fullstaff jumped right in. "Afraid not. I prefer potboilers and cookbooks."

"Oh," the master traveler answered, not quite sure as to whether to take the bear that walked like a man seriously.

"You don't do yourself justice, Honor," Chesslyn corrected, then turned to Volo and explained. "Honor has one of his aides read to him every night. He's read all of the major authors of the Realms."

Except me, Volo thought to himself.

"Well, time's a'wastin', and dinner should be on the table right about now. Hotspur has prepared something from this new Underdark cookbook that everyone is talking about," Fullstaff announced. His arm once again around the lovely Harper agent, they headed off toward the villa's entrance.

The blind swordmaster stopped for a moment, then turned back to face the quite confused master traveler.

"You're more than welcome to join us," Fullstaff offered. "And to answer the pertinent questions that are on your mind, so as not to delay dinner any longer: I recognized the gait of Chesslyn's mount and the scent of the soap that she uses on her saddle. As to knowing that you were not from these parts, I failed to recognize your cologne, and I am fairly familiar with the likes of such things that are available in these parts. Finally, no you don't have to worry about me. Chesslyn is one of my favorite former students, and she is like a daughter to me, and I am more than aware of her discreet assignations. The fact that this is an unplanned visit leads me to believe that she was purposely taking the back roads back to Mulmaster so as not to run into anyone. Ergo, discretion is required, so discretion will be maintained. So without further ado, let's eat."

With that, the master swordsman resumed his beeline to the dining room, Chesslyn still on his arm, and the master traveler following close behind.

The table was set for a feast, which had he not known better, Volo would have taken for a banquet party for ten.

Fullstaff took his place at the head of the table, with Chesslyn at his right hand. The master of the villa motioned that Volo should take the seat on his left. They had no sooner sat down than places were set for them by the omnipresent Poins and Hal, who were well accustomed to accommodating new arrivals at their master's table with little or no notice.

"Poins and Hal will prepare rooms for you after we dine," Fullstaff explained. "Make any wishes known to then and they will do their best to accommodate you."

The master swordsman was about to say something else when he cocked his head to the side as if listening for something. This was followed by the now audible sound of footsteps entering the room.

"How rude of me!" the gregarious host said in a self-deprecating tone. "In my enthusiasm for Chesslyn's unexpected visit, I have neglected my other guest for the evening. What a terrible host I am! Please forgive me."

Fullstaff stood up, and gestured to the other end of the table where a new visitor was approaching the table.

"Chesslyn, Volo, I'd like you to meet an old friend of mine, Mason McKern of Mulmaster," the gracious host boomed.

Volo and Chesslyn turned in the direction their host indicated. Both of the discreet travelers held their breath in sudden shock and surprise as the illumination from the table's candelabra revealed the face of their fellow guest at their host's evening meal.

Volo recognized him as the sour old geezer whose appointment he had usurped on his way to checking in with Thurndan Tallwand.

Chesslyn recognized him as one of the senior Cloaks.

The two travelers looked at each other in silent, controlled panic.

"Introductions accomplished," Fullstaff announced retaking his seat, "Let's dig in. Plenty of time to talk and get to know each other later."

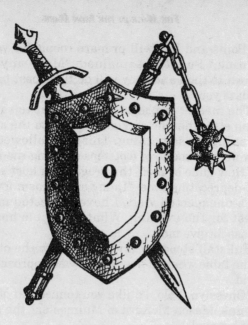

9

Dinner & Denouement

In the Dining Room of the Villa
of Honor Fullstaff, Master Swordsman, retired:

The tension in the air was palpable.

The stern man named Mage Mason McKern gazed ominously at the two travelers in shock.

Volo and Chesslyn exchanged looks, each indicating an instinctive combination of fear and readiness. They were both survivors and ready for any turn of events.

"Now, now, there is no reason for tension here," Honor instructed. "So, I committed a social gaffe. Wasn't the first time, and it won't be the last. Besides, it's my house and this is my table, and McKern, you know very well that dining at my table requires promptness. So eat."

"No," McKern answered, "please forgive me. I should have been on time. I had no idea that there would be other guests. Ms. Chesslyn Onaubra, I believe, of the Temple of Good Fortune."

The mage turned slightly to face Volo, and said, "And you are?"

Honor interrupted. "Eating!" he bellowed in a tone that could not be mistaken for anything but an order. "As you should be. There is plenty of time to exchange pleasantries with Chesslyn's young companion later. Besides that, it is impolite to talk with one's mouth full."

The blind swordmaster resumed the filling of his cheeks with delicacies from the table.

"Sor—" McKern began to say, but thought better of it when he felt Honor's sightless stare drilling an accusatory hole through him. Quickly, the mage began to partake of the feast.

Chesslyn and Volo exchanged glances again. Volo mouthed the words "Chesslyn's *young* companion?" to which the Harper agent replied with a suppressed giggle. Their silent exchange completed, both began to fill their plates, and, immediately afterwards, their mouths and stomachs.

The table was set with every manner of delicacy imaginable. Volo found it hard to believe that this was just an average meal at the table of Honor Fullstaff. In all his travels throughout Toril, he had never partaken of such a feast, and prior to this he had fancied himself an expert epicure. The plates were passed back and forth like cards at a gaming table, and Poins and Hal deftly retrieved, replaced, and refilled them with new contents as dispensed by the able hands of the dwarven cook Hotspur. Only once did a dish rest on the table for longer than a minute after it had been emptied of its contents while Hal and Poins fumbled with a particularly slippery soup tureen.

The host said, "Turnips," which were the contents of the empty bowl, and it was immediately refilled by the ever-ready Hotspur.

Volo was amazed at the sensory superiority of his host. Without the aid of sight he could still identify the contents of an empty bowl, perhaps by scent or by the sound it made when it hit the table or by the placement of the sound in relation to the other bowls on the table. The master traveler was awed, and now realized his folly in expecting that a swordsman such as Honor would have been forced into the atrophy of sedentary retirement by a mere inconvenience such as blindness.

The mage named McKern interrupted his masticating for a moment and asked, "Might I have a spot of wine, please?"

Honor stopped eating and cast his knife to the table, making a clang as it bounced off the side of the plate.

"I am appalled Mason! I will serve no wine before its time!" the host bellowed.

The servants and guests stiffened in silence. The host seemed honestly indignant and offended. Volo hoped that the swordmaster was not prone to violent outbursts over trivial matters such as this, as he had seen many age-demented warriors fall prey to in their declining years.

The master traveler's fears were unnecessary.

With all eyes upon him, Honor's stern visage stretched into the smile of a trickster, and a bold and boisterous laugh escaped from the venue that had formerly served as a way station for the delicacies of the table, on their way to the host's stomach.

"Ha, ha, ha," he roared, "but seriously Mason—only I get to call the great Mage McKern, revered senior Cloak of Mulmaster, by his first name—as I was saying, I have saved a marvelous after-dinner wine for dessert, and I have no desire to waste it on a palate that has already been plied by the pleasures of the fermented fluids of the grape."

The guests all joined in their host's levity with an unpracticed laugh in unison.

"Now," Honor ordered, "back to the matters at hand. Resume eating. Hopefully Mage McKern will not interrupt our gastronomic exercises and enjoyments again."

By the third course Volo realized that the only way to survive the opulent meal was to pick and nibble, rather than to fill one's plate and expect to empty it. Too bad Passepout isn't here, he thought. I bet he could give old Fullstaff a run for his money in the appetite arena.

A roar of thunder was heard outside, then a crash of lightning followed by another thunderous roar, and the sound of sheets of water being thrown against the roof high above their heads.

"I do believe it's raining," McKern announced in a manner more akin to a scholar positing a theorem than a dinner guest speculating on the obviously prevailing weather conditions.

"Mason, I shall not tell you again," Honor ordered, his clipped tones revealing the slight evidence of his irritation at the continued interruptions to the silent sanctity of supper time.

Honor had no sooner resumed eating when the sound of a door knocker resonated through the hall.

McKern was about to speak the obvious, as he was prone to do, when Honor Fullstaff saved him the trouble.

"Oh, let me guess, dear Mason," the host said, not even trying to hide the sarcasm from his tone, thus revealing the quick waning of his temper over the interruptions. "I bet you believe that there is someone at the door. Poins, please see who it is, and Hal, please set a place for them."

* * * * *

Passepout and Rassendyll had just made it to the edge of the grounds that surrounded the villa of Honor Fullstaff when the storm that had been following them announced its presence overhead, and let go its torrents of rain by the barrelful.

Passepout had been drenched before, and did not fear getting wet again. The thunder and lightning however spread fear throughout his very essence. At the first crack of lightning and roar of thunder, Rassendyll was quite surprised to see his rotund traveling companion speed forward in search of cover and protection from the louder and more destructive elements of nature. In the seconds it took for his eyes to recover from the lightning's flash, Rassendyll observed that Passepout had already gained the entrance to the villa.

"Yo, Rupert!" Passepout hailed. "You'd better get that coal bucket of a head over here. Aren't you afraid that it might attract a spare lightning bolt or two?"

Rassendyll hadn't thought of the danger inherent in his head gear and acquiesced to the suggestion of the rotund thespian, quickly joining him at his side, underneath the overhang that sheltered the entrance to the opulent, yet isolated villa.

The architecture of the stately villa reminded the masked escapee of the Retreat, and its isolated location, what Rassendyll reckoned to be a quarter day's journey from Mulmaster, probably lessened the risk of it being held by one of the High Blade's minions. Still, Rassendyll thought to himself, discretion was probably the safest course to take, as one could never be too careful.

"Wow! Get a load of this knocker!" Passepout announced, impressed with the door ornament. Before his companion could recommend the modulation of his tones, the stout thespian had already picked up the hanging gargoyle from its perch and mistakenly let it slip between his fingers so that it came crashing back to its place with a reverberating *thonk* that was doubtlessly resonating throughout the halls of the villa.

"Oops," Passepout apologized. "Well, with any luck someone will be home and be able to offer us shelter from the storm, and maybe even something to eat. It is about supper time after all, and I am famished."

Rassendyll was at a loss for words. He knew that he lacked the time to adequately convey to his traveling companion the dangers that might lurk within. The stout fellow was obviously ruled by his appetites, and had no idea that a death sentence probably awaited them both if they were to fall back into the clutches of the High Blade and his men.

Still, the villa was isolated, the masked escapee thought. Maybe it will be safe within. It might at least be safer than it was outside, given the thunder, lightning, and rain. Maybe we can wait out the storm here inconspicuously, and, when it passes, be on our way.

Rassendyll reached to finger his beard in contemplation when his fingers struck the barrier of the mask. "Damn!" he said out loud, and then thought to himself, well, so much for my hope of just passing for an itinerant traveler.

"What's the matter?" Passepout asked. "I think I hear someone coming."

A flash of inspiration struck Rassendyll, and out of desperation he decided to try his idea.

"Quickly!" he ordered. "Give me your blanket!"

"Okay," the thespian complied, a look of confusion on his face, "But I am sure that it will be warmer inside."

Rassendyll began to wrap the blanket around his head as if it was a combination turban, kerchief, and veil. He continued to wrap until only two slits for the eye holes of the mask, and one for the mouth managed to poke through. As he finished his wrapping he noticed the look of confusion on his companion's face.

"It's an old custom," he explained, making it up as he went along.

"From Zenda?" Passepout asked.

"I guess so," Rassendyll replied, frantically tucking the edges of the cloth into his shirt, around his neck, and down his back. "Uh, where I come from it is considered impolite to enter a stranger's house unless one has one's head covered with a veil."

"Oh, sure," Passepout said unsurely. "I've heard of that. By the way, where is Zenda?"

"Hush!" Rassendyll urged. "Someone is opening the door."

* * * * *

Honor's dinner guests could hear the voice of one of the new arrivals the minute the door was opened. The echoes of the halls and the noise of the storm outside, however, muffled and distorted the sounds before they reached the main hall.

As the new arrivals approached, the sounds of their steps became clearer and the voice of one became more recognizable. When the two drenched traveling companions entered the dining hall, Volo immediately recognized his old friend Passepout who he thought he had left back at the Traveler's Cloak Inn under the watchful eyes of Dela in Mulmaster. A flash of recognition was likewise immediately noticeable on the thespian's face.

A panicked revelation crossed the master traveler's mind. *What if my simple friend announces my presence in the company of McKern? Will this reveal more than Chesslyn desires and increase the risk of her exposure by the Cloaks?*

His fear turned out to be unwarranted.

Volo tried a preemptive strike.

"Passepout!" he hailed. "Have you eaten yet?"

"Vo—" the thespian began to answer, but quickly changed his priorities. "Food! And I am *so* hungry!"

Honor immediately interceded.

"You are both obviously hungry from your travels. We are eating, and meals are not meant to be interrupted, no matter what some of my house guests seem to think. Sit down and dig in. Poins and Hal will fetch you plates. I am sure Hotspur has prepared enough for all. Eat. We can get to know each other later."

Passepout and his facially turbaned companion dug into the meal.

Volo was relieved, having survived yet another hurdle in the challenge of maintaining his inconspicuousness. He marveled at Honor's immediate offer of hospitality to anyone who happened to drop by. Seeing that his old friend was enjoying the meal, he allowed himself another look at the old swordmaster, and noticed something.

While Poins and Hal had attended to the new arrivals, Hotspur had inconspicuously placed a sword and dagger well within the reach of their host. Even the gracious Blind Honor obviously didn't believe in taking too many chances.

Before returning to the gastronomical matters at hand, the master traveler also took a moment to visually examine Passepout's newly acquired traveling companion. The blanket veil gave the fellow—at least he appeared to be a fellow—a rather curious appearance.

I wonder who he is? the master traveler thought, and then resumed eating.

Honor ruled the dinner table like the family of Azoun ruled Cormyr: with great vigor, long reigns, and acquisitive tendencies. When his own plate was clean, and Hotspur's bottomless serving dishes empty, the otherwise gracious yet dictatorial host felt free to sample off the leavings of his guests' plates, much to the great relief of Chesslyn and Volo who found themselves full before the midpoint of the meal, and Rassendyll, whose progress was greatly inhibited by his turban-bound visage and the size of the mouth hole in the mask. Passepout and the mage Mason McKern gave the host a run for his money however, cleaning their plates with a gusto almost the equivalent of that displayed by their host.

When all the plates were empty, and Hotspur now occupied with the cleaning of the kitchen and the plates, Honor Fullstaff stood up and patted his firm yet expansive abdomen vigorously.

"Well done, Hotspur," Honor bellowed the compliment. "Well served, Poins and Hal. Well eaten, my esteemed guests."

Honor approached Passepout, and coming up behind him, gave him a firm, bearlike swat on the back.

"You have already earned my respect, good sir," the host complimented. "It takes quite a voracious eater to keep up with the likes of McKern and myself."

"Thank you, good sir," Passepout countered, "and thank you for your hospitality, but . . . when did you say that dessert would be served?"

Honor barked out another jovial laugh.

"Soon," the host replied, "soon. As I recall, your name is Passepout."

"Correct sir," the thespian replied, "Passepout, son of Idle and Catinflas, at your service. Perhaps you have seen me on the stage."

Volo inwardly groaned at his friend's faux pas.

"Afraid not," the jovial host replied. "I'm afraid that seeing anyone on the stage is one activity that is greatly hampered in its enjoyment by those with the misfortune of being blind, such as myself."

"You're blind?" the thespian said in astonishment.

"Afraid so, not that it seems to get in the way much," the host replied, not conveying any sense of embarrassment over his handicap.

McKern appeared on the other side of the still-amazed thespian.

"Tut, tut, my fine fellow," the Cloak said to the thespian. "No reason to be amazed. My friend Full-staff here is an accomplished fellow, no getting around it, but he is not that much an anomaly. My own brother is also blind as a bat, and is quite the master of magic metallurgy back in Mulmaster."

Rassendyll quickly drew in his breath in surprise. Could this be the brother of the one responsible for this infernal mask? he thought, bracing himself for further pertinent revelations in the evening ahead.

McKern scratched his head for a moment as if engaged in thought. "Passepout," he said out loud, repeating the thespian's name, "for some reason that name seems to ring a bell."

"Perhaps *you* have seen me on stage," the thespian asserted.

"No," the mage said, "seems to me I just recently heard your name around Mulmaster. Oh well, it couldn't have been important."

Passepout, slightly disheartened at the quick dismissal of his possible fame as a thespian, quickly reasserted his main concern. "You were saying about dessert, good host?"

"Oh, yes," Fullstaff replied. "It will be served in my study, a place of peace and quiet and contemplation where old soldiers and old mages such as myself and McKern can regale you younger folk with tales of past heroics and derring-do. The boys are fetching our puddings now. Shall we go?"

"I'm still waiting for my wine," a slightly cranky McKern reminded, adding, "It's time."

"Indeed it is," Fullstaff agreed. "To the study we go."

Passepout followed McKern as he hastened to the study to get a seat in one of the more comfortable chairs. Fullstaff followed, then turned back when he realized that the others were still rooted in their places at the table.

"Chesslyn, you know the way," the host called back. "Please show your friend, and Mr. Passepout's friend, the way."

"Sure, Honor," the Harper agent replied.

"Thank you for the splendid meal," Volo called after the host.

"Nothing of it, nothing of it," Honor called, already on his way.

"My thanks too, your lordship," Rassendyll chorused.

Fullstaff stopped in his tracks for a moment as if he had just thought of something, but then shook his head, and called back, "As I said before," and continued along the hallway.

"Shall we?" Chesslyn said, standing up.

"We shall," Volo agreed, taking her arm. "Care to join us, stranger?" the master traveler asked good-naturedly.

"Don't mind if I do," Rassendyll answered. "And the name is Rupert, Rupert of Zenda."

"Well met then, Rupert. I knew you weren't from around here," Volo replied.

"The face cover is a giveaway," Chesslyn offered.

Volo began to finger his beard, and said, "I've traveled a lot, and I can't say that I recall a place by the name of Zenda."

"I'm not surprised," Rassendyll answered, quickly changing the subject by saying, "I hear dessert calling. Shall we?"

"We shall," Chesslyn and Volo said simultaneously, then looked at each other and began to laugh.

The three set off after their dining companions.

* * * * *

Honor Fullstaff's study was far from what you would expect from a retired recluse's place of contemplation, but was in keeping with the remarkable abilities of their host, at least in the minds of Rassendyll and Volo. It was a veritable arsenal of bladed weapons, decorated with all sorts of military memorabilia and commendations tastefully arrayed in various display cases, mountings, and stands, complimented by several overstuffed chairs and numerous end tables that seemed to have been tailor-made for holding after dinner treats and cordials.

When the threesome arrived, the others had already settled into their chosen post-dinner modes. In the few minutes that had elapsed since the group had split in half, Passepout had already polished off two puddings, and had safely ensconced himself in an overstuffed settee that Volo assumed had been imported from far-off Kara Tur or possibly Zakhara to the south. The cushions reallocated themselves to support the thespian's bulk in such a way that no doubt provided the heavyset actor with luxurious comfort, but would also hinder him from being able to right himself later on. The master traveler anticipated more than a bit of huffing and puffing on his own part when Passepout called upon him for assistance. Mage McKern was sitting in a slightly more austere throne that might have at one time functioned as a sedan chair, and was sipping a glass of dessert wine, smacking his lips in zealous appreciation after each swallow.

Honor Fullstaff was not seated, and was instead pacing around the room juggling four daggers in the air while carrying on a conversation with McKern. Volo thought he noticed their jovial host cock his head to the side slightly when they entered the room as if to signal that he had indeed sensed their presence.

"Have a seat, have a seat," Honor heralded while not interrupting his juggling exhibition. "Anywhere will do. There's even a double, Chesslyn, for you and your friend, though I will not tolerate it if you two ignore the rest of us for the simple pleasures of each other's company."

Chesslyn looked at Volo and rolled her eyes at her teacher's misconception of their relationship, but nonetheless ushered the master traveler over to the double-seated couch.

"Pish tosh, Honor," McKern interjected, "leave them be. And besides, all eyes in the room are on you and your magnificent manipulation of the blades."

"Are they really?" Honor asked coyly, with a trace of a chuckle in his tone.

"Mmmmphyph," Passepout offered, his mouth full with the start of his third pudding.

"Agreed," said Honor, who shifted the orbit of the blades from in front of him to behind him and then back again without so much as a hesitation in his breathing.

"I am quite impressed," Volo said to the host, "and I've seen quite a bit in my travels."

"Oh, have you now," Honor responded. "Did you hear that Mason? The young whippersnapper claims to have been around. Maybe he's not necessarily the type of fellow who should be hanging around our Chesslyn."

Our Chesslyn, the Harper agent thought.

"Could be," McKern replied, and turned to face Volo. "You seem to be a bit familiar. Perhaps we have met before?"

"Perhaps," Volo replied carefully, adding, "after all I do get around."

McKern gave a hearty laugh at the witty rejoinder, and then turned his attention to Rassendyll. "I was just filling Honor in on the latest goings on in Mulmaster. Evidently a prisoner has escaped, two vagabonds are being sought, and there is rumor that there is unrest in the High Blade's marital chambers."

Honor quickly joined in.

"McKern here is one of Mulmaster's older Cloaks,"

Fullstaff explained, surreptitiously adding yet another blade to his juggling assortment. "We've known each other for years, and, in fact, both served under the previous High Blade."

"Selfaril's father," Chesslyn interrupted to annotate for Volo.

"Now *there* was a High Blade," McKern reminisced. "He wasn't the type to go off and marry some bald-headed sorceress from the east, of that I am certain."

"Indeed," Fullstaff concurred. "I miss the old devil."

The gracious and jovial host interrupted his juggling for a moment to quaff an entire goblet of the dessert wine that McKern had been slowly savoring. When the cup was empty, he removed two sabers from their stanchions and began to twirl them in close quarters.

"And you sir," Honor said to the seated Rassendyll as he resumed the show of his expertise, "by your tone, you are either quite congested or your head is bound in blankets. Which is it?"

"The latter, your honor," Rassendyll replied, "or at least something like that. It is the custom of my people."

Midway through Rassendyll's second sentence, a shocking thing occurred. There was the clang of steel on stone. Honor Fullstaff had dropped one of the blades, and was bracing the other, hilt in hand as if he was ready to deal some sort of mortal blow.

"What are you doing here?" Honor demanded of the masked and disguised escapee, the tip of his blade poised bare inches from his blanket-swathed head.

The others were speechless.

"I will not repeat the question," Honor said drawing back the blade as if readying a slash.

"Honor," the shocked Chesslyn asked, "what is it?"

"Yes, old boy," McKern added, standing up and hastening to his old friend's side. "What is the matter?"

Honor remained braced, and ready to strike. "I thought I was the only one blind here," the swordmaster declared. "Are you all deaf as well?"

"Again, I ask you," McKern repeated, concerned more for the agitation of his old friend than for the danger that loomed over the head of the turbaned guest, "what is the matter?"

Honor Fullstaff laughed out loud. This time however the tone was no longer jovial, and was, in fact, quite sinister.

"Why don't you tell them, Selfaril?" Honor said to the masked man.

"What?" the shocked escapee asked, as the onlookers stood by, puzzled at their host's actions and allegations.

"Surely I am not the only one here to recognize the High Blade through his tawdry disguise," Honor said firmly. "The custom of my people indeed. I'd recognize your voice anywhere. Prepare to die for the murder of your father."

To the shock of the others, Honor drew back the saber once more, and launched into a killing blow.

10

Reports, Instructions, & Revelations

In the High Blade's Study
in the Tower of the Wyvern:

"Permission to speak frankly, your highness," Rickman requested.

"What is it now?" the High Blade demanded.

"My men apprehended a felon by the name of James just before nightfall," the captain of the Hawks explained. "In addition to having claimed to have seen the travel writer named Geddarm when he left the city, he also claimed to have spotted two men who resembled drowned rats walking away from Mulmaster along the Moonsea shoreline. The description of one of them matches that of the itinerant thespian by the name of Passepout."

"Go on."

"At first we suspected that the other drowned rat was Geddarm, but James firmly denied this, saying that it was not the same person he had earlier encountered."

"Did he talk to the two, as you call them, drowned rats?"

"No, sire," Rickman explained. "He was hiding in wait for easier prey. He didn't like the odds of two against one."

"Indeed," Selfaril commented. "Maybe he was mistaken the first time. Perhaps the fellow that he previously encountered was not Geddarm. Maybe he was mistaken then."

"I don't believe so, sire," Rickman replied, reaching into his tunic and withdrawing a throwing dagger. "He claimed to have taken this off the first fellow."

The captain of the Hawks handed the dagger to the High Blade who drew it closer to examine it. Clearly etched into the hilt of the bladed weapon was the monogram VG.

"Two questions," Selfaril petitioned.

"Yes, sire."

"Where do you suppose this Geddarm fellow was heading after he left the city, and where do you suppose he is now?"

The captain was prepared with an answer.

"The felon pinpointed his encounter with the alleged Geddarm as taking place on a remote road that

I am not unfamiliar with."

"Oh?" the High Blade said, an eyebrow raised in evidence of peaked interest.

"It's the road to the Retreat," Rickman explained, "and as much as I was able to extract through our various means of persuasion, it was roughly within a few hours of when Wattrous and Jembahb were supposed to be there. I fear that this Geddarm fellow is the reason for their inability to find the bloodstained wand that would have implicated our friends from the east."

"The fools," Selfaril hissed. "The bleeding incompetents."

"Before he died, Jembahb mentioned that he thought the Retreat was haunted. Something about strange noises and such. Obviously this Geddarm fellow was in hiding and managed to trick the two half-wits. I fear that we have underestimated this clever travel writer."

"Do you believe him to be a Harper agent?"

"Perhaps, sire," Rickman answered. "Cyric knows they would love to have an agent in your city."

"You have already mentioned that Jembahb is no longer a risk, due to his incompetence. What about Wattrous?"

"An assassin has been dispatched," Rickman replied. "A reliable one, one of my best. Stiles should have Wattrous . . . *removed* by the end of the week. Our spies have already tracked him to Hillsfar where he is seeking an appointment. The only one he will receive is with our discreet executioner."

"Good," Selfaril said with a tone of demanding finality. The High Blade stroked his neatly-trimmed goatee in deep thought, then continued his inquisition.

"Were you able to get anything else out of James the felon?" he demanded.

"No sire," Rickman apologized. "I'm afraid that he lacked the constitution to survive our thorough cross-examination. Ironically, his body was disposed of at the same time as the late Jembahb."

"So we still don't know who the third conspirator is?"

"No, sire," Rickman replied. "I concur that Geddarm and Passepout are obviously in league with each other. The third fellow's identity is still a mystery."

"It would be just my luck for it to turn out to be my brother, back from the grave." The High Blade allowed himself a cruel laugh at his own absurd conjecture.

"Would you like to suggest a course of action, sire?" Rickman inquired.

"I want this Geddarm and Passepout brought into custody, but I don't want them killed until I know their whole plan. Understood?"

"Of course, sire."

"I need to know what they know about your men's visit to the Retreat, my brother, my wife, and anything else that might endanger the security of Mulmaster."

"Of course, sire."

The High Blade shifted in his throne and readjusted the sash of the silken robe that covered his dressing gown and protected him from the draughts of the Tower of the Wyvern. It was getting late and his bride awaited. As with all of the nights they shared together, it was an occasion that he looked upon in mixed proportions comprised of lust, self-loathing, fiendish delight, and suicidal bedevilment.

Readjusting his sash one more time, and without looking up at the captain of the Hawks, whom he regarded as the only person in the entire city that he fully trusted, he said, "You may go. The she-devil awaits."

"Permission to speak frankly, once again, sire," Rickman asked, adding, "just for a moment?"

The High Blade answered without looking up. "Yes?"

"I sincerely wish that I could remove the threat that exists for as long as you are married to that witch."

Selfaril looked up at his right-hand man, and said, "I appreciate your concern. She will no doubt try another ploy to subjugate me, but it will take time. At the present time we have the theoretical upper hand. In spite of the bungling of those below you, we are no worse off than we were before. At the very least we have foiled their plan, and removed a rival to my throne. For the present time, they are forced to accept the failure of their plans. Our stalemate is their defeat, at least temporarily. I intend to enjoy the respite that exists between plots in hopes of formulating one of my own that will give me Eltabbar, and from there, all Toril."

"Agreed, sire," the captain of the Hawks conceded, "it's just that I fear the danger that you place yourself in whenever you lay with her."

"I know, Rickman," the High Blade agreed, "but it excites me, and there is very little else that does anymore."

* * * * *

In the Apartment in the Tower of the Wyvern that the High Blade shared with his Wife:

In the spare hours since dinner, the First Princess once again sought the counsel of her half sister and Mischa was more than willing to lend her assistance and advice.

"Dear sister," Mischa cooed, the formality of titles ignored in favor of disarming familiarity, "what can I do for you?"

"It's not for me, Mischa," the First Princess corrected, "it is for our cause, and the will of Szass Tam."

"Of course, First Princess," the half sister replied.

"I will need your help in procuring the necessary means to enchant my husband. As always we must be discreet. He is very suspicious and not easily distracted."

"I will enlist the greatest of our wizards to the cause," Mischa replied, adding "Discreetly, of course."

"Everything must be prepared so that the spell may be consummated within these walls or else the Cloaks will surely detect it, and we will be doomed to failure."

"Might I recommend a distraction," Mischa suggested, "to occupy them elsewhere?"

"Fabulous idea," the Tharchioness replied, licking her lips and stroking her forehead tattoos with her exotically lacquered nails. "I know the perfect dupe. How about my roly-poly ambassador."

"A marvelous idea, sister."

"Once my husband's guard has been lowered, I will be able to conceive his child. If the High Blade is still willing to do my bidding afterward, so much the better. If not, he can be disposed of."

"And like his father before him, he can be replaced on the throne of Mulmaster by his own son," Mischa extrapolated.

"My son," the Tharchioness repeated, "the first of a long line of Thayan High Blades."

"Long may Szass Tam rule."

"Yes," the Tharchioness agreed, adding silently, "and myself as well."

* * * * *

In the office of the Thayan ambassador to Mulmaster:

The Thayan Ambassador wept at his desk.

"Why me?" he cried out loud. "I entered the foreign service to stay out of danger. I even picked Mulmaster because, through the First Princess's marriage, I was sure we would never be at war."

The note from the First Princess had been vague:

Worm,

The inefficiencies of yourself and your predecessor have caused us great discomfort.

Fear not. I have a plan by which you may redeem yourself, either through its success, or your martyrdom.

Long may Szass Tam rule.

This is your last chance.

—The Tharchioness

The wormlike civil servant picked up the official note from the Tharchioness and read it one more time. As he did, it burst into flames, singing his fingers.

The worm licked his burnt fingertips like a monkey who had tried to catch a flame.

Whatever the Tharchioness wanted him to do, he knew it wouldn't be easy, and he didn't like the mention of martyrdom. The sinking pit in his stomach soon sent chills throughout his body. Save for the trembling, he stayed petrified in place, waiting for further instructions from his princess.

* * * * *

*In the Bed Chamber of the High Blade
and First Princess of Mulmaster and Thay, respectively:*

The High Blade had begun to snore, signaling that he had entered a deep sleep.

Quietly and carefully, so as not to disturb her heinous husband, the Tharchioness stole from their luxurious bed, pausing only momentarily to wrap herself in a silken quilted robe to protect her body, still moist with perspiration, from the late night Mulmaster chill.

Listening for any change in the rhythmic rumbles of her husband's exhalations that would signal his awakening, she quietly tiptoed to her boudoir vanity and softly sat on its stool, careful to keep all noise to a minimum. Silently she picked up a silver cuticle file from its hiding place, and began to carefully remove the small flakes of her husband's skin from under her fingernails. With the precision of a surgeon or a gemstone craftsman, she placed the flakes in a small ivory pin box whose appearance innocently blended with the other decorative containers that lined the base of the mirror.

The snores of the High Blade grew louder as he sunk into an even deeper sleep.

Shall I chance it? she thought. Why not?

The Tharchioness reached under the vanity table and carefully extracted a crystal dagger from its hiding place. Running her finger gently and gingerly across the blade to ascertain that it was razor sharp, she crept back to the bed where her husband soundly slept, blissfully unaware of his helplessness, and the danger that hovered over him.

I never thought it would be this easy, she said almost silently under her breath as she raised the blade in preparation for its intended mission.

The High Blade's eyes fluttered for a moment and his lips curved into a sly smile.

He's dreaming, she thought, probably of the subjugation of myself and all of Eltabbar.

With all in readiness, she maneuvered the blade down, slicing at her spouse with care and accuracy.

The High Blade snored again, and turned over in his slumbers.

How fortunate, she thought. You've never been this accommodating before.

With two fingers of the hand that did not hold the crystal dagger, she carefully picked up the lock of her husband's hair that she had just snipped off with the blade.

Sure that she had not left any telltale hairs behind, she stole back to her vanity table, placed the hairs in the small box with the flakes of skin, then returned the box to its hiding place among the other knickknacks.

Her mission for the evening successfully completed, she returned to her place in the marriage bed, and gleefully went to sleep, dreaming of the successful fruition of her plans.

*   *   *   *   *

In the Villa of Sir Honor Fullstaff,
Swordmaster, retired:

The blind swordmaster was in the midst of his lethal swing when an invisible force came between him and the masked Rassendyll.

"Honor," the senior Cloak cautioned, "this is your

home, and in it we must follow your rules, but I will not stand idly by while you behead this fellow until you explain to us what is going on."

The enraged Honor tried to swing and strike again only to find the same invisible barrier. This only added further to his rage. Quickly he turned around to face Passepout.

"And you must be one of his Hawks, ready to watch his back, and follow his murderous orders. Well, at least I can rid the world of *you!*" the swordmaster yelled as he took a running start to strike and cleave the petrified and portly thespian in two. When he was a half-step's distance from the thespian, his blade was at the top of its arc and just about to start its deadly descent, when the dull thud of metal hitting skull was heard, followed by the thump and thud of Honor Fullstaff hitting the ground.

Volo thought he saw an oblong blur pass through the air as the long sword flew hilt over blade through the air on its intended course.

The swordmaster's former student replaced the long sword in its appointed spot on the mantle. Her expert aim, incredible ability, and indelible accuracy had guided the long sword as if it were a simple dagger as she threw it through the air. Her split second calculations had also enabled her to judge its path and orbit so that its heavy hilt would make contact with the blind man's head, knocking him out but leaving him relatively unharmed by the deadly blade.

Volo turned to the female Harper and whispered, "I heard you were an expert at heaving long swords but I never dreamed that you could pull off an incredible maneuver like that."

"Remember," she answered in an equivalent and hasty whisper, "don't believe everything you read. From what I understand, most writers are born liars."

By this time Poins and Hal had arrived, and, after assessing the situation, began to help their master into an upright position, and then onto one of the sturdy couches that was available. Slowly, the old swordmaster began to come around.

Passepout nudged Rassendyll, motioned toward the hall signaling that he was about to make a hasty escape, and turned to go, only to take a hastened step forward and immediately run into an invisible wall not unlike the one that had stopped the swordmaster's first blow.

McKern looked at Passepout and Rassendyll sternly and said, "Neither of you are going anywhere until I find out what is going on here, even if I have to call to Mulmaster for reinforcements, and something tells me that more than one person in this room would not be in favor of that."

"I don't know what got into him," Chesslyn told McKern. "Sure, I've seen him angry before . . ."

"Anybody who has known him has," the mage acceded.

". . . but such a rage," she continued. "Only once have I witnessed such animated anger from him, and that was after a night of too many libations and reminiscences of his days in service to Selfaril's father . . . but this time he hasn't had hardly anything to drink."

"It would appear that the reason lies beneath the turban," McKern observed. Turning his attention to Rassendyll, he instructed, "I have been forced to cast a spell against a dear friend in defense of your life. If you wish to keep that which I have protected, remove your mask."

Rassendyll realized that he had no choice. The old senior Cloak was a formidable opponent for the best of the wizards back at the Retreat, and without the use of his own powers, Rassendyll had very little recourse.

Shaking his head in resignation, he warned, "I will remove what I can," and began to undo the turban.

Volo inched over to Passepout, and whispered, "Who is this guy?"

"Rupert of Zenda," the thespian replied, then added, "and I thought that *you* were a barrel of laughs to travel with."

"Where did you meet him? I thought you were going to wait for me back at the Traveler's Cloak Inn."

"Dela and I had a lover's quarrel," the thespian extemporized, "so I temporarily became a dislocated person. I ran into Rupert on the Moonsea shore. I thought we were heading back to Mulmaster, but I guess Rupert had other ideas."

Chesslyn, feeling a little guilty for bludgeoning her former teacher, had joined Poins and Hal at Honor's side as the retired swordmaster gradually came around.

"What happened?" Honor asked groggily.

Poins looked at Chesslyn, then answered, "You hit your head, sir."

"On what?" he inquired, still not thinking quite clearly.

"On . . . something," Hal answered carefully.

"Oh," the swordmaster said, as if the question had been answered to his satisfaction.

Rassendyll had finished unwrapping one layer of cloth, and had begun to undo the second, under the watchful eyes of Mage McKern. As he unwrapped, the shape of the iron mask became more and more defined, until, fully unsheathed, the metal head cover was fully revealed.

"That's all I can do," Rassendyll stated. "I wish I could do more."

Mason carefully examined the metal handiwork

that adorned the man's head.

"Why does he have that on?" Volo asked Passepout.

"I asked him the same question," Passepout answered.

"And?"

"He ran afoul of a wizard," the thespian explained, "and now he can't take it off. Something about it being bound to his skull."

The master traveler, in his research for *Volo's Guide to All Things Magical,* recalled reading about such masks. If memory served him, he seemed to remember that they usually did more than just hide one's face, but also dampened one's ability to perform magic. Legend had it that in olden days such masks had been used on imprisoned wizards to render them vulnerable to torture and interrogation.

Honor had just fully regained his senses after the final covering had been removed from the mask. He sat quietly surveying the situation, the watchful and restraining presence of Hal and Poins supporting him on either side.

"Do you remember what happened?" Chesslyn asked her burly mentor.

"I remember being hit on the back of the head," he said with a twinkle, then added, "You're still pretty handy with a sword hilt, aren't you, dear?"

"I was taught by the best," she cooed.

"Indeed you were," he conceded.

"Stay right there or risk my wrath," McKern instructed Rassendyll, and then headed over to his old friend.

Honor saw him coming, and quickly put up his hand.

"I know, I know," the retired swordmaster said. "As senior Cloak you are bound by your office to protect the

High Blade, but I really thought you would be allied with me on this matter. Selfaril killed our best friend, and the murder of a High Blade must be punished."

"Be quiet, you old fool," the mage said in a derogatory tone that was obviously saved for only the best of friends. "What makes you think that this fellow is Selfaril?"

"I'd recognize that voice anywhere," Honor countered. "He sounds just like his father."

McKern scratched his head for a moment.

"Now that you mention it, his voice *is* awfully familiar," the mage agreed.

"It's Selfaril, I tell you!" Honor insisted, restraining himself from flying into the uncontrollable rage that he had previously allowed to overtake him.

"There is another possibility," Mason said turning to Passepout and Volo. "So, you two know each other?"

Volo answered, "You could say that."

"I remember clearly now," Mason stated. "The Hawks are looking for both of you. You are Volothamp Geddarm, a writer of some kind, right?"

"And if I am?"

McKern just shook his head, saying, "Let us not waste time with such foolishness. Neither of you has anything to worry about from me. Though I am sworn to protect the High Blade, I have no desire to do his dirty work. If he has dispatched the Hawks to find you, you can be guaranteed that it is dirty work indeed."

"Why are they looking for us?" Volo asked, his eyes surreptitiously darting across the room to make contact with Chesslyn. She was equally attentive for the answer.

"I'm not quite sure," McKern replied judiciously. "Something about an escaped prisoner."

"That would be me," Rassendyll confessed, seeing

no reason to continue the charade. "My name is Rassendyll, formerly a student at the Retreat."

Chesslyn jumped into the conversation. "The Retreat," she offered. "That's where I met Mr. Geddarm here. We decided to travel together back to Mulmaster out of concern for our own safety."

"Why?" the senior Cloak asked with all the delicacy and demanding nature of a grand inquisitor.

"Because of what we found there," Volo answered.

"What did you find there?" Rassendyll interjected, more scared than he had been since he left the Retreat.

"Everyone was slaughtered," the master traveler explained. "Not a single person was left alive. We found a blood-encrusted crystal wand that was left behind."

"Thayan raiders, no doubt," McKern observed. "No doubt the High Blade's men will deal with them."

"That's what we thought," Chesslyn inserted, "but while we were there, we observed two of the Hawks apparently looking for the wand as if they knew what to look for. Neither of them seemed even remotely concerned about the dead bodies or what had taken place there. It was as if they already knew that it had happened."

"Indeed, that is odd," McKern agreed. "As of this morning, there was no word about an attack on the Retreat, and, given the concerns of the Cloaks, that is extremely odd indeed. No doubt if it had been an attack by Thayan raiders certain political concerns would have brought it to our attention."

"Maybe the Tharchioness had arranged a cover-up, or perhaps the High Blade was withholding the information from the public until his bride had once again returned to the east," Chesslyn posited.

"Or maybe the High Blade himself was involved,"

Honor added with a sense of knowing finality. The blind swordmaster then turned his attention back to Rassendyll. "You there," he said. "If you are a student mage of the Retreat, why were you spared, and imprisoned?"

"I have no idea," Rassendyll replied. "The best that I can remember is falling asleep on watch, and then waking up bound and blindfolded in transit. My abductors were then attacked on the road by those who I initially thought to be my rescuers. As it turned out, they were the High Blade's men, and bore me away to prison where a blind mage put this accursed mask of iron on me."

McKern interrupted, his eyebrow arching in interest, "Did you say a *blind* mage?"

"Yes," Rassendyll replied. "He did as he was told, under the watchful eyes of the High Blade. When he was done, I could no longer remember a single spell, let alone wield my magic."

McKern approached Rassendyll and examined the collar piece of the mask carefully.

"I thought it looked familiar," the mage replied. "It is my brother's handiwork. What else do you recall?"

"Only that the High Blade seems to be my twin."

Honor stood up, pushed McKern out of the way, and confronted the seated Rassendyll directly. A quick scan by Chesslyn revealed that he had left the numerous bladed weapons out of hand, and therefore probably did not intend a repeat performance of his prior attack.

The blind swordmaster stared with unseeing eyes into the iron-masked face of Rassendyll, and said, "What do you mean 'twin?'"

"We look exactly alike, save for his trimmed hair and beard. We are dead ringers."

Honor chuckled. "Indeed," he said, "this resemblance would have undoubtedly led to your death."

"He said that I would eventually choke on my own beard," Rassendyll recalled.

"No doubt an appealing thought to our esteemed High Blade." Honor turned toward the direction from whence he had last heard Chesslyn's voice, and said, "Chesslyn dearest, would you please bare our masked man's shoulder please."

Chesslyn complied without asking why. The sane and knowing Honor Fullstaff who had been her teacher had returned, replacing the rage-driven mad swordsman who had made an appearance earlier that evening. She knew that he had a reason.

When Honor heard her completion of the deed, he turned toward Mage McKern and said, "Do you recognize that birthmark in his armpit?"

"But I thought he was . . ." Passepout said, none too discreetly.

"I am, my fine epicure," Honor retorted. "I have no need for the use of my eyes to validate that which I now know to exist."

McKern raised the masked man's left arm, and gasped.

"It is the birthmark," the mage confirmed.

"I thought so," Honor said, and extended his hand to the masked man. "You have my sincerest apologies. I could have borne you no greater insult than to mistake you for your brother."

"My brother?"

"Yes," Honor said, "you are the other son of Merch, my dearest dead friend, the former High Blade. You are, therefore, the heretofore unknown twin brother of the ruthless murderer Selfaril."

Honor took a step back and called to his men. "Hal and Poins, get Hotspur and fetch us a keg of my best Halruaan ale. We have much to discuss this night!"

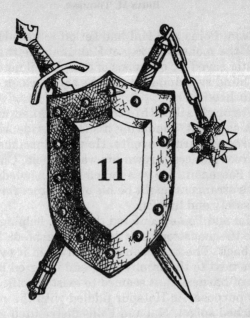

Tankards of Memories

11

At the Villa of Honor Fullstaff,
Swordmaster, retired:

As they waited for the ale to arrive, they splin-
tered off into separate groups. Volo introduced the
very confused Passepout to Chesslyn. The master
traveler was careful to conceal the young lady's
Harper affiliation as he was more than acquainted
with the chubby thespian's pronounced lack of dis-

cretion. Poins and Hal had set off to help Hotspur
with the monstrous keg of Halruaan ale that their
master saved for occasions of exceptional note, while
the blind swordmaster and the senior cloak argued
in hushed tones.

Through all of this the iron-masked man remained silent, pondering his fate, his identity, and
the recent turn of events. He was conscious of the
discreet glances thrown his way by Volo, Chesslyn,
and Passepout. He was forced to acknowledge that
these strangers might be his only chance for reaching safety and freedom.

Hal and Poins reentered the room, helping to balance the monstrous keg that the dwarf cook bore on
his back. The threesome maneuvered it over to a
place next to the trophy wall, and inserted it into a
sort of harness that seemed to exist specifically for
this purpose. As Hotspur fiddled with the recently
attached spigot, Hal and Poins distributed mugs to
the rest of the group and each became filled with the
delicious libation from the Shining South. By the
time everyone had been served, Honor and Mason
had reached some sort of agreement, and had taken
their places in the impromptu circle of chairs that
had formed around Rassendyll.

Accepting his tankard from Poins, Honor downed
it in a single quaff and wiped away the foam from his
bearded jowls.

"Ahhh!" the blind swordmaster said in appreciation as he handed the empty tankard back to his servant who immediately set off to refill it. "You can't
beat the Halruaans when it comes to ale, a fact that
I am sure you are more than aware of, Mr. Volo's-
Guide-to-Wherever."

The master traveler was slightly startled, then
amused at the sudden reference to his reputation and

repertoire made by their host. Indeed, he thought, our host is quite cagey and knows much more than he lets on—about a lot of things.

"I agree," the master traveler concurred aloud, "though I personally prefer the brew from a different part of the south, Luiren."

"Ah, but too many halflings can spoil the brew," Honor replied, accepting his second brimming helping.

The masked man's fear and uncertainty gave way to his own impatience.

"All this talk of halflings and brew is well and good," Rassendyll said with impertinence, "but I really do wish you would get on with whatever you plan to get on with."

Honor stiffened, and Passepout feared that the swordsman was about to enter into another rage. His fears were quickly allayed when he saw the wide grin spread across their blind host's face.

"Told you," Honor said to McKern. "Even has his father's lack of patience."

"Indeed," the senior Cloak concurred. "More and more, I am inclined to agree with you, and set aside my own misgivings."

"I knew you would, old friend," the blind host said, then turned his attention to the rest of the group. "I'm sorry. Please forgive us. Old men are prone to share old times and memories, both the good ones, and the bad, whenever the opportunity arises, no matter how discourteous it happens to be. Still, that is no excuse, and I beg that all of you will accept my apologies on behalf of Mason and myself."

Honor downed his second tankard of ale, once again emptying it in a single quaff, whispering instructions to send his appreciation to Hotspur for a job well done, as he went about deftly refilling his own mug. Refilling it faster than a Baldur's Gate bartender, he strode over to the seated mage in the iron mask who was the focus of all their attentions, and said, "Most of all I beg your forgiveness, and request your indulgence for just a little while longer. You are among friends now. Mason and I will protect you, as we should have protected your father."

Rassendyll felt the gentle bear paw of the blind swordsman on his shoulder, and looked up into his unseeing eyes. For some reason, he felt a profound sense of security. He believed the words that the generous host spoke.

Honor gave Rassendyll's shoulder a gentle squeeze, much as a teacher would give a star pupil to signal some private affection, and took what would have been considered a sip in comparison to his earlier draughts from the brimming tankard, only draining it of half its contents. He then returned to the tap to top it off, and took his place back in the circle.

"Mason," Honor said, "why don't you fill everyone in on our friend's background? I'm sure they will find it quite interesting."

"Agreed," the old mage replied, then added, to the masked man, "I am sure that you would like to know a little about your parentage, wouldn't you?"

"Of course," Rassendyll replied. "Of the many things I learned at the Retreat, that was not one of them."

"Well, old friend," Honor encouraged Mason McKern, "get on with it."

* * * * *

In the Thayan Embassy in Mulmaster:

The worm of an ambassador had not expected to be summoned so soon after receiving the note from the First Princess. He was even more surprised to be approached in his chamber by the Tharchioness's sister.

"The Tharchioness instructed me to come to you immediately, as you are her only hope," Mischa Tam explained in tones of hushed urgency.

"Of course," the ambassador said, beaming with pride, relieved at Mischa's message, eyes glued to the curves of her body, which were subtly visible against the silken robe that barely concealed her nakedness. "The First Princess knows that she can call on me at any time, day or night . . . as I invite you to do also, my dear Mischa."

Mischa Tam maintained her composure while burying a shudder of revulsion that ran through her inner core at the advances of the wormlike ambassador. She was sure that until her arrival, he had been dreading the next contact with the Tharchioness, anticipating a suicide mission of some type.

Even though he did not realize it, his initial anticipations were more than accurate.

"My dear ambassador," she cooed, "I wish I could take you up on your generous offer, but my pragmatic nature, I'm afraid, gets the best of me. You know how jealous the First Princess gets. She would have my head or worse if she caught me giving undue attention to one of her favorites."

One of her favorites, the ambassador thought, I should have known. I never dreamed that she felt that way about me. Obviously she is a woman prone to sadistic affections toward those who strike her fancy. If necessary, he mused, I could get used to that.

"Time is fleeting, and I owe it to the Tharchioness not to dally unnecessarily, even if it does prolong my time with you," the First Princess's half sister whispered, her ironic tone lost on the corpulent and soft civil envoy. "Here is the packet of information that I promised to deliver for her. She so wants you to clear your name, and the successful completion of your mission will do more than that. After all, a Thayan hero would make a perfect First Princess's consort. Don't you think?"

The slow-witted ambassador became confused.

"What hero?" he asked. "And what about the High Blade?"

"Why *you* will be the hero, of course," she cooed, kissing him gently on his doughy, bald pate, and then, with a sigh, adding, "I'm sorry. I just couldn't control myself."

"Quite all right," the blushing, lusting ambassador sputtered.

"And the High Blade," she concluded. "Well, that is what is probably in the message. I must go now."

"No," the ambassador urged, "surely you can stay awhile. The Tharchioness need not know."

"As much as I would love to," she countered, "I really can't. Nothing must deter you from the planning of your mission."

The ambassador looked at the unopened message that had been handed to him, and said resignedly, "Oh, yes, my mission."

"And when it is over, no one will deny you anything, not even the Tharchioness."

"Indeed," he replied, his greed overcoming any fear about the prospective contents of the packet.

"It is the will of Szass Tam," she said, as she slinked out the door of the ambassador's suite.

"Indeed," he repeated to himself, trying to savor the image of Mischa and combining it with that of a similarly compliant First Princess. "Indeed."

Had the ambassador escorted the Tharchioness's half sister to the door, he might have been able to hear her derisive laughter once she turned the corner down the hall.

Looking down at the packet in his hand, and with a gradual return of the anxiety that churned in the bottom of his stomach, he began to open the seal so that he could learn of the fate that awaited him.

The pervasive terror returned as he finished the missive which burst into smokeless flames no sooner than he had fully digested its contents, incinerating the instruction on the spot.

The despair that he felt more than distracted him from the painful searing of his fingertips.

* * * * *

At the Villa of Honor Fullstaff,
Swordmaster, retired:

Drinks refilled, the blind swordmaster sat back in his chair, and began to tell a tale.

"Everyone hereabouts," he began, with a quick nod to Volo, "and thereabouts, who might have done their research, knows that I was the captain of the Hawks under the former High Blade. You might all have by this time made the correct assumption that it was during that tour of duty that I first became acquainted with my good friend Mason McKern, now senior Cloak, then just a plain old mage who lived with his brother, known throughout the inner circles of the Moonsea region as mage smiths of inordinate skill and mastery."

"Once again my good friend is overly generous in his praise," McKern interrupted. "It has always been my brother who possessed the mastery of forged metals. I am, and have always been, but a simple caster of spells."

Honor directed an unseeing glare toward the senior Cloak.

"I am the one relating the pertinent history at this time, and it is only my opinion that matters. I would greatly appreciate it, old friend, if you would maintain a courteous conduct of silence, for I would experience no pleasure in physically encouraging you to do so by giving you a fat lip, if you get my drift."

McKern was about to reply, thought the better of it, and instead embraced the silence that was requested.

"Now, as I was saying," Honor continued, "these things are easily known by many, as is the heinous fact that Selfaril killed his father in order to succeed him on the throne with the same amoral, opportunistic glee with which he entered into matrimony with that sorceress bitch from the east, the First Princess of Thay."

Passepout leaned in close to Volo and whispered, "I guess there is no question about our host's feelings toward Mulmaster's incumbent administration."

"I might add at this point that I would have no trouble dealing with new friends in the exact same manner as I would old friends," Honor said pointedly, but without changing his storyteller tone, pausing just a moment to take an uncharacteristically small sip of his ale.

Even the sometimes dull Passepout, for whom matters of subtlety were usually matters of mystery, understood his meaning and joined the others in the reverential silence of attentive listening.

"But what of Selfaril's father?" Honor continued. "From whence did he come, and where are the tales of his heroics? It is almost as if all trace of the glory that was Merch Voumdolphin has been expunged from public record. And what of his wife, the mother of Selfaril? Whatever became of her?"

Volo felt that he was sitting in on a hard-sell session by his publisher to some unenthusiastic bookseller. He wished that he could take out his handy notebook, but thought better of it. Though it sounded as if the makings of a bestseller were about to be laid out before him, he realized that this was neither the time nor the place for such whimsical maneuvers of ambition, and a quick glance at the iron-masked man reminded him that this was indeed a matter of life and death. What good would a bestseller be if the author never lived to see its completion, submission, or publication.

Honor took a more ample drink of ale, and wiped his jowls with his sleeve in a somewhat vulgar manner that at once conveyed his appreciation of the drink and affirmed to the crowd at hand that this was indeed his home and thus he could do as he well pleased.

"Now that I have your attention, and I thank you for your indulgence of a blind old man, I will answer the aforementioned questions."

"Merch and I shared our early years of formative education, for he too was a graduate of the Hillsfar gladiatorial arena. Though I led the revolt, he planned it, preferring to leave me the glory and gusto of leadership. Once we had escaped, I founded our mercenary band while he took advantage of his less notorious persona to insinuate himself into merchant society by romancing a certain Mulman aristocrat's daughter. In no time they were married, and Merch had safely slept his way up the ladder of Mulman high society.

"There was only one small problem: unbeknownst to him, he had already fathered two sons from a slave girl he had lain with during off hours at the arena, and these offspring were still imprisoned back in Hillsfar."

"It was I who first found out about these two infants that had just been born on the wrong side of the blanket, and I hastened to Mulmaster to alert Merch. Needless to say, he was horrified, torn by his duty to his newly-acquired wife—who was already pregnant—and the illegitimate spawn of his loins."

Mason McKern lightly tapped his friend on the arm, and politely asked, "May I fill in for a few moments?"

Honor smiled.

"Of course, old friend," the genial host replied, "you've more than earned that right."

McKern cleared his voice and continued the tale.

"At that time," the senior Cloak said, "there was a pair of very young mages-in-training in the employ of the household into which Merch had married. They had pledged their services to the head of the household in return for certain financial endowments that had been bestowed upon their other brother, a high-level mage by the name of Loyola who wished to start a private refuge and place of study."

"The Retreat," Volo inadvertently blurted aloud.

"That's right," the senior Cloak acknowledged, adding, "and you need not fear a 'fat lip' from me. If nothing else, old age has at least given me tolerance."

Honor harumphed.

"That said," Mason segued. "I shall continue. Over the years of his employment in the household, the younger of the brothers, the sighted one as he was known, had also become the confidant of the young lady of the household."

Honor took this opportunity to take up the tale. "Merch decided that duty demanded that he rescue

his sons from the futile doom of being raised in the
slave pits of Hillsfar where eventual death in the
arena was considered to be one of the more favorable
options. He told his pregnant bride about his sons,
and she approved of his desire to return with his old
comrade-in-arms to retrieve them. But she feared
that he was ill-prepared to return to the life of a warrior after having spent several months without the
practice of a blade at hand."

McKern again took over.

"So, she asked the two mage brothers to forge an
enchanted weapon that would imbue its bearer with
great facility and lethal mastery of the bladed arts.
The brothers complied, forging a weapon whose
blade was combined from the melted-down blades of
several of Mulmaster's veteran swordsmen, includ-
ing that of the bride's father, whose title of Blade be-
spoke more of his own experience with one than such
a title conveys today."

"When your father took the blade in hand," Honor
interrupted, directing his words at the iron-masked
man, "he became a swordmaster the likes of which
Mulmaster had never seen. Together with his old
comrade-in-arms, Honor Fullstaff, he returned to
Hillsfar, raided the slave compound, and rescued his
infant sons, who at the time were still less than two
months old. Triumphantly, he and his comrade returned with the babes in hand to a prearranged spot
where they could meet up with his bride and her
trusted confidant."

McKern resumed his telling of the tale.

"The rendezvous took place as planned and Merch
was reunited with his bride who accepted the twins
with open arms. Honor and myself decided to leave
the happy little family some time to get acquainted.
Unfortunately, the young mother-to-be fatally mis-

carried while we were absent, leaving the soon-to-be High Blade grief stricken, but with two small sons from a previous affair."

Honor picked up the chronology from there.

"On that very night a plan was hatched. Merch remained in the safe house for another month. Mason was dispatched back to Mulmaster with news of the premature birth of a son. We considered it to be too risky to pass both the twins off as her issue, so you were sent into hiding. A trusted ally was sent to bring you to the safety of the Retreat where you would be cared for in secret until your father cemented his position in Mulmaster. Later, the body of our ally, your guardian, was discovered on the shore of the Moonsea. We assumed that you were borne off by outlaws, and never conceived of the possibility that you made it safely to the Retreat."

"Loyola was always closemouthed about arrivals, or at least so we later learned," Mason amended. "Honor and I now believe that he planned on keeping your existence a secret until such a fortuitous time that he needed more leverage in Mulmaster. Apparently he died with his ace in the hole still a secret."

"Selfaril," Honor continued, "was assumed by his father's in-laws to be the son of their daughter's union, and he was raised with all of the privileges of an heir to a Blade. I remained at your father's side, as his second in command, and trained the army that he raised to lay siege, unsuccessfully of course, to the Zhentarim and other less than cooperative Moonsea states. I was even your brother's tutor in the way of the sword, though I now curse the day I first laid eyes on him."

The tale had come to an end, and silence pervaded the room, until the opening of the door signaled the return of Poins and Hal, who came to inquire if another keg was going to be necessary.

Honor broke the awkward silence.

"It is late," the blind swordmaster said, "and we all have much to digest. Poins and Hal will escort you to your rooms. Mason and myself still have some matters to discuss. We will see you all at breakfast."

Rassendyll raised his hand, as if requesting permission to proffer a question. Realizing that the blind man was unable to see him, he said loud and clear, "Sir, if I may. . . ."

Honor strode over to the source of the question while it was still in progress and, putting his arm around the iron-masked man, interrupted, "I realize that I have probably just set your mind reeling in all sorts of directions. Poins and Hal will provide you with a sleep draught so that you may rest." Turning his attention to the rest of the group, he added, "All of you . . . we will have much to discuss tomorrow. Rest now, while you can."

Volo looked at Chesslyn, then at Passepout and Rassendyll, and shrugged.

Chesslyn smiled, took the master traveler's arm, and set off down the hall to the room she usually stayed in. She knew that Poins, Hal, and the others would be following shortly.

* * * * *

In the Thayan Embassy in Mulmaster:

From her hiding place down the hall, Mischa Tam patiently waited for the maggot-like ambassador to begin carrying out the instructions detailed in the note.

Her patience was soon rewarded. She spotted the quivering and shivering gelatinous mass of a wizard leave his apartment and set off down the hall, the fear of damnation and torture in his eyes. His lips were moving as he muttered some incomprehensible prayers to save his miserable excuse for a life.

When he was well out of sight, Mischa slinked back to the door of his apartment, and carefully let herself in. The door was unlocked, which was no surprise given the man's incompetence.

A quick look around the rooms immediately drew her back to the place he had been standing when she had left. Casting her eyes down to the carpeted floor, she found what she was looking for—the pile of ashes from the note she had brought. Extracting a small brush and a sheet of paper from a pocket in her gown, she proceeded to bend over and carefully brush up the ashes onto the sheet of paper. When she was positive that she had indeed recovered every single ash, she set them onto a bare spot on a nearby desk. Muttering the words of a spell of reconstitution over the ashes, she stood back and watched the note reform.

The original note now intact, she placed the other sheet of paper on top of it, passed her hand over it, and once again removed the paper. The note appeared as before with one minor alteration: the signature at the bottom having changed from that of her half sister to that of the ambassador's predecessor. As the High Blade's men were unaware of his recent demise, no questions would be asked of its validity.

Mischa Tam smiled and licked her lips as she examined her handiwork. The note contained clearly written plans for the ambassador to assassinate the High Blade. The discovery of this would clearly obfuscate their more subtle plans of the gentle sorcerous coopting of Selfaril.

Mischa laughed softly. 'Tis a pity, she thought, that my sister's name has been removed, but it would not suit Szass Tam's goals at this time to point fingers at her. It is important that this plan be attributed to a splinter faction led by intransigent ambassadors who are opposed to the coming together of the two great powers. My sister will get her just desserts eventually.

Mischa looked around the room for another moment, and softly said aloud to herself, "Now, where would a great master of deceit like that worm dispose of confidential papers."

Laughing one more time, she crumpled the reconstituted and altered note, and threw it into the wastepaper basket, then, after peeking through the peephole of the door to make sure that the coast was clear, she picked up the trash basket and left the apartment, setting the container with its crumpled evidence in its appointed place for pickup.

A fast look in both directions assured her that she was alone, and once again licking her lips in anticipation of the rewards for a job well done, she hastened back to her own apartment.

12

An Evening's Just Rewards

At the Villa of Sir Honor Fullstaff,
Swordmaster, retired:

"Hey, Volo," Passepout called after his friend,
"wait for us."

"Damn!" the master traveler cursed under his
breath, thinking, just inches from a clean get-
away!

"Your friend seems eager to talk to you," Chesslyn

said, unentangling her arm from that of the master traveler.

The roly-poly thespian caught up to them, quite out of breath, and was followed closely by the iron-masked man named Rassendyll.

"We were just on our way to bed," Volo said, trying to give his former companion of the road a subtle wink.

"How did you know the way to the bedrooms?" asked the very dense Passepout.

"Oh," Chesslyn explained, "I've been here before, and I was showing Volo the way."

"Oh," answered Passepout, the stars of infatuation beginning to twinkle in his eyes.

Rassendyll put his arm around the thespian. "I'm sure that Poins and Hal will be along shortly. We can wait for them to show us the way."

"Here they are, now!" Passepout exclaimed, "just in the nick of time."

Poins approached Chesslyn, saying officiously, "Miss Chesslyn, the master has instructed that you should enjoy the comforts of your usual room. Mister Geddarm and the others will share the students' quarters."

"But . . ." Volo began to protest, but was cut off by the secret Harper agent.

"It's all right," she said softly. "It's late, and Honor was quite specific that we should all get a good night's rest, because tomorrow will be quite busy. It's for the best."

"I guess," Volo said, unsure.

" 'Til morning," Chesslyn replied, giving Volo a light peck on the cheek.

"What about me?" the thespian asked moonily.

"Of course," Chesslyn said, giving him a quick peck as well, and offering the masked man a quick handshake in lieu of a kiss against the metal barrier that obscured his cheek. With a quick wave, she disappeared down the hall.

"This way gentlemen," Poins said, starting down the hall in the opposite direction in which the young lady had gone.

The threesome followed the servant of Honor Fullstaff, eager to get started on a well-earned rest.

The room they arrived at resembled the typical barracks quarters of a young students' hall. The three quickly found suitable accommodations on beds that were only slightly smaller than their adult-sized bulks. Passepout accomplished this by putting two of the cots together.

Poins gave each the promised sleeping draught, and turned the light off as he left.

Volo was just about to pass into slumber when he heard his friend whisper his name.

"What?" the master traveler answered, trying not to be too terse.

"You know that Chesslyn?"

"Yes," Volo answered, not really wishing to be reminded of the company that he would have preferred to be sharing at this very moment.

"I think she likes me," the clueless thespian said.

Volo just rolled his eyes, and replied, "How could she not?"

After less than a moment's pause, and in the middle of a yawn, the thespian concurred, "I guess you're right."

Passepout didn't see Volo shaking his head in disbelief, as he turned over and embraced a deep slumber.

* * * * *

*In the Office of the Captain of the Hawks
in Southroad Keep:*

After two hours of unsuccessful tossing and turning, Captain Rickman returned to his office to do some paperwork, considering that to be a more productive alternative to lying sleepless in his bed. The halls were empty, and the chill of the Moonsea winds brought a coolness to his chambers that necessitated his drawing a blanket around his shoulders to keep warm. The single candelabrum that provided enough light to work by could not possibly also adequately heat the room.

"Brrr," the Hawk captain said aloud as he settled into the chair behind his desk, his mind not really on the paperwork that lay before him.

For months now, Rickman had been growing progressively more worried about Mulmaster's stability. The rebuilding of the navy was proceeding at a slower pace than even he had anticipated, and there was talk of civil unrest among the common folk, who still had not accepted the desirability of their alliance with Eltabbar.

For many, the diplomatic incentive of this alliance was overshadowed by the misalliance that was construed as the High Blade's marriage.

Initially, Rickman had every confidence that Selfaril knew what he was doing. The plot for the annexation of Eltabbar, and the subjugation of the Tharchioness, had seemed both sound and desirable, but now the captain of the Hawks was beginning to feel uneasy.

Rickman did not like the game of cat and mouse that the High Blade seemed to enjoy playing with his bride. Everything would have been much easier had he just confronted her with his knowledge of her treasonous plans, forcing her to abdicate to him the throne of Eltabbar . . . just before her execution for treason; but the High Blade had decided against this pragmatic course of action, and as a result that which had been a winning endgame was left as a fool's stalemate with both sides at the same point they were when the game started.

Eventually, Rickman realized, Selfaril would come to his senses and look for a scapegoat, and no minor functionary like Wattrous or Jembahb would do. The captain of the Hawks knew that his days as the High Blade's right-hand man were numbered, and, therefore, his days among the living were equally numbered. He only hoped that a plan for his own salvation would present itself.

His prayers (perhaps to Cyric, perhaps to Bane) were answered with an unexpected knock on his chamber door.

"Come in," he responded, his voice gravelly with night congestion.

The door opened and a spineless informant that Rickman recognized as his man in the Thayan embassy entered.

"Sir," said the man, whose name was Lendel, "I came by to drop off some recently acquired intelligence of great importance. I was going to drop it off at our usual place, the Warrior's Arena, but decided it couldn't wait. I had hopes of leaving it under your door so that you would see it the first thing tomorrow morn, but when I saw the light flickering under your door. I felt that it was best to deliver it to you personally."

"What is it?" the captain demanded. "Even though it is late, I hope you took precautions to avoid being followed. It would serve Mulmaster naught if we were to lose our ear within the enemy's embassy."

"I took every precaution I could," Lendel said obsequiously, "but I felt that this was worth the possibility of blowing my cover. Even so, I am fairly sure that I have managed to arrive here unobserved."

The captain of the Hawks stood up and said, "Then what is it?" at the same time noting to himself that perhaps the security around his own office should be increased.

"Here," Lendel said, taking a step forward and proffering his hand, which held a crumpled up note. "I found it in one of the ambassadors' trash."

Rickman read the note with great interest. "Do you believe it to be authentic?" he demanded.

"Yes, captain," Lendel answered. "This particular ambassador is not what anyone would call very bright. His carelessness is Mulmaster's gain."

"Agreed," said Rickman, tapping his forehead with the note as a plan began to present itself. "Remind me, Lendel," he asked, "who is your contact within the Hawks?"

"Lieutenant Wattrous, sir," Lendel replied.

Rickman walked around the desk and put his arm around the spy's shoulder. "And other than him," the captain inquired, "who in Mulmaster knows your true affiliation?"

"Just yourself, sir," Lendel replied officiously. "I have been very careful about that."

"Good," the captain of the Hawks replied, patting the spy on the back. "You have done well, and in doing so have made things much easier on me."

With another pat on the spy's back, Rickman silently withdrew his dagger, and quickly slashed the throat of the surprised and shocked Lendel, who tried to gurgle a protest, a question, then a scream, but to no avail. His throat was already clotted with blood.

"Sorry about that," the calm captain apologized. "In another time and in another place you would have gotten a commendation. Unfortunately at this time, and in this place, you are a liability. Rest assured, however, that the new High Blade will look upon your memory fondly . . . as I take the throne."

The slain spy slid to the ground, as the captain of the Hawks returned to his desk. Quickly, Rickman took the crumpled note and set it next to one of the candelabrum's flames. When it was aflame, he carefully set it in a dish where it safely converted itself to smoke and ash.

Rickman began to talk to himself out loud as he practiced his explanation. "Imagine my surprise," he said. "When I returned to my office, I found this Thayan lying in wait for me. It was only through sheer luck that I was able to dispatch him before he me. I'm afraid that I have many enemies in the Thayan camp, unlike our High Blade . . . the High Blade . . . oh, I see no reason to alarm him. It's not as if *his* life were in any danger."

The Thayan bastards would carry out their assassination, and Rickman would be ready with a few trusted men, to seize the throne in the name of Mulmaster, ending this eastern affair once and for all. The First Princess and her lot would be executed for treason, and he would ascend the throne.

"Mulmaster needs a High Blade who will think with his head, the way you used to, Selfaril," Rickman declared to the empty room. "Mulmaster needs me, and I will graciously serve."

Blowing the ashes out the window, Rickman took several short, fast breaths, disheveled his robes, and set off down the hall to alert the night watch about the altercation that had just occurred in his office.

PART THREE

**The Plan,
the Plot,
&
the Ploy**

Morning Maneuvers

*In the Villa of Sir Honor Fullstaff,
Swordmaster, retired:*

Eventually exhaustion had been sated, and the
sleeping draught began to wear off. Rassendyll
drifted into a lighter mode of sleep that was disturbed every time a movement would upset the center of balance of the heavy mask that encased his
head. Despite the fact that he could not recall having

ever slept in a more comfortable bed (for his quarters
at the Retreat had always been in keeping with the
ascetic ways of the older contemplative mages), he
was unable to find a position that would allow him to
return to the arms of Morpheus.

Realizing that he had received about as much rest
as he was going to, he sat up in the bed and waited
'til he heard footsteps in the halls outside, before
leaving the room that he had shared with the world-
traveling Volo and the snoring Passepout. Making as
little noise as possible, he opened the door and made
his way down the corridor to the main hall in which
dinner had been served.

The hall was empty, though he could hear the clat-
ter of pots and pans in the nearby kitchen, where
Hotspur the dwarf was undoubtedly making preparations for breakfast. Most of the torches from the
night before had almost burnt down to their holders,
which common sense told the masked man meant
that sunrise would be upon them at any moment.
Having nothing better to do, and not wishing to disturb his slumbering companions, Rassendyll re-
traced his steps to the foyer where he and Passepout
had first entered the villa and stepped outside to
watch the golden dawn.

As he walked out to the gate, a blanket held
firmly around his shoulders to protect him from the
dawn's early chill, he looked off to the horizon where
he saw the beginnings of a new day. Odd, he thought
to himself, less than two days ago I despaired of ever
seeing another sunrise . . . now here I am, and it is
beautiful.

So engaged in the rising of the sun was Rassendyll,
that he did not even hear the telltale approach of
footsteps coming up behind him. The senior Cloak
McKern, aware of the seemingly oblivious state of

concentration of the iron-masked man, decided to announce his presence more forcibly.

"Young fellow," McKern hailed before he had reached the subject of his and Fullstaff's private conversation the night before, "mind if I join you in your enjoyment of one of Toril's early morning attractions?"

"Not at all," Rassendyll replied. "Isn't it picturesque?"

McKern recognized the tone the young man had adopted in his admiration for the sun's wonder—the same tone taken by his own brother when he reminisced about his sighted days.

"Indeed," the mage replied, putting his arm around the young mage's shoulders to try to set him at ease. So entranced was Rassendyll with the morning sun, that extra becalming efforts by the mage were completely unnecessary.

"So you were a mage-in-training at the Retreat?" McKern asked.

"More than in training," Rassendyll corrected. "I was more than qualified to leave the Retreat as a full mage, had I so desired."

"Or if such an opportunity had been offered to you?"

Rassendyll closed his eyes in realization. His teachers had never presented him with the option of leaving. Had the events of the past few days not come to pass, he would probably have spent the rest of his days engaged in study at the Retreat.

"Even if it hadn't been," Rassendyll said haughtily, "I was more than a match for other mages of my age."

The iron-masked man immediately became deflated when he realized what he had said. "I was," not "I am." All of his years of study had come to naught, unless. . . .

"Good and gracious sir," Rassendyll beseeched of the senior Cloak, "can you help me to retrieve the spells and powers that I seem to have lost? I studied for so long, and so hard. All I was ever taught was to be a mage, and I would no longer have a reason for living if I have to consider a life as anything else."

McKern chuckled. "No longer have a reason for living?" the senior Cloak repeated. "What about the sunrise and her sister the sunset? Are they not reason enough? The world has much to offer even the simplest of men, let alone someone with your lineage."

Rassendyll did not have a reply for that common sense wisdom.

The senior Cloak put his arm around the masked man and said, "I am afraid that no one can undo what the mask has already done to you. Everything that you have learned through your studies, the proficiencies that you acquired, the spells you learned to cast, the incantations that you had memorized, have all been leeched out of you by the magical conductivity of the iron mask."

"Then all is lost," Rassendyll said in despair and resignation. "I am now useless. I would be better off dead."

Mason McKern gave the young man an encouraging squeeze as one might do with a discouraged brother. "Yes, that which was there before is now lost," the mage conceded, "but look at it this way. Think of a bottle of fine wine, properly aged, and cared for. Imagine that the seal on the cork breaks, and slowly, because of the angle the bottle is stored at of course, the contents of the bottle, the finest wine in the land, is allowed to leak out, and evaporate."

Rassendyll turned his head so that he could look into the mage's eyes through the narrow eye-slits of the mask, as he did not see how this story was supposed to be encouraging.

"Now, the wine steward discovers what has happened," Mason continued. "The wine is gone, the bottle is empty."

"So?" Rassendyll asked still failing to see the point that the mage was trying to make.

"What about the bottle?" the mage asked. "Is it not still a bottle?"

"Well yes, but . . ."

"Can it be refilled and resealed?"

"Well, yes, but . . ."

"True, it would take time, more wine of course, and a desire to maintain the usefulness of the bottle, but would it not be possible?"

Rassendyll tilted his head down and looked at the ground, and conceded the mage's point with a slight nod.

"It's your choice," Mason acknowledged. "There is nothing to prevent you from starting again provided you want to, and I advise you to think about that. You never really chose to become a mage; the Retreat made that decision for you. For the first time in your life, the choice will be yours."

Rassendyll kept staring down at the ground, and asked woefully, "But what about the mask?"

"We will see that it is removed," Mason replied. "I recognize the mark that designates it as being the handiwork of my brother. He will remove it quite easily."

Rassendyll brightened slightly, but still did not look up.

Mason continued, "And I guarantee that we will have it off long before your beard causes you more than a minor irritation."

"It already does," Rassendyll pointed out.

Mason chuckled. "Well, at least you're not choking on it, as your brother desired," the senior Cloak countered. "Stop looking at the ground. You are wasting the sight of a beautiful sunrise. Choose to enjoy it now, and afterwards we shall dine."

Rassendyll looked up and enjoyed the rest of the dawn's early light, feeling a bond of closeness with the old senior Cloak that he had never felt with his teachers back at the Retreat.

*   *   *   *   *

When Volo awoke he discovered that Passepout was still sound asleep and snoring loudly, while their iron-masked roommate had apparently already risen. Pulling his pack together, he followed the scent of freshly baked muffins, and arrived back at the dining hall where Chesslyn and Fullstaff were just beginning their breakfast.

"Morning," he hailed as he once again took a place at the table right next to that of the secret Harper agent.

"And to you, sir," Honor replied, seemingly oblivious as Chesslyn and Volo exchanged smiles and silent greetings. "I trust you found your accommodations acceptable."

"Better than some," Volo replied, and with a wink to Chesslyn added, "and not as good as others."

"Oh, that's right," the host replied, "you are a travel author after all, and therefore always ready to rate the rooms, so to speak."

Volo thought carefully, and quickly adding, "I meant no disrespect, sir. I apologize if I might have seemed overly critical."

Honor belted forth a hearty laugh that immediately set the gazetteer at ease.

"No offense taken, my boy," Honor boomed. "Chesslyn was right. You are a well-mannered sort."

A groggy Passepout entered the room, wiping the sleep from his eyes.

"And good morning to you, oh master thespian of the heavy-stepped gait," the host haled. "Your breakfast will be here momentarily."

"Uh, yeah," Passepout acknowledged, "thank you." The thespian took a seat across from Chesslyn and Volo and quickly brightening for a moment, added, "and a good morning to you, fair maid."

Chesslyn rolled her eyes, and secretly squeezed Volo's hand under the table.

"I trust you slept well," Volo said to his old friend. "You seemed to be out like a light when I got up."

"Indeed, I was," the thespian replied, "until the booming sounds of good company encouraged my wakefulness."

"Not to mention the roar of a stomach tempted by the aroma of early morning muffins," Honor observed. "Dig in, dig in. The bowls will be replenished as the need arises, my portly friend, and there is more than enough for everyone."

A full mouth and a swallow later, Passepout garbled, "Ufgphmmp."

"Come again?" Volo asked.

"He asked where Rassendyll and McKern were," Honor translated, and then turned in the direction of the young thespian. "They should be here shortly. Mason always was a sucker for an early morning constitutional, and I assure you he's never made a practice of missing breakfast. It is the most important meal of the day you know, provided you don't sleep through it."

"Aghmphlghj."

Volo and Chesslyn once again turned to Honor for

the translation while the portly thespian continued to feed his face.

"Well, of course Rassendyll is probably with him," the blind swordmaster replied. "You might not realize it, but they do have a lot in common. Wait! I hear their approach now."

All seeing eyes in the room turned to the empty doorway. Ten seconds later Rassendyll and McKern entered.

Volo shook his head in astonishment, and whispered to Chesslyn, "How does he . . ."

". . . do that?" Honor finished. "My hearing is quite acute. The wise men say that when you are deprived of one of your senses, it is easier to develop your others. Let's do an experiment while Poins and Hal bring some more muffins so that the sun-gazers can sustain themselves as well."

Honor quickly stood up and strode to a set of foils that were hanging on a wall fixture in crossed-swords fashion. Taking one in each hand, he called out, "Mason!"

"Over here, old boy," the senior Cloak answered.

Turning slightly, the blind swordmaster said, "Then you must be there," tossing the foil directly to the slightly bewildered Rassendyll whose catching of it was more a tribute to the swordmaster's precise aim, than to any quick thinking on the young man's part.

Mason took a step away from the masked man just as Honor shouted, "On guard!" and rushed toward the surprised Rassendyll.

The iron-masked man held the foil up in front of himself and protested, "No! You don't understand. I've never been trained in swordsmanship or anything."

"Of course, you haven't," the blind swordmaster

retorted, using the iron-masked man's voice to zero in on his position, while carefully sensing with the foil as if it was some sort of divining stick. "Up until this point you've been a wizard-in-training, and swordsmanship would be grossly inappropriate."

"I am a mage, not a wizard-in-training," Rassendyll protested loudly, his foil just barely deflecting a shadow thrust from the master, "and wizards and mages don't use swords or foils, not even in jest."

"Who's jesting?" Honor said, in a tone markedly more serious than the one he exhibited while he had been seated at the dinner table on the night previous. "Since your head has been shelled in that cast-iron insulator, you're no longer a mage, if you ever were one, that is. All you are now is a marked man whose brother, and several others, I'm sure, want dead. Defend yourself!"

Honor lunged just slightly to the left of the terrified Rassendyll, the blade of his foil just making slight contact with that of his intended prey.

Rassendyll leaped back and held the foil forward, allowing himself more space between himself and the blind predator. Turning his wrist slightly without even realizing it, he adjusted his grip a bit to allow for a little more control of the foil.

Volo, remembering the uncontrollable rage that their host had exhibited on the night previous, moved to intervene, only to be stopped by a firm hand on his shoulder. Quickly turning to see the source of his restraint, he was surprised to see that it was Chesslyn.

The look in her eyes told him to hold back, Honor Fullstaff knew what he was doing. A scan to his left showed that Mason had further withdrawn to a more advantageous place for observation, and a scan to his right indicated that Passepout had interrupted his meal, and seemed to be frantically looking for a way out that would not put him any closer to the sword fight. Instead of approaching the duelists, Volo instead sidled over to his former traveling companion, and making eye contact, nonverbally advised him to stay in his place.

Passepout complied, but was so uncomfortable, he did not resume his meal.

With a series of pokes, prods, and slashes, Honor Fullstaff had maneuvered Rassendyll to a spot in the room from which, unnoticed by the spectators or the other participant, Hal and Poins had cleared away all furniture that might interfere with their movements. Fullstaff obviously had the playing field memorized, and wished nothing to get in the way of the test that he had planned.

When all had reached a certain point that Fullstaff had set, he lunged forward and with a loud cry, began to attack with full slashing fury.

Rassendyll, despite his lack of training, parried back as the sightless swordsman rallied a nonstop series of attacks, slashing the foil through the air as if it were a saber.

Chesslyn joined Volo on the other side of Passepout and whispered over the thespian's head and into the master traveler's ear, "He's just testing him. Had old Blind Honor really meant business, he wouldn't be treating his foil as if it were a saber, and I assure you he more than knows the difference."

"I don't doubt you," the master traveler replied, "but testing him for what?"

"I'm sure we will find out," the Harper answered.

"Indeed, all three of you will," interjected the senior Cloak who had joined the onlooking threesome, "but for now, just enjoy the show."

Volo could not help but be impressed by the pure

artistry of the blind man's swordsmanship. Each attack was calculated to make its appearance within the visible sight limits provided by his opponent's mask, while never appearing to be anything artificial or staged. As Rassendyll parried and launched counterattacks, Honor deftly blocked each thrust, miraculously anticipating the path of his opponent's foil without the benefit of sight.

Even Passepout was eventually impressed. "He's pretty good for a blind man," the portly thespian commented as he began to sneak bites of hot muffins that had just arrived at the table.

"There never was any question of that," Chesslyn countered, "but watch Rassendyll."

Volo immediately noticed what Chesslyn was referring to. The iron-masked man was more than rising to the occasion. His awkward blocks and haphazard attacks had been replaced by more organic moves, mirroring the fluidity of his opponent. As Honor upped the degree of difficulty of each attack, Rassendyll countered, reclaiming lost territory, and gradually forcing the swordmaster back to the center of the room from which he had originally started.

"Enough!" the master swordsman announced, dropping his guard for a moment, and then quickly raising the foil in a salute to his opponent before turning to the left and the waiting hands of Poins who returned the foil to his proper place. "Back to breakfast. My keen sense of smell has determined that the second round of succulent muffins has indeed been delivered."

A quick glance to the left by the breathless Rassendyll revealed the presence of Hal who quickly recovered the foil from his hand, and placed it in its matched home next to Honor's.

"Come, come!" Honor ordered with nary a shortness of breath. "Breakfast is waiting, and believe me there is nothing that stirs the early morning appetite like a gentle workout with an evenly matched opponent."

The exhausted Rassendyll returned to the place at the table that he had occupied the night before, and after wiping the sweat from his brow with a towel provided by the ever-present Hal, he took a long swig of juice and reached for a muffin to sate his recently incited appetite.

* * * * *

In the High Blade's Study in
the Tower of the Wyvern:

"Ah, Rickman," Selfaril said as the captain of the Hawks entered the High Blade's private refuge, "I understand there was a bit of a problem last night." The High Blade had summoned Rickman at the same time that he had ordered his breakfast and, true to form, the captain of the Hawks had beaten the morning tray by a matter of seconds.

"A problem, sire," replied Rickman, adding, "I'll take that," as the valet entered the study. Slater bowed slightly and handed the tray bearing the High Blade's breakfast to the captain of the Hawks, then quickly retreated from the study.

Rickman placed the tray in front of his sovereign, and removed the napkin that covered the tray of tasty early morning delicacies.

"Care to join me," the High Blade asked in an uncharacteristically jovial tone. "Slater can easily fetch another tray."

"No, thank you, sire," Rickman replied, "I have already eaten, but thank you for your generous offer, and, if I might say, you are in a fine mood this morning; rested and renewed, if I do say so myself."

"Do you really think so?" the High Blade said. "I must say that it was a most satisfying night, if the Tharchioness's scratches on my back are any evidence. And as they say nothing stirs the appetite like . . ."

". . . the rest of the virtuous and pure?" Rickman offered.

Selfaril, his mouth full of pastry and jam smiled, swallowed, and agreed. "But of course. But this is not why I summoned you. Slater informed me that there was a trespasser in High Road Keep last night."

"Really nothing to concern yourself with, sire," the captain of the Hawks assured, making a mental note to be more wary of the High Blade's valet. "I am afraid that I may have made myself a few too many enemies among the Thayans. One such fellow was lying in wait for me in my office, but I dispatched him easily."

"Really?" the High Blade said, "I am impressed."

"Nothing, really," Rickman replied, and began to relate his carefully constructed explanation that interweaved truth with his own clever fabrications.

"A few weeks ago I ran into this Thayan at the Warrior's Arena tavern, at least I assume he was Thayan by the tattoos and such. He claimed to be a civil servant of some sort working for the embassy. I didn't think much of it at the time, though as I recall he did seem to be trying to bait me into an altercation. Mindful of your concerns for the delicacy of diplomatic matters, I let his remarks roll off my back."

"Well done," the High Blade remarked. "All of our opposition to those bald-headed barbarians must be done in secret."

"Of course, sire," Rickman agreed, then continued

with his fabrication. "Well, last night, not being able to sleep, I decided to go back to my office and get some work done, when lo and behold I found the Thayan lying in wait for me. With a cry of 'This will be for the insult of the other night, and for all my people,' he came at me with a dagger. I reacted quickly and killed him first. The body has been discreetly disposed of to avoid any diplomatic unpleasantries. It was all nothing really, though I do admit that I am more than a little surprised that word of my minor altercation has already been detected by Slater."

"Yours are not the only set of ears in service to the High Blade," Selfaril commented. "So you don't attach any significance to the event."

"None, sire," Rickman said confidently. "I have in the past, and probably always will, attract my fair share of enemies, in bars as well as on the battlefield. I can take care of myself."

"I'm glad to hear that," the High Blade replied. "Many of the Blades and the Cloaks fear for my wellbeing, particularly due to the presence of so many Thayans in town. Tomorrow night, the First Princess and I will be hosting a public reception, for soon she must return to Eltabbar for something to do with that earthquake. I would hate to have to postpone the reception and her departure for security reasons."

"I really don't think that will be necessary," Rickman replied. "This was only an isolated and personal matter, nothing that should concern a High Blade."

"Well then, you may go," Selfaril said. "It would appear that the unpleasantries and worries of the past few days have fairly faded away, and I can get back to the more personal matters of state."

"That is the High Blade's duty," Rickman said deferentially, adding silently, and you won't be troubled by it much longer.

* * * * *

In the Dining Hall
of the Villa of Sir Honor Fullstaff,
Swordsman, retired:

As Poins and Hal began to clear the table, and Hotspur the dwarf began the neverending task of preparing the next meal, Honor Fullstaff leaned back in his chair and rubbed his stomach vigorously as if to outwardly encourage the inward savoring of the breakfast feast that he had just devoured.

The group had been strangely quiet since the unannounced exhibition of Rassendyll's swordsmanship. Even Passepout seemed cowed into silence, managing to avoid any embarrassing remarks that might get him in trouble, or, even worse, make him the object of some other previously unannounced test from the swordmaster. Once, during the end of the meal, he stole an encouraging look at his former companion Rassendyll, but gave up trying to make contact as the presence of the mask seemed to make such contact impossible.

Volo continued to take in the entire scene. Throughout the meal Honor and Mason occasionally exchanged some meaningless banter on the good old days, and the good lives that they had led up to this point. The master traveler looked at Chesslyn as if to ask, what are we waiting for, which was only met with a shrug by the secret Harper. He was about to ask that same question of their host when the awkwardness was interrupted by the arrival of a fourth heretofore unseen servant who arrived in the dining hall out of breath, and hastened to deliver a folded piece of parchment to the master swordsman.

"Thank you, Bardolph," the blind host said as he

accepted the message. "You may rest now. You've had a busy night."

"Thank you, milord," Bardolph said, bowing slightly and hastening out of the hall to his quarters for a well-deserved slumber.

Honor Fullstaff unfolded the note, and gently passed his fingers over its surface as if trying to detect any imperfections in the grain with his fingertips. "Yes, yes," he said aloud as his fingertips did their slow-paced dance on the parchment's surface. "It is as we discussed, Mason. Though Bardolph was unable to locate your brother, my friends in the Company of the Blind have indeed confirmed the matters at hand."

Volo looked to Chesslyn as if ready to ask a question.

The secret Harper beat him to it.

"Who are the Company of the Blind, Honor?" Chesslyn asked her former teacher.

"Surely you don't wish to know all of my secrets, young lady?" the host answered coyly. "They're just a useless bunch of sightless men who provide the ears for certain concerns in Faerûn who are willing to pay for their services. Occasionally I broker some information through them, for them, or from them. Those who are deprived of sight must stick together."

Volo was impressed. An entire network of sightless spies and informants that was previously unknown to him, the greatest gazetteer in all Faerûn. He could already see his publisher, Justin Tyme, salivating at the exclusive news that would be trumpeted in his next guide book.

Rassendyll stood up and reached across the table to pick up the recently delivered note to scan its contents for himself. Honor offered no objection as the iron-masked man took it from his hand.

"It's blank!" exclaimed the surprised Rassendyll.

"Not really," Honor explained. "The message is imprinted for unseeing eyes alone. Feel the little bumps on the parchment. There is the blind man's message."

Rassendyll ran his fingers over the parchment, his fingertips sensing the irregularities in its surface, yet unable to decipher the subtleties of its message.

"What does it say?" Rassendyll demanded.

"I think that we have kept these youngsters waiting long enough," Mason pointed out.

Passepout, Chesslyn, and Volo all looked at each other, the same thought emblazoned on their minds. Indeed, it had been quite a long time since any of them had considered themselves to be youngsters.

"In a moment," Honor said, delaying just a while longer.

Honor stood up from his place at the table and approached Chesslyn, his hand affectionately seeking out her cheek.

"Chesslyn, my favorite student, I have no desire to set you at risk," the swordmaster stated.

"What do you mean, Honor?" she asked sweetly.

"Unlike the other youngsters here, you are a citizen of Mulmaster."

"So?"

"The penalty for treason, or even conspiracy to commit treason, is death by torture. I will understand it if you feel that your obligations to the state prevent you from taking part in what I am about to propose."

"Treason?" she repeated incredulously.

"Yes," Honor said. "I realize that you are apolitical, and though skilled with the sword, you have chosen to make your way in as quiet a manner as one who lives by the sword can. If you wish to excuse yourself before I bring the conversation at hand to the forbidden subject of treason, I will understand. You have chosen to live in Mulmaster after all."

Chesslyn looked at Volo as if to send a silent message, as if to say, see, he doesn't know everything about me, and then said to her former teacher. "You have taught me well in the past. If the lesson in now treason, then let's make the most of it."

"Good!" Honor exclaimed. "Then treason it is, and as for the rest of you, have no worry. The penalty for conspiring to overthrow the High Blade is merely death, minus the torture. In that regard it is sometimes better *not* to be a citizen."

Rassendyll, Volo, and Passepout all had one question on their minds, a mixture of disbelief, confusion, and terror (in the case of Passepout) more than evident in their thoughts.

What have we gotten ourselves into?

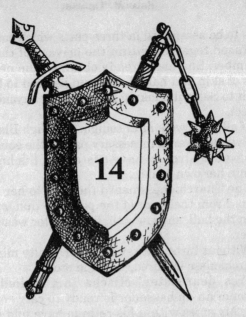

14

Treason, and Making
the Most of It

*In the Private Quarters of
the First Princess of Thay
in the Tower of the Wyvern:*

The Tharchioness had just begun her day-long
preparations for the reception that was being held
that evening, and for the very important night that
would follow thereafter. The charm with which she
intended to enslave her husband and his kingdom

was to be assembled in three parts which could then be fused together within the privacy of their bed-chamber. She had already obtained the necessary bits of skin and hair that would be used to bind the spell to Selfaril, making it harder for anyone else to detect.

If all went well, after tonight the High Blade himself would be an unnecessary part of the equation as she would already have custody of his heir deep within her own womb.

The Tharchioness heard the door to her boudoir open. From the scent of the perfume that wafted in from the hall, she knew that the visitor was her half sister.

Without turning away from her vanity mirror, the Tharchioness inquired, "Is all in order?"

"Yes, dear sister," Mischa Tam replied. "That worm of an ambassador is ready to carry out your will. My spies within his retinue have told me that he has managed to obtain access to a secret passage to your husband's private study where he will be able to lie in wait for him after tonight's reception. I have also taken the liberty of ascertaining that the captain of the Hawks has the same information, so if by chance the worm should actually pose a threat to dear Selfaril, his right-hand man will be able to intervene. The captain—"

"His name is Rickman," the Tharchioness interrupted.

"Uh, yes, First Princess," Mischa acknowledged, "was attacked himself last night, and will obviously be on the lookout for further attempts."

The Tharchioness turned to face her sister. "I don't recall ordering an attack on him," she said severely.

"We didn't," Mischa explained, "though rumor has

it that it was indeed a lower-ranking member of our embassy staff. It would appear that it was merely a personal matter between the two men."

"I see," the Tharchioness replied. "It is nice to see that other members of my retinue share my feelings for my husband's lackeys."

The Tharchioness returned to her cosmetic concerns. "Will all be ready with your part of the piece?" she inquired.

"Of course, First Princess," Mischa replied, the hatred of her sister growing even stronger due to the dismissive manner of her half sister.

"I will send Elijakuk to fetch it after the reception. I will then be ready to help my dear husband relax after his narrow brush with death."

"I await, and serve," Mischa answered.

"You may go."

"Thank you, First Princess," she acknowledged, bowing as she backed out of the apartment, thinking silent curses condemning her half sister to neverending torture.

* * * * *

At the Villa of Sir Honor Fullstaff,
Swordmaster, retired:

Honor looked at the expressions of disbelief on the faces of his guests, with the exception of Mason McKern, with whom he had drawn up the plan of action.

"There is to be a reception tonight honoring the High Blade and his bride, and as a distinguished veteran of past defenses of Mulmaster, I have once again been invited to attend, and as has been the case with all previous receptions, so has my dear friend senior Cloak Mason McKern. Unlike those previous occasions, however, this time we will actually attend, and in my company will be my latest star pupil in the ways of the sword," explained Honor, with a tip of the hand to Rassendyll who started to protest only to be silenced by a gesture from the swordmaster.

"Allow me to continue before I entertain questions," the swordmaster instructed, pausing just a moment to clear his throat with a sip of juice from a mug borne by the ever-attentive Poins who appeared out of nowhere to heed his master's wishes.

"My good friend Mason will cast a disguise spell on the iron mask worn by Rassendyll so to all outward appearances it will look like a dress helmet for an obscure order of knights in whose employ I have occasionally served, as a teacher to their squires. I have the rest of the dress uniform available here so that the disguise will be complete."

Fullstaff paused for another drink, and then shifted slightly in his chair so that he was more or less facing Passepout, Volo, and Chesslyn.

"You, Mister Geddarm and Mister Passepout, will be turned in to the city watch as there is a warrant out for your arrest. Miss Onaubra will do the honors, in disguise of course. I have no desire to put her at risk."

I wish you could say the same for the rest of us, Volo thought, deciding to hold his tongue.

"You will undoubtedly be incarcerated in Southroad Keep, probably on the same level that previously housed Rassendyll."

"Wonderful," Passepout replied sarcastically, "I was wondering when I could go back. The Mulmaster jail has so much to offer."

Volo jabbed his traveling companion in the ribs

with his elbow. The chubby thespian got the message, and kept his comments to himself.

"Given all of the affairs of state that have to take place at the reception tonight, I am sure that Selfaril will not be able to get around to tortur—I mean, *interrogating* you until tomorrow, by which time Mason here will have already rescued you with the help of his brother, whose apartment is within the dungeon of the keep itself . . . so that he can be available for any smith work that might require a resident wizard."

Volo couldn't help noticing that the blind swordmaster had once again made dismissive allusions to the possibility of torture for himself and his companions.

"Mason will then lead you two to a subterranean chamber where Rassendyll and myself will rendezvous with you. There are secret tunnels and passages throughout the city, several of which lead directly to the High Blade's private study. We will proceed to that location, where we will await the arrival of the High Blade and force him to turn over the throne to Rassendyll."

The man in the iron mask glanced at Volo, Passepout, and Chesslyn. Though his face was obscured, they surmised that his expression mirrored theirs—being one of astonishment.

Mason interjected himself into the presentation at this point.

"You have to understand," the senior Cloak began, "we only have the best interests of Mulmaster at hand. Patricide is not a legitimate means of ascension to the throne, and it has succeeded in tainting the current High Blade's entire reign. This absurd matrimonial union with that beastess of Thay, his wanton and ill-advised offensives that have destroyed our navy, and this reign of fear that has pervaded the inner circles of the court, Hawks, Cloaks, and Blades alike, all have weakened Mulmaster's defenses so that it is now both vulnerable and detested.

"It is not too late to change this course," he continued, "and with Rassendyll on the throne, most of the harm can be undone." Mason then turned and directed his comments directly to Volo and Passepout. "Should Mulmaster fall to that she-witch, the Tharchioness, there will be nothing to stop her and her infernal Red Wizards from laying siege to all Faerûn, at which point Mulmaster's problem becomes shared by all of Toril."

Volo listened earnestly to the old mage, and realized, despite his melodramatic presentation, that he had a point.

Passepout was about to once again declare a stance of passive and uninvolved neutrality when the master traveler stifled him with a hand across his mouth. The hand contained a hard roll which, under the circumstances, the corpulent thespian began to devour as he was now unable to speak.

"All Chesslyn has to do is turn us in to the city watch, and you'll do the rest?" the master traveler asked.

"Now, Volo," Chesslyn began, "you know I can take care of—"

"That is all," Honor assured. "If there was a way that we could engineer this coup without your assistance we would, but unfortunately we are a bit shorthanded at the moment, and a blind old man and a decrepitly ancient wizard can't do it all themselves. You and Passepout are our inside reinforcements. Unless we are able to remove the mask from Rassendyll here, all will be lost. No one will learn that he is the High Blade's brother, and he will die a miserable death, choking on his own beard."

Volo looked at Rassendyll, then at Chesslyn, and then at Passepout, before saying, "All right, we're in."

Passepout looked at Rassendyll anxiously, but didn't protest, though Chesslyn did here him mutter a sarcastic, "wonderful" under his breath.

Mason then went over a preliminary map of the keep to acquaint Volo and Passepout with the intricacies of the architecture. The two were then washed and bathed by the able-handed Poins and Hal, fed, and dispatched to Mulmaster in the custody of an old crone with a crossbow who sounded, to the very discerning ear, suspiciously like Chesslyn Onaubra.

* * * * *

On the Road Back to Mulmaster:

"Why do you and I have to be the reinforcements?" Passepout asked his boon companion. "Why couldn't Fullstaff have sent Poins, Hal, Hotspur, or any of his other lackeys?"

"Probably," the master traveler of all Toril answered, "because he didn't want to risk anything happening to them."

Volo and Passepout's hands were tied to the saddles of their horses in such a way that unless they sat perfectly upright and still, they would fall off and be dragged under the hooves of the surefooted stallions of the stable of Honor Fullstaff, whose servants did the binding, in Honor's words, to make their captivity convincing.

Chesslyn's long sword was hidden on a pack mule that followed closely behind so as not to arouse the suspicions of the guards at the gate, and in its place was a modified crossbow.

Along the way, Volo passed the time with stories of exploits similar to his own that he had picked up in various taverns around Toril. Chesslyn's weapon at hand reminded him of one that he had heard recently.

"I remember an article a while back that I read about a man with a crossbow who searched all Faerûn in hopes of finding the meaning of life, but instead found love, laughs, and friendship," he began.

"What was it's title?" Chesslyn asked.

"*On the Road with Crossbow, Hope, and Lamour.*"

"Lamour?" she queried.

"It means female love interest in some foreign tongue."

"Oh," she replied wistfully.

Volo could almost make out the towers of Mulmaster peeking up in the distance, and rashly chose this moment to make his move.

"Speaking of love, laughs, and friendship," he said quickly, slurring over the first "l" word, "when this is all over I was wondering if maybe you and I could spend a little more time getting to know each other."

"What do you have in mind?" she asked coyly.

"Maybe dinner?" he asked carefully.

"I have an even better idea," she countered, "how about . . ."

The *tête-á-tête* of the two travelers was interrupted by a loud snore issuing forth from the unconscious Passepout, who, despite the bumpy road had somehow managed to fall asleep in the saddle. Chesslyn and Volo turned in his direction, and in doing so noticed an advance squad of Hawks approaching, no doubt a patrol for the city watch.

Chesslyn put a finger to her lips, indicating discretion, and whispered, "Later."

It was the last word to pass between them, as the oncoming Hawks took possession of the two prisoners, promising their old crone captor that she would be notified when the reward for their capture could be picked up.

The two Hawks talked about how they planned to split the reward between themselves as they rode into Mulmaster with the bound Passepout and Volo.

In less than an hour the two travelers were sharing a dark and damp cell in the bowels of the dungeon of Southroad Keep.

* * * * *

In the Villa of Sir Honor Fullstaff, Swordmaster, retired:

Mason worked his magics on the iron mask that encased Rassendyll's head. When the spellcasting was complete, a mirror was brought out of storage so that the masked man could admire the handiwork that had been performed.

Gazing into the mirror, Rassendyll couldn't believe his eyes. He immediately raised his hand to the mask, to feel whether it had tactually changed as well.

It hadn't, but to all outward appearances the flat, stark, blank face of the mask's surface had been transformed into an ornately engraved faceplate on an even more elaborately emblazoned helmet.

Honor approached the still bewildered former mage, ran his fingers over the mask's surface, and turned toward the direction of Mason McKern.

"You're slipping," the blind swordmaster commented, "it feels the same."

"True," the senior Cloak replied, "but to the naked

eye, it is now a work of art. The glamour surrounds the surface of the metal, without ever making contact with it."

"Then it will do," Honor acknowledged, and called to Poins. "Are his tabard and leggings ready?"

"Indeed, milord," Poins replied, and began assisting Rassendyll in the donning of the uniform of a Knight of the Order of the Hard Day.

Moments later, Rassendyll was completely masked in his knightly disguise.

"Only one last touch remains," Honor said aloud, turning slowly to accept a locked case from the arms of Mason.

Honor held the case out flat, and placed it into the outstretched arms of Hal who acted as a podium stand for the heavy box, his hands and arms stiff and unwavering under its oaken weight.

Carefully and gently, Honor opened the case and withdrew a samite-draped object which, with the gentle assistance of Mason, he began to unwrap.

"This was your father's sword," the blind swordmaster explained. "No one else has used it since the day he died. It has been waiting for you. Hold it, use it, and it will remember."

Rassendyll gripped the sword, gently swinging it through the air in a wide arc as the memories, abilities and skills of its former owner coursed through his body.

Rassendyll was still absorbed in his gentle practice when Mason turned to Honor and whispered, "We should be getting changed for the reception. Let's leave them alone to get acquainted."

15

Guards, Guards, & Custodians

*In the Dungeon of
Southroad Keep:*

"So these are the two aliens that we have been looking for," stated Rickman as he looked into the dark and dank cell that housed Volo and Passepout.

"Yes, Captain," the guard replied. "The fat one has been here before."

"Then he must be the vagrant Passepout," Rickman said. "Are they alone in there?"

"I believe so, captain," the guard answered.

"You *believe* so?" Rickman replied, on the verge of rage. "What do you mean 'you *believe* so?'"

"Well you see, captain," the guard explained, "the cell has been vacant for a few weeks, but the last prisoner we left in it was never found."

"Did he escape?"

"No, captain, we believe an unusual fungus ate him. There is something growing in the back darkness and, as best we can determine, it is carnivorous. The last we heard from the previous inhabitant was a scream in the darkness. By the time we got some torches to investigate, all that was left in the cell were his boots . . . and that fungus."

"How amusing," Rickman commented.

"Captain," the guard inquired as the captain of the Hawks turned to leave, "should I warn them to stay away from the dark parts of the cell?"

"Don't bother," Rickman instructed, not even bothering to turn around. "It will just mean less work for the torturer tomorrow, that's all."

* * * * *

"Did you hear that?" Passepout whispered frantically to his friend.

"Indeed I did," Volo replied, apparently unperturbed by the fungoid threat that lurked in the darkness.

"I thought I noticed some mushrooms back there, and was just about to treat myself to some for dinner."

"Well, then," the master traveler offered cheerily, "it's a good thing you didn't. A mushroom meal is what you wanted, not to be a meal *for* a mushroom."

Volo heard a nervous titter of laughter from the

unamused thespian, who moved as close as possible to the door, as both prisoners sat and waited for their rescue.

* * * * *

The Reception Hall
in the Tower of the Wyvern:

Fullstaff and Rassendyll had just reached the end of the receiving line to greet the High Blade and First Princess when a herald announced that the affair was coming to an abrupt end.

Honor tapped the shoulder of one of the guards in attendance, and asked him what was going on.

"Golly, I'm really not sure, sir," the guard replied, recognizing the decorations on Honor's tabard as belonging to a veteran of the Hawks. "Both the High Blade and the First Princess seemed rather preoccupied to begin with. You know, as if they would rather be doing something else."

"Imagine that," Honor muttered, trying to mask his concern over the change in plans.

"Then Captain Rickman arrived and told the High Blade that two wanted criminals had been captured, and that they were scheduled to be tortured tomorrow."

Honor heard Rassendyll draw in his breath.

"And then the High Blade seized the opportunity to leave, and announced that he would take care of all of the arrangements himself."

"Did the High Blade, perchance, mention when he planned on doing this?" Honor asked.

"I think he is on his way over there now," the loquacious guard added. "Captain Rickman said that he was otherwise engaged, but the High Blade didn't seem to be concerned, and left muttering something about if you want something done right, you might as well do it yourself."

"I see," Honor replied, keeping a firm grip on Rassendyll's arm to keep the disguised twin from panicking. "Thank you for all of your assistance. What is your name so that I can put in a good word for you with the High Blade."

"Well, golly," the guard drawled. "That would be mighty nice of you."

"Not at all," Honor replied quickly, getting ready to turn and leave.

"The name is Nabors," the guard answered, "but my friends call me by first name which is GoMar."

"Indeed," Honor replied, shaking the young man's hand, and then quickly turning to usher himself and Rassendyll out of the Reception Hall.

"We will have to move fast," the blind swordmaster instructed, as they hastened down the corridor. "We're just lucky that I know a shortcut."

* * * * *

In the Staff's Quarters
of Southroad Keep:

Mason McKern knocked on the door to his brother's apartment and was instantly alarmed as the door swung open, apparently unlatched.

How odd, the senior Cloak thought. Normally my brother is a stickler for security.

The appearance of the room was even more unsettling. Even to the least observant visitor, it was obvious that the room had not been occupied for at least a day. The pallet had not been slept on, the hearth was left untended, and a half-eaten meal that looked as if its diner had been disturbed in midbreakfast had crusted over. Next to the meal's bowls and plates was a book of some kind which Mason assumed was his brother's spellbook or personal journal.

In reality it was both.

Mason was about to open it when a voice from behind him called.

"You there! What do you think you're doing?"

Mason turned around to confront the interloper who immediately recognized him.

It was Dwight Wrenfield, Southroad Keep's custodian.

"Oh, I'm sorry, sir," Dwight apologized. "I didn't know it was you."

"My apologies," Mason said calmly, "I should have stopped by your cell to let you know that I was here."

"Oh, that's all right," Dwight replied, "I was just collecting spiders before dinner, and saw that the door was ajar, so I decided to check things out. I assume you are here to pick up your brother's personal effects."

"Uh, yes," Mason answered guardedly, picking up the volume that lay open on the table.

"It was a shame about his accident and all," the wide-eyed and slow-witted caretaker consoled.

Mason's heart sank. Something must have happened to his brother, but since time was of the essence he would have to wait to find out what happened.

"Uh, yes," Mason said softly, as he hurried to his prearranged meeting place. "I will have to return later to attend to the other matters at hand."

"No problem, sir," Dwight replied. "You and your brother always treated me like gentlemen. I will . . ."

Mason McKern chose not to hear the last words of the custodian as they formed a cacophony with the pit-pat of his own steps on the stone floor.

16

Fungus, Fugitives, & Fencing

*In the Dungeon of
Southroad Keep:*

Volo heard the approach of guards, their boots
making a distinctive military sound on the stone
floor. He nudged Passepout into consciousness.

"What?" the groggy thespian inquired.

"Either our rescuers are coming in disguise," Volo
whispered, "or something has gone very wrong."

The master traveler and his longtime companion heard the bolt and locks being undone on the door. Quickly Volo took to his feet and, grabbing Passepout by the scruff of the collar, retreated into the darkness of the unlit part of the cell.

"What about the fungus?" the thespian desperately implored, only to be shushed by the gazetteer.

The door to the cell opened, and Volo recognized the backlit silhouette of the guard that he had heard talking earlier in the day.

"The High Blade has decided to move the interrogation up to tonight. I understand that he plans to torture them himself. They must be hiding back there somewhere," the guard asserted to his junior officer. "Go get them."

The junior officer, obviously blissfully unaware of the dreaded fungus, proceeded into the darkness-obscured rear of the cell, where he tripped over the cowering body of Passepout.

"I found one," the younger guard called back, still backing up, not realizing he was quickly approaching the fungus-encrusted wall of the cell. "The other one has to be—"

The young guard's report gave way to a scream of outrageous pain and surprise. As the guard's backward journey brought him into contact with the wall-anchored fungus, it had latched onto his unsuspecting body and stubbornly refused to let go. The young man screamed again as the fungus began to dissolve any living tissue with which it came in contact.

The senior guard stepped forward to help the junior officer, but quickly thought better of it as the young man's screams turned to a horrible sound that could only be described as a sickly combination of sucking and chewing. He turned to fetch reinforcements.

Frantic to make his own escape, Passepout bolted forward like a charging bull. The force of his bullet-like flight literally bowled the still-turning senior guard over, tossing him in the air, and causing him to follow a head over heels path that sent him rolling back into the sucking fungus, right past the watching eyes of Volo. Before he knew it, the senior guard had joined his junior as wall's the main course.

Passepout, meanwhile, still not looking where he was going, collided with Mason McKern who was just entering the cell. The senior Cloak saw him coming, managed to brake his stride, and braced himself against the door frame, blocking the stout thespian's charge of egress.

Volo stepped forward, out of the darkness. "What kept you?" the master traveler queried.

"Something must have happened to my brother," the mission-obsessed mage replied, "but I found his spellbook. I am sure the key to releasing the mask from Rassendyll's head is in here somewhere."

Mason opened the book, and his expression immediately darkened.

The pages were all blank.

* * * * *

Selfaril strode through the subterranean halls of the dungeon of Southroad Keep, muttering to himself.

"Why didn't Rickman alert me the minute that they were apprehended?" he asked himself, his gruff tones echoing off the stone walls. "Perhaps he has finally outlived his usefulness. A position such as his might lead to a lust for more power, and acting on such a desire would not be convenient for me. . . ."

The High Blade knew the subterranean passageways by heart, having played beneath the city during his carefree childhood years. He often found the below-the-surface byways to be a much more agreeable method of getting around town, as it limited the necessity of his interaction with the common rabble. Without retinue or bodyguard, he traveled with confidence, safe in the security and protection afforded by his own dagger and sword, one in a concealed holster, the other bouncing in its scabbard at his hip.

A few minutes' walk, and two turns to the left, then up a staircase, and he should arrive at the cell.

"I hope that they will have the prisoners ready for me," he muttered. "Incompetence always puts me in a bad mood."

* * * * *

Volo ran his hand over the pages of the blank book.

"Just our luck," Passepout said, regaining his composure after the unsettling chain of events in the cell. "I guess we won't be able to get the bucket off his head."

"No," Volo corrected, "we will just have to take the book to Honor so that he can translate it for us. I can feel the letters of the language of the blind imprinted on these pages. We'd better make for the rendezvous point."

"What were the guards doing here?" Mason asked.

"Apparently Selfaril was bored and decided that a little entertainment would do the trick, so our interrogation was moved up to tonight."

"Then we will have to hurry," Mason said urgently. "He's probably on his way as we speak."

Mason led the way down farther into the bowels of secret passages that existed beneath the keep's

dungeon. The senior Cloak was in the lead, Passepout close behind, and Volo brought up the rear.
They had just descended a torchlit staircase when
Volo heard footsteps approaching from above. The
master traveler paused for a moment to look back,
and saw Rassendyll and Honor about to descend the
staircase after them.

Volo called to their co-conspirators and waved, but
unfortunately due to the iron mask that covered
Rassendyll's face, couldn't see the look of concern on
the secret twin's face. He turned back toward his
traveling companions to alert them of the arrival of
their allies, when he felt a sharp blow to the top of
his head as the hilt of the High Blade's sword came
crashing down on top of his beret clad skull.

The master traveler blacked out, his legs going
limp, and his body rolling down the stone stairs like
a broken puppet, his limbs all akimbo.

* * * * *

Rassendyll saw his evil twin brother gaining on
the unsuspecting Volo and tried to warn him, but it
was too late. Thinking quickly, he drew his father's
sword from his scabbard with one hand, while extracting Honor's side foil from its holster as well.

Honor was a bit startled at first, but quickly realized that they were under attack, and flattened himself against the wall until he got his bearings on the
battleground and the attacker. He did not even feel
the removal of his side-arm due to the twin's preter-
naturally light touch.

Selfaril stood his ground, not aware that the hel-
meted knight was indeed his twin brother. The High
Blade assumed him to be just the latest mercenary
sent to train under Fullstaff, and decided to offer the

stranger an opportunity to change sides.

"What ho, fair knight," Selfaril hailed, "I have no gripe with you. Throw in with me and I'll guarantee you a commission in the Hawks."

Rassendyll advanced down the steps, keeping silent.

"Well," the High Blade replied, "if that is your decision."

Selfaril lunged forward, charging forward over the body of the fallen Volo. Rassendyll excellently parried with one rapier, while attacking with the other. The High Blade dodged at the last possible moment, losing his footing slightly, and slipping to the bottom of the staircase.

"Well done, Sir Knight of the Hard Day," Selfaril taunted as he backed away from the foot of the staircase. "The blind old man has taught you well."

Rassendyll joined him on the stone floor, Honor creeping behind him to stand alongside Mason, while Passepout rushed up the stairs to aid the fallen Volo.

The two swordsmen crossed swords again with Rassendyll thrown off balance by a slashing blow of steel to the side of the mask.

"Maybe that lesson rings a bell," the High Blade jested evilly.

Rassendyll righted himself quickly and responded. "I have never taken a lesson in the ways of the sword," he replied. "I've inherited all of my moves from *our* father."

The High Blade's twin set upon his brother with the fury of a whirling dervish. Selfaril had to use all his skill and cunning to parry each move.

While the two brothers fought, Mason handed his brother's spellbook to Honor who scanned each page with his hand until he came upon the spell to unmeld the mask. Finding the proper spell he quickly told the procedure to Mason who ran to the still-fighting Rassendyll, and placing his hands on each side of the mask, said an incantation, and quickly removed the two pieces that had been melded to the young man's skull.

Rassendyll was relieved to finally be free of his burden, but had no time to enjoy his release, for while Mason had worked his magics the evil High Blade had taken off down one of the subterranean tunnels.

Rassendyll turned to assist Volo who was just coming around when Honor yelled at him sternly. "We'll take care of him," Honor boomed. "Go after your brother."

Not pausing for a response, Rassendyll rushed into the darkness in hot pursuit of his murderous brother.

17

Just Desserts

The Tower of the Wyvern:

Selfaril raced through the subterranean tunnels deep beneath Mulmaster until he reached a side passageway leading upward. A few steps inside, he felt against the cavern wall until he touched what to the naked eye would have been a long-abandoned sconce. Gripping it firmly, the High Blade turned it to the left. The sound of a pulley creaked into reluctant compliance, opening a hidden door that revealed a ladder hanging from above. Turning the iron sconce back to its original position, Selfaril hurried inside and began to climb upward in the darkness, not even noticing that the secret door behind was still slightly ajar, held open by some inward mechanism of the pulleys that had jammed after years of limited use and zero maintenance.

When some previous High Blade had this passage installed, he probably intended to use it as a possible escape route from the sanctity of his study, Selfaril thought. Isn't it ironic that my first use of it is for the exact reverse?

The murderous High Blade climbed further onward and upward through the secret space that existed between the walls that separated the rooms within the Tower of the Wyvern, occasionally scuffing his boots against the tunnel wall.

Anyone on the other side of this wall, he thought, will probably complain of hearing rats or vermin scurrying in the night. I'll assure them that they will not be bothered again.

The ladder was anchored to a ledge upon which the High Blade hoisted himself. Not pausing to rest for even a second, he crawled forward through a curtain obscured from view by the tunnel's darkness, and entered his study on hands and knees through a false wall inside the hearth that was used to heat his inner sanctum.

It's a good thing I didn't order Slater to have a fire set before the reception, he thought with a chuckle, then set his mind to the matters at hand. I'd better summon Rickman and his Hawks to rid the tunnels of my verminous brother and his cohorts before anymore mayhem is started.

Standing up, and stretching for just a moment,

Selfaril closed his eyes and took a breath.

Just a little out of shape, Selfaril realized, but then again even my best Hawk would be out of breath after such a workout.

The High Blade relaxed for a moment and pulled the bell rope that would send a signal to Rickman's quarters (which, unbeknownst to the High Blade, were quite vacant), then plopped himself into his chair to await the arrival of his right-hand man.

No sooner did Selfaril issue a sigh of relief at having finally arrived in the safety of his sanctuary, than he was greeted with a shock. The wormlike Thayan ambassador stepped from behind a set of curtains and reached forward, thrusting a crystal wand into the High Blade's chest that severed his heart in twain.

The last thing he remembered in his life was the distinct taste of the blood filling his windpipe and mouth, and a feeling of dampness on his breast as his silken tunic failed to absorb the onrushing blood from the pump within his chest that had not yet realized it should stop beating.

* * * * *

Rassendyll raced after his murderous brother in the darkness, relying only on his hearing to guide him in the proper directions. The cool air from the tunnel felt good against the skin of his face, luxuriating in the absence of the metal second skin that it had become accustomed to.

The formerly iron-masked man stopped short. He no longer heard the skit-skat of running steps in front of him.

Remaining absolutely silent, even holding his own breath, Rassendyll listened carefully for any new sounds.

A new noise had been added to the subterranean cacophony of plips, plops, and echoes . . . an irregular scuffling sound like a spoon scraping against the inside of a jug, or a muffled striker making occasional contact with the inside of a bell. As he listened, the sound seemed to be getting farther and farther away in a seemingly upward direction.

Silently and carefully as possible, so as not to lose the trace of the new sound, Rassendyll backtracked along the passageway, his hands searching and sweeping along the wall for some variance in the tunnel's make up.

He stubbed his finger on the still unrighted sconce, and noticed the barest of crevices in the wall. Reaching inside he forced the door open further, and feeling around, immediately discovered the ladder.

He quickly pulled back his hand as the ladder continued to dance back and forth for a few seconds, before coming to a hanging rest.

Whoever was just using this seems to have arrived at his chosen destination, Rassendyll thought.

Still in hot pursuit, the High Blade's twin brother paused for a few seconds more, listening for new movements on the ladder, then proceeded to climb upward to where he now knew his brother had fled.

* * * * *

Rickman watched the assassination of High Blade Selfaril from his safe haven of the closet through which he normally entered the High Blade's sanctuary when the utmost secrecy was required. The ambassador had hidden himself behind Selfaril's chair, barely obscuring himself from view with the help of a hanging tapestry that provided a barrier of insulation between the seated High Blade and the cold and drafty stone walls of his chambers.

The stupid ninny, the captain of the Hawks thought. Selfaril will certainly notice the unusual tumor that seems to have grown on the wall behind the tapestry. If he sees that worm, I may have to lend a hand in his disposal.

Rickman thought that he knew all of the secret passages in and out of Selfaril's study until he saw the High Blade make his entrance on hands and knees through some passage within the hearth.

I will have to have the local engineers make up a floor plan for all of the entrances and exits to this room once I become High Blade, he noted mentally, adding as an afterthought that they would have to be executed when it was completed.

Selfaril was out of breath and distracted as if he had been in a chase and was only now able to take a rest. As a result he failed to see the tumorous bulge against the wall that was the more-or-less concealed assassin.

A feeling of warmth and joy entered the captain of the Hawks' heart when he saw the wormlike ambassador plunge the crystal wand into the High Blade's heart, recognizing it as the twin of the one that had been left at the Retreat barely a week ago.

The High Blade is dead! Long live the High Blade! he thought, his own dagger ready to silence Selfaril's assassin. Next he would sound the alarm, alerting Mulmaster to the tragedy that had occurred; that an agent of the First Princess has killed her husband.

Just as he was ready to make his grand entrance, the sound of scuffling came from the hearth, and a second figure entered the secret chamber.

* * * * *

Rassendyll felt the slickness of sweat on his face as the exertion of the past few hours began to take its toll. All of my training in the Retreat never prepared me for this, the High Blade's twin thought, pausing for only a moment to get his breath. Holding the ladder firmly with one hand he wiped the perspiration from his brow and face with the other, simultaneously slicking down his recently unshorn whiskers with the discarded sweat before resuming his climb.

Another few steps upward, he felt the end of the ladder and carefully pulled himself up onto the ledge to which it was anchored.

Fighting the desire to stop and rest again, Rassendyll frantically scanned the darkness for some indication of where to go next. A hint of a crack of light to the left provided the only clue so, carefully feeling forward on hands and knees, he crawled to it until he felt the fabric of a curtain, which he lifted up just enough to slip under it.

Rassendyll crawled forward, momentarily blinding himself with the light of the High Blade's study. Withdrawing back slightly into the shade of the hearth, he allowed his eyes to adjust for a moment before once again penetrating the room.

When he opened his eyes he saw the feet of a robed individual standing by a great desk. Carefully and silently he took to his feet, ready to do battle if necessary.

* * * * *

The wormlike ambassador turned when he heard the noise from the direction of the hearth—only to confront the man he thought he had just killed bearing down on him with a sword.

The ambassador looked at the figure slumped in

the chair, the crystal wand still embedded in its chest, and then back at the apparition approaching from the hearth.

They are one and the same! the Red Wizard realized. He has already come back from the dead to acquit his honor!

Frantically, the portly and soft Thayan civil servant retreated to the place on the wall against which he had previously hidden, but was unable to slip back behind the tapestry. He thought for a moment that perhaps he could extract the wand from the corpse's chest, but quickly realized that it would do no good against one who had already been killed; and besides that, the corpse's double was already upon him.

The wormlike ambassador embraced the darkness of fear and panic and fainted dead away, falling to the floor inches from the feet of the approaching twin of the High Blade.

* * * * *

Rassendyll glanced down at the pathetic heap of flesh that was his brother's assassin, and then looked to the corpse of his brother, the stain of blood slowing in its spread across his chest.

"I only wish that it had been my own hands that had the honor of taking your life," Rassendyll said out loud to his unhearing twin.

A voice from behind the nearly exhausted Rassendyll replied, "I am sure you do, and, I assure you, you aren't alone in that wish."

Rassendyll spun around, careful not to become entangled in the mass of flesh that was the Thayan ambassador's unconscious body, and immediately recognized the figure stepping out of his closet hiding place as the man who had accompanied the High Blade on the night upon which the events that would forever change his life had begun.

"We meet again," Rickman said acidly, "and might I say the beard becomes you much more than the mask your brother insisted upon."

* * * * *

Far below the High Blade's sanctuary, four figures pressed onward through the darkness, trying to catch up with the twins. Without the benefit of a torch, or even the fleeting traces of sound left by the one being pursued, the party was unable to keep up given the lead and pace that the younger men possessed. The four hastened guardedly through the black of subterranean night.

Honor led the group, who linked hands in order to stay close together. The blind swordmaster used his acute senses of hearing and touch, and his excellent memory of years earlier to retrace the route he took along these paths many years ago.

"Merch was always fond of these tunnels as a means of getting around Mulmaster without being seen. If I know his damned son Selfaril, and I believe I do, he will no doubt be heading to the High Blade's study," Honor asserted, his voice echoing through the underground chambers.

"Don't you think you should lower your voice?" Passepout said in a hushed tone.

"No," the blind swordmaster replied, "I am using it to help keep my course. Given the shape and width of the tunnel around us, I am fairly certain that we are going in the right direction as the echo of my voice is traveling further to our rear than it is in front of us."

Volo thought he understood the principle that the aged Fullstaff was using and decided to make a mental note that he should study and experiment with it before undertaking his *Guide to the Underdark*.

"Now if memory serves," Honor instructed, "there should be a ladder hanging against the wall to my left."

"Here it is," Passepout announced proudly.

"Good," Honor replied. "Now up we go."

"Up?" asked the stunned thespian.

"Indeed," the blind swordmaster confirmed. "Now scoot. The High Blade's study awaits at the top of this ladder, and Rassendyll may need our help."

Passepout paused for a moment to look up. The fact that he couldn't see the top of the ladder frightened him to death.

"*Now!*" Honor insisted. "We're burning daylight!"

Passepout shot up the first few steps of the ladder at a speed that surprised the rest of the group, causing Volo to chuckle at both Honor's jibe, and the panic that had urged the thespian into action.

"I'll go next," McKern replied, pausing only long enough for a body length to separate him from Passepout before joining the climb upward.

"Now you," Honor told Volo, "and don't look down. I'll see you upstairs."

Volo waited for the prescribed body length to separate himself from the old mage, and joined the climb, proceeding accordingly.

The progress upward continued slowly, with the older mage and the corpulent thespian stopping every few steps to take a breath. On one of these intervals Volo paused for a moment to look down at Fullstaff, who he was sure would be climbing right behind him.

The ladder below the master traveler was completely empty.

* * * * *

The wave of exhaustion Rassendyll felt from his ordeal thus far threatened to envelope him, as he fought to remain alert and conscious in the presence of this new threat. With false bravado, he brandished his father's sword.

Rickman laughed.

"That's funny," the captain of the Hawks retorted. "I always thought that mages were forbidden to handle such vulgar and impure weapons as a saber— oh, that's right . . . your brother already took care of that little detail. You are a mage no more."

Rassendyll took a step forward, careful to disentangle his feet from the body of the Thayan coward, his saber ready to strike.

The captain of the Hawks laughed again.

"Oh dearie me!" Rickman exclaimed sarcastically. "A simpleton new to the sword is coming at me. I must defend myself."

Faster than the weary Rassendyll's eyes could follow, Rickman leaped and pivoted at the same time, and proceeded to hurl himself against the wall of the study. In the blink of an eye the human projectile had landed on the edge of the hearth, grabbed a pair of crossed swords from the wall, and propelled himself back in the direction of the High Blade's twin.

Rassendyll ducked barely in time to avoid being skewered as part of the villainous Rickman's acrobatic act.

"Well done!" the knave hailed. "I don't want this to be too easy. After all it isn't every day that I get to kill the two assassins who plotted against and killed my liege."

Within a second, Rickman launched himself back at Rassendyll. The High Blade's twin raised his father's saber to deflect both blades, parrying the first while blocking the second with the hilt.

"Not bad for one so new to the artistry of the blade," Rickman jeered. "If you weren't so obviously tired you might actually make a worthy opponent."

Rassendyll shook his head quickly, trying to clear the cloud of exhaustion that pressed down upon his entire being.

"Come, come," Rickman offered sarcastically. "Why don't you attack this time? Maybe I should mention that your beloved Retreat is no more. All of your brethren were slaughtered. And shall I mention that I was the one who ordered their deaths?"

Rage gripped Rassendyll as a new rush of adrenaline sent a lightning bolt of energy through his entire body. With all the fury of a berserker in a blood rage, he leaped forward, blade slashing through the air that separated him from the object of his fury.

Rickman was prepared for the attack and sandwiched the saber's slicing strike between his own two blades, deflecting the efforts of the novice swordsman, and sending him spinning to the side. The captain of the Hawks could not resist further toying with his prey, and booted him in the rear as he spun by, sending the brother of the High Blade sprawling, Rassendyll barely held on to the sword of his father.

"So sorry you tripped," Rickman mocked. "Killing well takes practice. Now let me see. Over the past few days I have killed a Thayan traitor . . ."

Rassendyll scrambled to his feet.

"Ordered the deaths of the entire inhabitants of a monastery . . ."

The High Blade's twin thought he detected a sound from the hearth through which he had entered the room, but kept his eyes focused on the purveyor of bladed destruction in front of him.

"Ordered the deaths of some of my own men, just to keep a few things secret . . ."

Rickman sprang forward again, slashing at his prey, the tip of his blade nicking Rassendyll at the edge of his scalp.

"How clumsy of me!" he taunted. "I bet you wish you had that iron mask on now."

The captain of the Hawks hesitated for a moment as a new thought just crossed his mind.

"Oh dear!" Rickman mocked. "I seem to have lost count. Did I mention that I also killed another of your kind? The blind wizard smith who fashioned that mask for you!"

"*No!*"

The shout from the hearth startled both of the duelists, as McKern tried to race into the room having just climbed up the ladder moments in time to hear the taunting admission of Rickman to murdering his only brother.

Rickman spun toward the hearth, ready to slice and dice the Cloak who was frantically trying to enter the room and extract his own vengeance. The captain of the Hawks was focused on this latest intruder, but failed to observe the now-prostrate form of Passepout, who had fallen forward at the mage's scream. The thespian had had the misfortune of being in front of the now enraged wizard and had belly-flopped out of the hearth and onto the carpet directly in front of the rampaging swordsman, catching Rickman's foot in his wake.

Rickman realized this latest obstacle too late to stop himself from pitching forward. His frantic attempts at regaining his balance only succeeded in making his head come into contact with the hearth ledge, knocking him out. Both of his swords fell point first beneath him, skewering the prostrate form of the helpless Passepout as Volo peeked out from the secret entrance to observe the unfortunate proceedings.

"*No!*"

The master traveler now cried in vain. He could not stop the body already in motion.

18

Covering Tracks

In the High Blade's Chambers
in the Tower of the Wyvern:

Volo rushed to the side of his impaled friend, scrambling past the equally horrified Mason McKern, and around the other two prostrate forms that littered the floor near the hearth. The master traveler unceremoniously cast the groggy form of Captain Rickman off the body of his obese and decidedly prone boon companion.

Rickman began to groan; the concussion of the contact of his head against the hearth only succeeded in knocking him out for a moment, and in no time he would be in a groggy state of consciousness. "Oh, my head!" he mumbled as his hands vainly tried to make their way off the ground and up to his pate. "Ohhhhhh."

Volo ignored the blackguard's cries of pain, and knelt by his boon companion, trying desperately not to look at the hilts of the duelist's two swords that swayed like flagpoles on the mountainous summit that was the body of his beloved Passepout.

"Oh, son of Idle and Catinflas," the master gazetteer cried.

The thespian opened his eyes, and a grimace of pain immediately passed over his face.

"You are alive old friend!" Volo said softly, not yet sure how serious the thespian's wounds were.

"Just barely," the son of Idle and Catinflas replied weakly.

"Is there anything I can do, old friend?" Volo asked.

"No, dear Volo," Passepout said a trifle dramatically. "Just allow me to pass from this life, here and now, in this pool of blood."

Volo felt on the verge of tears, and held the dying thespian's hand up to his face. "Courage, dear friend," he implored. "You are still warm, perhaps McKern can save you."

"No," the master thespian insisted, "I already feel death's cold shadow as my heart pumps its last few ounces of blood into the river that feeds this pool of blood."

Pool of blood, the master traveler thought to himself, it sounds so familiar.

Volo looked down at the area around his bisected friend. The floor was dry, and nary a trace of blood was visible.

Quickly the master traveler cast back the cloak from his prostrate friend's body, and observed the placement of the two blades, one sandwiched between two tree-sized thighs, the other nestled in the right armpit. In both cases, the thespian's skin was barely nicked.

The master traveler laughed.

"It serves me right, you lucky knave," the master gazetteer replied, as his thought-to-be-dying friend sat up with great vigor.

" 'Twasn't luck, 'twas skill," the thespian replied. "It is imperative that a skilled actor know how to avoid an oncoming blade in a dying sequence if one wishes to have much of a career on the stage."

"*Pool of Blood* was the title of one of the plays in your repertoire, if I recall correctly."

"Indeed, it is," the thespian replied, "*Ward's Folly*, also known as *The Pool of Blood,* a real slaughterfest of a show."

Out of the corner of his eye, Volo saw McKern. The old mage was still staring at the slowly recovering form of the captain of the Hawks, muttering under his breath.

"You killed my brother," he murmured. "An honest man, a craftsman, a humanitarian. He served Mulmaster as best he could, trusting his superiors, and now he is dead. He never saw it coming. My name is Mason McKern. You killed my brother; prepare to die!"

As the grief-possessed mage rambled on, his rage increased, his fingers began to flex, and his exclamations of grief dissolved into arcane incantations.

Rassendyll immediately recognized what was happening. "Back off Volo, Passepout!" he ordered.

"Get away from the bodies!"

Volo sprang to the side, while the chubby thespian responded with a quick roll to the right, seeking shelter behind a chair.

The High Blade's twin approached the mage, who was in turn approaching Rickman. "Calm down, McKern," Rassendyll urged gently, trying not to notice the smoke that seemed to be coming from the old wizard's fingertips. "This is neither the time nor the place for a fireball."

"Leave me be," Mason said sternly. "Your father's killer is dead, and my brother's killer should join him."

For the third time in less than half an hour, a person announced their presence to the inhabitants of the room with a loud, prohibitive command.

"*No!*"

The mage, former mage, gazetteer, and thespian turned toward a sideboard located on the other side of the room which had just started to swing forward to reveal yet another secret passage, out of which stepped the imposing figure of the blind swordmaster, Honor Fullstaff.

"The sentence of death will be carried out, old friend," Honor Fullstaff said with great certainty, "but not just yet. I am afraid that he might still be of use to us for just a little while longer."

McKern was torn between his desire for vengeance and the common sense preached by his old friend. The stern look on his old friend's face cast the deciding vote, as the old mage had no desire to cross Honor Fullstaff when he had already let his position be known.

"Agreed," the old mage assented. "What's our next move?"

* * * * *

*In the Apartment of Mischa Tam
in the Thayan Embassy in Mulmaster:*

Mischa Tam was beginning to get nervous.

The cat's-paw who had been dispatched to attempt the assassination of Selfaril should have botched the job by now, she thought. Even if he had somehow managed to surprise the High Blade, surely he would not have been able to overpower him. And what about the Hawks? She had made darn sure that Rickman was aware of the plot as well and would be able to intervene and arrest the quivering maggot.

A heinous thought crossed her mind.

What if, somehow, the incompetent had succeeded?

The First Princess would surely have her head, that is, if any of the Thayans managed to make it out of Mulmaster alive.

Though the death of Selfaril was undoubtedly the eventual goal, timing was of the essence, and at the present, the time was not right.

Mischa removed a talisman from inside her robe, and stared into its multi-faceted surface.

"Do I dare to see through the eyes of the worm?" she whispered.

She had to know.

Mischa took out a piece of skin that had formerly belonged to the ambassador and placed it on the talisman. She paused for a moment, reliving the disgust she felt at the measures that she had to take to obtain this living souvenir of the maggot, shuddered, and placed it onto the orb.

The skin immediately melted into the talisman's surface.

Wasting no time she held the orb up to her eye, and looked into its opaque surface as if it were a magnifying crystal.

All she saw was darkness.

Mischa considered the possibilities. *Perhaps he is already dead, or unconscious . . . but unfortunately that still doesn't solve the problem.*

Concentrating with all her scrying powers, she once again looked into the orb, trying to backtrack through the images that had been recorded by the maggot before he had been enveloped by the darkness.

The shadows gradually cleared. First she saw a dishevelled and unkempt High Blade . . . a hearth . . . the High Blade better groomed, but obviously fatigued . . . a crystal wand striking home into the heart of the mortally wounded Selfaril!

Mischa dropped the orb in a panic.

The fool actually succeeded in killing my sister's husband!

A knock on her chamber door interrupted her panic.

"Who is it?" she said with mock calm.

"It is I, Mischa," announced the messenger, "Elijakuk."

Mischa opened the door to allow in the Tharchioness's chancellor.

"What is it?" she demanded, still trying to hide her own uneasiness.

"The First Princess sent me for your part of the project," he said gravely. "I believe she desires to use it tonight. She fears that our window of opportunity is rapidly diminishing."

Mischa stifled a laugh at the inadvertent irony of the chancellor's last statement, and thanked Szass Tam for the news.

My sister does not yet know of the fate of her husband! she thought in exultation. *There may be a chance for me yet.*

Maintaining her composure, the Tharchioness's

half sister went to her vanity table, reached into a secret compartment, and extracted the disk that she had treated with the appropriate oils and herbs to accomplish her part of the spell. She wrapped it in a silk scarf and handed it to the chancellor.

"Her desire is my command," she said reverently. "My part is now complete."

"The First Princess will be pleased," Elijakuk acknowledged her with a bow that included a pause to appreciate the Tharchioness's sister's ample cleavage. "Szass Tam be with you."

Mischa cracked her best seductively serpentine smile.

"And with you," she said sweetly, "but tarry no longer. We mustn't keep the First Princess waiting. She knows best. If she believes that time is of the essence, then who are we to dispute it?"

"Indeed!" the chancellor agreed, a satyrlike smile on his lips. "Shall we go?"

"No," she countered with a touch of mock regret. "You will travel faster and more discreetly, on your own. I will wait here to carry out any further orders from the First Princess should she desire me to do so."

"I will return with further instructions," the chancellor said, giving Mischa's hand a quick kiss accented with a touch of the tip of his tongue, adding, "with great haste."

"I will await," she responded with mock eagerness, as she closed the door behind him and let out a sigh of relief.

Collecting her thoughts, her composure regained, the Thayan sorceress set about gathering her things, for she had no intention of being around when the detritus flew from the waterwheel.

"My sister will need a scapegoat and I have no intention of being available for that honor," she said aloud.

In a matter of moments she had packed all she needed, and within the hour she had already stolen herself from the city of Mulmaster like a thief in the night, hoping to make the court of Szass Tam in enough time to state her case before the Tharchioness had issued her death warrant.

The chancellor was quite disappointed later in the evening when he returned to her chamber having completed his appointed mission. When she failed to respond to his gentle taps on her door, he increased the force of each of the blows until he became afraid that he would wake up a neighboring minister before arousing the lovely Mischa. He quickly concluded that she must have already fallen into a sound sleep, and that a good night's rest would do him good as well, so that he would be amply refreshed when they resumed their *tête-à-tête* on the following day.

Unbeknownst to him, he had missed the lovely Mischa by mere moments, and would never have the pleasure of seeing her again.

* * * * *

In the High Blade's Chambers
in the Tower of the Wyvern:

Honor took Mason aside and exchanged furtive whispers with him as the others looked on, assuming that he was trying to calm his old friend down.

Rickman, who had almost returned to consciousness was encouraged to remain out cold by Passepout, who utilized a firm blow to the captain's head with a ceramic bust that had been resting on a table near the mantlepiece. The portly thespian, unfortunately misjudged the trajectory of the bust's blow, and nearly broke his own toe when its deflected path caused it to impact his foot.

Volo and Rassendyll shared a stifled grin at their friend's minor misfortune, and then quickly moved to his side to console him and applaud his fast efforts in dealing with the deceitful Rickman. By the time the three had finished ascertaining that Passepout's foot was not even sprained, nor very badly bruised, McKern and Fullstaff had finished their exchange, and asked for all of their attentions.

"Our paths herewith must diverge," the blind swordmaster maintained. "With Selfaril dead, we must quickly move to put Rassendyll in his place as the new High Blade of Mulmaster. What better way to do so than by having him assume Selfaril's identity?"

"But . . ." Rassendyll began to protest, but quickly hushed when Honor's upraised hand signaled him to wait a minute.

"Mulmaster without a High Blade in place would be easy prey for all takers in the Moonsea region, let alone the imperialist hungers of Azoun in Cormyr, and the residential threat of the Thayans, who already have exerted undue influence in our fair court."

Rassendyll nodded in agreement, realizing that the older swordmaster was indeed correct in his assessment of the situation.

"Therefore, we must slip you into his identity as quickly as possible," Mason added. "Honor and I will be right at your side all the time."

"What about us?" Passepout interjected with a gesture indicating that he was referring to himself and Volo.

"Indeed," Mason acknowledged with a nod.

"Indeed," Honor seconded, and began to relate the second part of his plan. "In order for our plan to work, Mason and myself will have to be at Rassendyll's side at all times, in case anyone should question him on some matter of state or of Selfaril's own business or history that our dear former mage may not be acquainted with. Unfortunately this leaves us with a task that we will be unable to perform. We beg that you please take care of it for us."

"What is it?" Volo inquired, not sure that he could really trust that Honor had not already triaged his and Passepout's survival as being detrimental to the future greater glory of Mulmaster, as he so eloquently seemed to term it.

"The body of Selfaril," Honor instructed, "must be disposed of so that no one ever discovers that the now former High Blade is dead."

Passepout began to turn green at the thought of having to carry the body of the man who just earlier that evening had tried to kill him and his friends.

"What do you propose?" Volo pressed, certain that Honor had already formulated a very specific plan.

Volo was not disappointed.

* * * * *

*In the Tharchioness's Boudoir
in the Tower of the Wyvern:*

"As you requested, First Princess," said a minister by the name of Greenstrit, having received the disk from Elijakuk. He handed the remaining part of the enchanted amulet to the Tharchioness.

"Where is Mischa Tam?" she inquired, as she placed the disk into its proper setting. Separately the parts held little magic beyond the typical glamour spell that was an inherent part of all of the jewelry of Thayan noblewomen. "I thought for sure that she would want to be present for the total conjugation of all our efforts."

"Elijakuk said that she awaits your bidding in her chambers," said the obsequious minister. "After all, we can't be present for the *full* implementation of the spell."

The Tharchioness cast a stare at him that could only be described as a death look. The minister embraced silence, and quietly prayed that his life would be spared.

The amulet took on a subtle aura indicating that its empowerment was complete and the Tharchioness smiled, momentarily forgetting the minister's transgression.

"The plan really was quite inspired," the Tharchioness admitted. "The fusing of several spell parts together—a glamour aura, a fertility orb, and a will binder, each developed in isolation so as to not attract the undue attentions of the infernal Cloaks . . . but not even they can secure Selfaril's own bedchamber from my magics. Since the will binder, anchored to my dear husband by the flakes of his own skin that were obtained during the height of passion at no undue expense of my own, never left our apartment, in its weakened, solitary form, there was no reason for anyone to be suspicious. I assure you no one will have the opportunity to detect it before I have put it to good use, which should be in a matter of minutes if I know my infernal husband."

"Then I will leave, First Princess," Greenstrit said, turning to exit before another thought had entered her mind. With an obsequious bow, he hastened from the room.

"Indeed," the Tharchioness replied absently, then added with a smile, "we can deal with your transgression later."

The minister was no longer within earshot of the issuing of his death warrant.

* * * * *

Selfaril's Study
in the Tower of the Wyvern:

Honor spoke with confidence, assurance, and authority. It was obvious to all present that he had no intention of considering anything less than the complete acceptance of his plan.

"As Mason and myself must remain with Rassendyll to assure the success of his masquerade, I am afraid that the task of disposing of the body in question must fall to you two non-sons of Mulmaster."

"What about them?" Volo asked seriously, nudging the bodies of the wormlike ambassador and weasel-like captain of the Hawks who were both still enjoying the oblivious state of unconsciousness.

"They must remain here," Honor said emphatically. "Mason will temporarily befuddle their brains with a feeblemind spell. They can then both be turned over to the proper authorities and charged with attacking the High Blade. No one will question the veracity of that story, and no one needs to know that they succeeded, since an attempt at the act itself commands the same sentence as its successful completion."

Not even Passepout had to question what that sentence would be.

"Okay," said Passepout agreeably, "we need to get rid of the body. I'm sure that Volo can manage that with no problem on his own. He is very resourceful after all. He and I can meet up later at some tavern or other. Yes, indeed, that sounds like a good plan, so I guess I can be off and running. This entire ordeal has increased my already ample appetite."

Volo chuckled. He knew that Honor had other, more definitive plans in mind.

"Surely you will not leave your friend on his own to complete this task?" Honor said sternly.

"He doesn't mind," Passepout answered quickly, turning quickly to Volo. "Do you?"

"Well . . ." the master traveler began to answer.

"See," said the corpulent thespian. "Now if you will excuse me—"

"*Enough!*" ordered the blind swordmaster. "Precautions must be taken. Both of you are to ferret the body back through the tunnels from whence we came, to the room in which we removed the iron mask from Rassendyll's head. You are then to carefully place the halves together around the head of our now deceased High Blade. It will weld itself back together, and this well-known face will be permanently obscured until normal decomposition takes its toll."

Passepout began to interrupt. "But . . ."

Honor proceeded as if he hadn't heard the objection.

"You will then carry the body out the other door of that chamber. Not the door that you entered, mind you, the other door. Follow the tunnel 'til you reach what appears to be a sewer hole. Drop the body down there. The current will bear it out to the bottom of the Moonsea in no time, far from prying eyes and dangerous minds."

Rassendyll shuddered at the memory of his own journey through Mulmaster's sewer system.

"From that point on, you two can find your way to the surface and do as you wish," Honor concluded. "Your services will no longer be required by that point."

Volo fingered his beard for a moment to contemplate the alternatives. There weren't any. He had no desire to incur the immediate wrath of Mason and Fullstaff who seemed to have taken charge of the matters at hand by protesting the proposed plan of action. In order to prevent total anarchy, or worse yet, the further spread of Thayan tyranny, Rassendyll had to ascend to the throne. Honor's plan was sound, and no other choice was available for himself or Passepout.

"The plan sounds fine," Volo finally concurred, "but how will we find our way? You were our guide on the trip to get here and, though I'm not a bad trailblazer if I do say so myself, I'm afraid that along the way I failed to notice any telltale signposts in the darkness, if you know what I mean."

"We've already thought of that," Mason replied, reaching into his tunnel-soiled robe and extracting an orb of luminescence. "This will light your way. As long as it glows gold, you will be on the right track. If it begins to fade, double back until the glow is restored to its previous luminescence, and then choose a different route. I am sure that you will be able to follow its guidance."

Passepout snatched the orb from Mason's hand and volunteered, "I'll carry the orb, you carry the body."

Volo chuckled. He had forgotten how fast the pudgy fellow could move when encouraged by hunger, fear or self-preservation. He concurred, and began to ready the body for transport.

"Mind if I wrap the corpse in the curtains?" the master traveler asked. "It will make it easier to carry and a lot less messy. Bloodstains are so hard to get out of cloaks these days."

"As you will," Honor replied, his tone dead serious.

The master traveler began to wrap the corpse, then paused a moment, and turned back to the blind man who had taken charge.

"Just one question, Honor," Volo added. "How did you get up here so fast? You didn't take the ladder we did. I looked back while climbing and you weren't there."

"My good friend Merch had installed a pulley-operated lift on the other side of the chamber that let me off on the other side of the wall of that closet. Unfortunately it can only carry one at a time, and time was of the essence, so rather than fighting over its use, I sent the rest of you up the ladder and employed it myself."

"Does that mean we can use it instead of the ladder?" Passepout asked hopefully, remembering his own feelings of vertigo during the ascent.

"I'm afraid not," Honor replied with out a trace of regret in his voice. "The pulley automatically resets itself, and dispatches the lift back to the bottom of the shaft."

"Wonderful," the chubby thespian said dolefully.

"You'd better be off," Honor instructed, adding, "good luck."

"And to you as well," Volo returned, tarrying a moment to specifically single out Rassendyll with, "and especially to you."

"Thanks," the former mage-in-training acknowledged, "and thanks for your help."

"Don't mention it," the master traveler replied, hoisting the curtain-wrapped body of the dead High Blade over his shoulder like a sack of potatoes. As he left he couldn't resist adding, "and give my best to the Tharchioness."

A look of panic crossed Rassendyll's face at the thought of what he was about to do, but neither Volo or Passepout saw it, as they had already begun their descent back down the ladder to the bowels of Mulmaster.

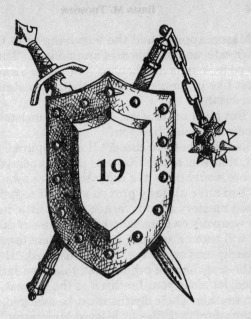

Changing Blades

In the Study of the High Blade
in the Tower of the Wyvern:

"Now get a hold of yourself," Honor told Rassendyll. "Mulmaster needs you."

"But I am not High Blade material," the former mage-in-training insisted. "A week ago I was just another scholastic at the Retreat, learning the wizardly craft."

Mason approached the surviving twin from the other side, and put his arm around him. "Those days are gone. You have taken up your father's sword, and must live up to his legacy, rather than stain it like your brother."

"But all of my studies," Rassendyll insisted. "I was to be a mage just like you."

"Is that what you chose?" Honor inquired. "As I recall, that was a fate that was thrust upon you. Now, as fate would have it, a different future awaits you."

"You have already proven yourself as heir to the sword mastery of your father, with a little help from the weapon's own memory of course. Soon that training will become as much a second nature to you as the wizardly arts once were," Mason assured. "It was due to the treachery of others that your own father was killed, let alone your brethren at the Retreat, and my own brother. Their deaths must be avenged, against all who dare to defile our beloved Mulmaster."

Rassendyll looked at the two old men in whom he now had to place his trust. Both had been friends of his father, and both put Mulmaster and its glory above all else. He had to admit that neither quality was anything less than admirable, and that their sole objective was just.

Mulmaster needed a High Blade, and he was the only one who would be capable of pulling off the masquerade.

"I know what you are thinking," Mason said, "and you are right except in one respect. This will no longer be a masquerade. You *are* the High Blade, the son of Merch Voumdolphin, and Lord Protector of Mulmaster. The masquerade took place while your brother held the throne. Your father would have wanted you to succeed him; why else were you sent to be schooled in secrecy if not to one day return and succeed him?"

"What about the Tharchioness?" Rassendyll asked, absently cooperating with Mason as he began to undress the surviving twin. One of the High Blade's robes and a basin of water had been readied while they were talking.

"She is to all outward appearances your wife," Honor admitted, "but such matters of diplomacy as your marriage must be dealt with gently."

"I hate her, and all that her Red Wizards stand for!"

Honor and Mason looked at each other and smiled. "That is good," Honor admitted, "and it will be my job, with Mason's help, of course, to make sure that you continue to think so clearly, for the good and solidarity of Mulmaster, let alone the entire Moonsea."

Rassendyll nodded in agreement, but repeated his question. "But what about the Tharchioness?"

"I am sure you will be able to deal with her," Honor assured. "After all you are the High Blade, aren't you?"

"Indeed, it appears so."

Honor smiled. "Let us call your valet," Honor instructed. "You should be well cleaned up by the time he arrives. The two assailants can be turned over to him, and you can launch your new life."

Mason put his hand up to the surviving twin's head, and muttered a few words. Instantaneously, Rassendyll felt the onrush of a cacophony of unrelated messages.

"There," Mason said, "just a little background to help you along. I'm sure you can pick up the rest *in medias res*."

Rassendyll reached across the desk, and felt for a stud that was hidden between the drawers. He pressed it to summon *his* valet.

"And so it begins," the High Blade said, already

beginning to feel the weight and responsibilities of office that had not been shouldered for a very long time.

Then a new thought crossed his mind.

"What about Volo and Passepout?" he asked evenly.

"They will not be a threat, I assure you," Honor replied.

"I don't want them harmed," Rassendyll ordered, "unless it can't possibly be avoided, and then only if the security of Mulmaster is in jeopardy."

"Agreed," the two elder men said in unison, neither wishing to clarify their answer.

* * * * *

Beneath the city of Mulmaster:

The normally indefatigable Volo began to tire of carrying Selfaril's corpse and opted to drag it after several wrong choices in the darkness had caused them to backtrack several times.

"Maybe I should be the navigator," Volo offered to Passepout. "I am the master traveler after all."

Passepout considered the offer for a moment. The slight bit of appetite that he felt back in the High Blade's study had metamorphosed into a ravenous hunger, and he had no desire to delay its satiation any longer than he had to, nor did he want to carry the body either.

"Why don't we just leave it here?" the pudgy thespian suggested. "No one will find it. We don't even know where we are."

"That's the exact reason why we can't leave it here," Volo answered. "That light in your hand is programmed to lead us on a certain path. Do you want to risk running afoul of a powerful mage's magics?"

Passepout didn't have to answer and returned his focus to choosing yet another underground corridor, hoping desperately that the orb would not begin to dim once again.

* * * * *

The two travelers and their deceased burden finally found their way back to the room in which Mason had removed the iron mask from Rassendyll's head. The two halves of the magically insulating/leeching metal were still right where they left them.

"Well, we certainly took a roundabout way to get here this time," Volo concluded. "That which took us bare minutes before, seems to have taken hours now."

"My stomach feels like it has been days," Passepout said, as he went to fetch the halves of the mask.

"Careful," Volo advised sharply.

"I know, I know," Passepout said with a pout. "I have to keep the two halves of the mask apart until we have them in position around the stiff's head."

"That's not what I was referring to."

The exasperated Passepout turned around and placed his hands on his ample hips, and said in his most long-suffering voice, "Well, what then?"

"The luminescent orb," Volo replied. "Keep it away from the mask. We don't want our only source of light to go out on us do we?"

"I didn't think of that," the thespian admitted, and carefully placed it on the ground between them. As Volo unwrapped the head of the corpse, Passepout brought the iron mask's two halves over to him, one at a time.

"Would you like to do the honors?" Volo asked, already knowing the answer.

"No," the thespian replied with a shudder.

"Well, I'll need your help anyway," Volo countered. "I'll lift the stiff's head off the ground. You set the mask half underneath it. Then I'll lower its head back down, and place the other half on top. Agreed?"

"Agreed," Passepout said reluctantly.

Like clockwork the two went through the procedure as outlined by Volo. Though Mason had clearly told them what would happen when the two parts were placed in contact with each other, both of the travelers were awed by the magical glow that began to permeate the metal and fuse the two halves together.

Once the glow had dissipated, Volo lifted the corpse into a sitting position to observe their handiwork.

It was then that the two travelers noticed that they had put the iron mask on backwards with the sight and breathing holes affording them three clear little windows to the back of the dead High Blade's head.

Volo looked at Passepout, who returned his scathing look.

"Well, it's not like he's going to need to do much seeing or breathing," the thespian offered, "given his current condition and all."

The master traveler chuckled. His friend did indeed have a point. Taking a deep breath, he heaved the now heavier corpse back onto his back, and the two travelers set off through the door that they had not used to enter the chamber.

* * * * *

As luck would have it, the traveling twosome made the right choices in the dark, and in a matter of minutes they had located the open hole to the sewer.

"Whew!" Passepout said aloud as he looked down the hole. "This really stinks."

"Then this must be the place," Volo replied, unceremoniously dropping the iron-masked corpse down the hole. After a few seconds they heard what sounded like a far-off splash, at which point they knew that the man whose last goal had been the rebuilding of the Mulmaster navy, was embarking on his final journey out to sea.

"Where to now?" Passepout asked. "I'm hungry."

"Back to the surface, I guess," Volo said guardedly.

The master traveler was not surprised when, seconds later, the orb's luminescence went out completely. It was possible that the spell that Mason had cast on it had been adversely affected by the magic-leeching mask . . . or perhaps it had simply fulfilled the task that had been assigned to it.

Volo turned his attention to keeping his frightened friend from panicking, and frantically tried to formulate a plan that would return them to the daylight and salvation. The master traveler had no desire to spend the rest of his days in total darkness, no matter how few they might turn out to be, but there was equally no sense in wandering around in the dark without the benefit of a torch or talisman.

As Passepout began to cry, the master traveler tried to think harder for a possible solution.

* * * * *

In the Bedchamber Shared by
the High Blade and the Tharchioness,
in the Tower of the Wyvern:

Rassendyll entered his brother's bedchamber, prepared for the next trial of the neverending night.

"I've been waiting," the Tharchioness said seductively, "and you know how I hate that."

"We have a slight problem," he said, still no more than a step inside the chamber. "I was attacked in my study."

The Tharchioness drew her hand up to the talismanic brooch that rested nestled between her silken breasts. "Are you all right?" she asked, her voice the epitome of concern.

"Yes," he replied. "I was meeting with an old associate of my father whom I have decided to take on as an advisor. Together, we subdued the blackguards."

The Tharchioness's ears perked up at the word "blackguards."

"Did you say blackguards, as in more than one," she inquired.

"Yes," Rassendyll replied, "one of mine and one of yours."

The Tharchioness's fingers began to massage the broach in a nervous, rhythmic pattern. "What do you mean?" she asked, her voice breaking slightly.

"It appears that one of your ambassadors and the captain of the Hawks seemed to have been planning a coup," Rassendyll replied, repeating the story that Honor and Mason had advised him to tell.

"Are you sure you are all right?" she asked, kneeling up on the silken sheets of their marriage bed. "I don't know what I would do if you had been killed."

"I'm just a little winded and a bit tense from the ordeal," he replied, "so I think I will be sleeping alone tonight."

The Tharchioness thought quickly and knew the proper response.

"I understand," she said sweetly, "but will you at least kiss me good night?"

Rassendyll assessed the shapely form of the woman who was his brother's wife, his eyes immediately drawn to the talismanic brooch that seemed to be casting off an aura of some kind.

She noticed his eyes' fixation on the brooch, and said, "Do you like it? I had it specially made."

"It's very nice," he replied, wondering what the focus of its enchantment was, "but I should be going."

The Tharchioness pouted, and said, "The kiss?"

"Of course," he replied, stepping forward to comply.

The Tharchioness stood before he could bend over, and quickly enveloped him in a total embrace, her lips locked on his, her tongue dancing into his mouth. He tried to match her passion touch to touch, pausing for a lingering moment as if he actually loved her and was trying to prolong the interval before they had to part. He felt her firm and ample bosoms rubbing against the chest that she had discreetly bared by pulling his robes apart, the metals of the amulet making contact with his skin.

They parted after a moment, and he opened his eyes.

The Tharchioness was smiling, confident of her victory. On the matrimonial battlefield of wills and diplomacy, she would emerge the victor. Mulmaster would be hers.

"Well, I'll see you in the morning," he replied, and began to head toward the door.

The Tharchioness was momentarily speechless.

"Don't you want to stay?" she sputtered, trying to understand what could have gone wrong with the spell.

"Of course I do," he replied, "but I have much to attend to tomorrow." Rassendyll paused for a moment, and added sharply, "and I am tired, I thought I had explained that!"

"Yes, my High Blade," she said instinctively.

Rassendyll left the chamber. He correctly surmised that the brooch that she had been wearing must have had some charm spell attached to it that was designed to work on his brother. He made a mental note that he would have to be especially careful in dealing with her sorcerous ways in the future.

Once the door had closed, the Tharchioness let loose with a string of obscene epithets directed at the incompetence of all of her ministers. The amulet had not worked and they would pay!

Little did she realize that it would be the last time she would see the man she thought to be her husband in the privacy of their bedchamber.

*   *   *   *   *

Beneath the City of Mulmaster:

Volo put his arm around his corpulent friend. The grown man had stopped crying and seemed resigned to the fact that the two of them would die together in the darkness. Despite the telltale rumblings of his impatient stomach, nary a complaint or whine issued from his lips.

Idle and Catinflas would be proud, thought the master traveler.

Volo passed the time with his friend relating tales of his expedition to the Underdark. What seemed like hours passed, and still the master traveler was without a plan. The irregular contours of the ground and walls, and the frequent underground cliffs overlooking bottomless pits made groping around in the dark unadvisable. Had he had ample time to prepare for this excursion in the darkness, there would have been numerous precautions against situations such as this that he would have taken, but unfortunately such was not the case.

The master traveler's thoughts drifted back to Honor Fullstaff and Mason McKern. He was still not quite sure if they had planned for this to happen once he and Passepout had fulfilled their mission, but was quite confident that neither member of the old guard of Mulmaster had the least bit of concern for himself or his friend's lives now that their task had been performed. In fact, to a certain degree, they might even be more comfortable with their now assured permanent silence on the matters that had recently transpired.

Volo sighed, but Passepout seemed not to notice, having slipped into an almost catatonic state of despairing acceptance.

The master traveler was fairly confident that he could find their way back to the sewer hole and would have been willing to accept the risks involved in surviving the subterranean trip out to sea, had he not also been confident that his dear friend would never have survived such a journey.

If no alternative came to them shortly, they would have to take the risk.

Passepout bolted upright, his nose sniffing the air. "What's that?" the portly thespian asked urgently.

"What's what?" the master traveler responded.

"I smell breakfast rolls," Passepout replied.

Volo sniffed the air, but was unable to detect a change in the aroma of their locale. He feared that his friend was beginning to hallucinate, until he heard what seemed like the soft patting of slippered footsteps on the underground path.

"Well, can you smell it?" the thespian asked desperately.

"Hush!" Volo commanded. "I think someone is coming."

"Friend or foe?" Passepout asked in a quivering whisper.

"I don't know," Volo answered, "but we'll find out soon enough. Whoever they are they're coming closer."

Volo looked in the direction that he and his friend had come from, and saw the beginnings of a torch's glow entering the chamber in which they now sat, soon followed by the silhouette of either their savior or the latest threat to their existence.

"Well, it's about time I found you two," Chesslyn said, a bit of good-natured impatience in her voice. "Breakfast is almost stone cold."

The Harper secret agent reached into her pack, and handed the two travelers breakfast buns. Passepout devoured his immediately, and looked longingly at Volo's. The master traveler gladly offered it to his friend, who gratefully accepted.

Volo stood up, and hugged their savior.

"What took you so long?" he said happily.

"I'm a good tracker," she replied, "but not that good. Honor sent a message instructing me that what had transpired over the past few days had never taken place, and that it was only because I had been his favorite student that he knew that I would understand. He then made mention of his being grateful for my part in the beginnings of the restoration of Mulmaster to its former glory. That was it."

"I see." said Volo cautiously.

"Since he never mentioned you or Passepout, I naturally assumed something had happened," she explained, "and since you still owe me that chance to get to know you better, I decided to trace your steps from where I left you the other night and, *voila,* here I am."

"In the nick of time, I might add," Passepout interjected. "I had despaired of ever eating again."

Chesslyn handed him another breakfast bun and turned her attention back to Volo. "Do you think it's safe for us to return with you to Mulmaster?" the master traveler asked guardedly.

"I think so," Chesslyn answered. "Though Honor might allow you to disappear without a trace, I don't think he would actually lift a hand to have you removed, given the current business in court. It might attract too much unwanted attention. You should be safe around town for at least the next few days."

"Just enough time for us to get further acquainted," the master traveler offered.

"My thoughts exactly," she agreed with a smile.

The two held romantic eye contact in the shadowy subterranean chamber, until Passepout once again injected himself into their conversation.

"Do you think you can show us the way out of here?" he asked.

"Certainly," she replied, handing him the last of the buns, "just let me rearrange my pack and we can be on our way."

"Wonderful!" the chubby thespian replied.

As the Harper secret agent attended to her preparations, Passepout turned to his traveling companion and whispered assuredly, "See, I told you she liked me."

"Indeed," the master traveler replied, giving his friend a good-natured pat on the back. "Indeed."

"Wonderful!"

Epilogue

Over the previous few days Mulmaster was a flurry of activities. Two different executions were held with the normal accompaniment of festive fanfare.

Former captain of the Hawks Sir Melker Rickman was executed for conspiracy to incite treason. He was hung from the scaffold in front of the keep that had housed his offices. The customary last words of the accused were dispensed with as the prisoner's tongue had been removed immediately upon his incarceration. His lifeless corpse was allowed to hang in state for a full day before the annoyance and public health concerns necessitated it be removed.

Farther down the road, and a day later, the Thayan embassy added to the festivities when the Tharchioness hosted an execution of her own as former ambassador and envoy, Joechairo Lawre, a wormlike politician of the worst sort, was publicly incinerated at the stake by a fireball cast by the First Princess herself. The crowd that gathered was quite impressed since nary a cry of mercy or anguish escaped the Red Wizard's lips as the flames engulfed him, the crowd being quite ignorant that his tongue, also, had been removed upon his arrest. As he was a Thayan national, he was thus executed by a duly empowered representative of Thay, and it was not necessary for him to be charged, or the execution justified. Among the members of the court, there was rumor that the charge was similar to that of Rickman; or perhaps it was just, according to those who knew the ambassador, simple incompetence. The Mulman mob didn't really care about justifications or the whys and wherefores—they just turned out for an afternoon's entertainment.

Curiously enough, the High Blade and his bride presided over both occasions.

The crowds interpreted this as further evidence of the diplomatic alliance that began with their nuptials, a sense of mutuality of their governmental responsibilities, and the development of a further closeness between the leaders whose marriage of diplomatic advantage may have evolved into something deeper between the two individuals. Rumors abounded among the mob that they had mutually agreed that the time had come for them to assume the responsibilities of parenthood.

Those closer to the respective thrones thought otherwise. The paradoxically amorous/antagonistic dynamic that had existed between the two had seemed to vanish overnight, and with its departure came several noticeable changes in their retinues. In addition to the arrests of Rickman and Lawre, both entourages underwent a change in personnel. A blind old swordmaster and former Hawk by the name of Fullstaff was appointed as chief advisor to the High Blade, and an equally geriatric mage by the name of McKern was appointed first consul, much to the chagrin of Senior Cloak Thurndan Tallwand. The overnight ascension of these two former retirees was looked upon with some amazement by the High Blade's court, particularly since both individuals, though officially still citizens of Mulmaster, had had next to no involvement in the government for more years than anyone seemed able to remember.

The changes to the First Princess's party were mostly in the form of deletions. Mischa Tam, as well as several ministers who had formerly been considered among the First Princess's inner circle, were noticeably absent. The ministers had evidently opted to return to Eltabbar at very short notice, while the Tharchioness's half sister felt the need to avoid that domain and seek the counsel of the great Szass Tam instead, a move that those in the know realized to be tantamount to choosing between the lady and the tiger. A new ambassador of obviously weak character had made an appearance, and the lower level Thayan functionaries were already taking bets on his life expectancy.

The third day of festivities was brought to a close by a public address by the High Blade himself in which he swore to return Mulmaster to its former days of glory. He then went on to announce that due to the priority of accelerating the rebuilding of the navy, the city would be unable to offer any financial assistance to Eltabbar during their recovery from their devastating earthquake. The needs, security, and goals of Mulmaster were always to be the first concern, and it was his intention that nothing was to get in its way on its chosen path to become the power center of the entire Moonsea region.

The crowd cheered, failing to notice the icy glare that the Tharchioness cast in her husband's direction.

He then went on to declare that the First Princess would indeed be cutting her conjugal visit short so that she could attend to her own matters of state back in Thay. He pointed out that it was important that all realize that matters of state must come first, and that in all things the glory of Mulmaster was to be his number one concern,

Fullstaff and McKern exchanged a secret wink and a conspiratorial grin between themselves as they saw their long-term goals and wishes finally coming to fruition.

The crowd cheered again, and no one noticed that the Tharchioness and her aides had quietly left the stand and were probably already on their way back to Mulmaster. Over the past few nights the First Princess had had more than enough time to pack, as the High Blade had chosen his private quarters to spend his nights in solitude.

Though Selfaril had commanded the respect of the mob on numerous occasions, no one could recall a time when he had earned as much acclamation as the High Blade did on this day. Worries of the encroachment of Thayan interests on Mulmaster's sovereignty were put to rest at last.

The High Blade went on to conclude that the following day would also be a holiday in honor of his father, the former High Blade, for whom respect and praise was long overdue. The next day would begin their journey onward to the glory of all Mulmaster.

The High Blade took a seat, exhausted at the emotional speech he had just given. Fullstaff and McKern gave his shoulders a subtle squeeze of encouragement and affirmation. Rassendyll knew that he had a tough job ahead of him, but that was the least a High Blade owed his city.

* * * * *

"I never thought of Mulmaster as much of a party town," Passepout said. "I guess first impressions can be misleading, especially when your first night is spent in jail."

The master traveler chuckled and replied, "I have to remember to put that in my next book under 'extremely useful axioms for travelers.'"

Passepout laughed, adding, "And of course I will be given proper attribution."

"Of course," Volo replied. "Maybe I can talk my publisher into another book. *The Words, Wisdom, and Observations of Passepout, son of Idle and Catinflas.*"

"The Famous Thespians," the rotund actor corrected. "It has to be Idle and Catinflas, the Famous Thespians."

"Of course, old friend," Volo said, slapping Passepout on the back just as he was about to quaff yet another tankard of ale. "How else will anyone know which Passepout we are talking about?"

"Or which Idle and Catinflas," the rotund actor added. Changing the subject just slightly, the thespian asked, "Do you really think Tyme Waterdeep, Limited would publish it?"

"I don't see why not," the master traveler said, holding back a fiendish grin so as not to betray his levity. "They seem to have done well with *The Underdark Diet,* and given the scope of the contents of the book we are now discussing, it's not as if it will require a huge investment in paper or printing time, it being such a short book and all."

"Agreed," said Passepout in all seriousness, "and if it doesn't cost them that much to do, they will be able to pay me more."

"Of course," Volo replied, adding a single sticking point, "once you've turned the book in."

"You mean I have to *write* it first?"

"Of course."

Passepout became visibly disheartened, refilled his tankard, and turned his attention back to the merriment at hand.

Speaking of books, Volo thought, I'd better make sure that my notes are properly in order. Instead of my guide to the Moonsea, a book-length expose on the goings-on in Mulmaster will no doubt top the charts and line my pockets with gelt in no time.

The master traveler's dreams of wealth were interrupted by the arrival of Chesslyn with whom he had shared almost as many festivities as he had the risks, dangers, and adventures of the days previous.

"Volo," she said sweetly, "may I have a word with you?"

"But of course," the master traveler said guardedly. He had no desire to break the poor girl's heart, but figured that the time had come to let her know that he wouldn't be sticking around, and that, though he would always cherish the memories, he didn't believe in making any commitments that would result in the diminishing of the options that might make themselves available to him.

The master traveler put his arm around the secret Harper, and the two wandered away from the crowd. Volo looked back, saw that Passepout was making conversation with yet another serving wench, and decided that his traveling companion would be safe for at least the next few minutes.

Arriving at a tree whose branches managed to droop in such a way as to provide an enclosed and secluded seating area for those agile enough to maneuver themselves within, the two settled in away from the mob for their *tête-à-tête*.

"Will this do?" the master traveler asked, brushing a lock of the swordswoman's hair away from her face with the back of his hand.

"Looks good to me," Chesslyn replied. "Secluded, private, just the thing. The locals call it the Necking Tree."

The master traveler sighed. He really didn't want to hurt the feelings of his latest conquest, but all unfinished business had to be resolved before he moved on. In his best helluva guy tone, he began to let her down easily.

"You know, Chesslyn," he started, "we have shared some times that many would be jealous of, and I would like to think that we have grown close enough that we can tell each other anything, and that is why I must . . ."

"My thoughts exactly," Chesslyn interrupted, "and that is the only reason why I feel that I should be the one to let you know what has been decided."

"Now I know that . . ." The master traveler was startled. "Decided? Who decided what?" he asked, shaking his head to try to make sense of the situation.

"My superiors, back in Shadowdale," she replied.

"That's the who," Volo said tentatively. "What's the what?"

Oh no, she didn't, the master traveler thought to himself in a panic he managed to keep secret from Chesslyn. I've always heard the rumor that Harpers had to ask their superiors for permission to marry, but. . . .

"Now, Chesslyn," Volo said cautiously, "I hope you didn't rush into anything. I always prefer to proceed with caution in all matters, looking before I leap, etc."

"That's what I figured," Chesslyn said confidently, "that's why I knew you wouldn't mind if I sent a message to Storm back in Shadowdale about your involvement in the goings-on and all in case there were any concerns that you should be made aware of before even considering doing a book on Mulmaster."

"What?"

"The what is your book," she replied seriously. "My superiors, and indeed Elminster himself, feel that you should forget that any of the events at hand ever happened."

Volo shook his head in confusion.

"I don't understand," the master traveler replied. "I thought . . ."

". . . that it would probably be the basis of a great book," Chesslyn interrupted again, "and it probably will, but for the sake of the balance of power in the Moonsea region, and perhaps all of Faerûn for that matter, it is a story best left untold. To everyone but those who were involved, and my superiors of course, nothing has happened."

The master traveler's head was still buzzing in confusion.

"But I thought," he sputtered, "you wanted to talk about us, and . . ."

". . . that I would intercede for you," Chesslyn interjected, "and I did, but balance is more important than personal gain. Surely you agree, don't you?"

"Well, yes, but . . ."

Chesslyn stopped for a moment as if a new thought had just occurred to her. Her expression softened. "That is what you were referring to," she said softly, "about us?"

Volo leapt at the opportunity to save face.

"Of course," he said in mock confidence, quickly averting his face so that she couldn't look in his eyes. "Still, you have to admit that such a book would have great potential."

"Enough potential to get you in even more trouble than you were over *Volo's Guide to All Things Magical*," she pointed out, "and I was instructed to point that out to you."

"Point made," Volo acknowledged, his voice showing the dejection he felt.

Chesslyn put her arm around the depressed author, and kissed him lightly on the cheek. "Don't be so glum," she said. "You can still do the book that you originally intended to, and you have to admit you enjoyed some good times while doing the research."

Volo quickly regained his composure, and with a bit of false bravado, responded, "Agreed. Maybe not the best of times, but certainly not the worst of times."

"Well, I had a good time," the Harper admitted.

"And I did too," the gazetteer assented, "and now it's time to move on."

"Agreed."

The two shared a quick kiss in the privacy offered by the Necking Tree, and then returned to the hustle and bustle of the mob to rejoin Passepout.

As they walked back, Volo shared a few softly voiced thoughts with the Harper agent. "You know," he pointed out, "there is no guarantee that Rassendyll will make a more peaceful High Blade. With all that talk of returning Mulmaster to its former glory, who knows what can happen?"

"Agreed," Chesslyn answered.

"And Fullstaff and McKern are both nice guys and all, don't get me wrong, but they aren't exactly the type of guys who aren't willing to have the end justify the means."

"Why do you think I didn't let them know of my Harper affiliation?" she pointed out. "Even though Honor was my nearest and dearest teacher and mentor, I only share that little secret tidbit with those nearest and closest to my heart."

Volo brightened for a moment, and immediately hid his reaction, as there were some things the master traveler felt embarrassment about acknowledging.

As they approached the spot from whence they had come, Volo saw Passepout get slapped by a serving wench and saw a burly bouncer about to add his own two cents' worth of contusions to the beleaguered thespian.

"Duty calls," Volo replied, as he set off to help his friend.

"For both of us," Chesslyn answered, squeezing the master traveler's hand. "Farewell."

" 'Til we meet again, and may it be soon."

"Agreed."

With nary another kiss the two parted, and set off to right the matters at hand, Chesslyn back to the temple where she worked, and the master traveler to aid the about to be assaulted Passepout, his boon companion, and once again, friend in need.

If you enjoyed *The Mage in the Iron Mask,* and would like to pursue the further adventures of Volo, the master traveler of all Toril, some of his other exploits are detailed in . . .

Once Around the Realms
Brian M. Thomsen
A grand tour of Faerûn as only Volothamp Geddarm and his erstwhile companion Passepout can make, proving once and for all who is the greatest traveler on all Toril!

. . . and the anthologies
Realms of Magic
edited by Brian M. Thomsen & J. Robert King
What's all this about a guide to all things magical . . . ?

Realms of the Underdark
edited by J. Robert King
. . . and you thought Mulmaster was the City of Danger . . .

For more swashbuckling adventure, try such other books in the Nobles series as . . .

King Pinch
David Cook
Meet Pinch, a man of many titles: scoundrel, thief, criminal extraordinaire . . . heir to the throne?

Escape from Undermountain
Mark Anthony
Getting into the mysterious labyrinth under the city of Waterdeep will be the hardest thing Artek the Knife has ever done. Getting out may prove to be impossible!

Welcome to the FORGOTTEN REALMS, the largest and most detailed of TSR's fantasy worlds.

Look out from the high walls of Waterdeep, the sprawling, cosmopolitan City of Splendors. Beyond lies the Savage Frontier: the rugged mountains and endless forests of the Sword Coast, wilderlands that cloak the crumbling ruins of fallen kingdoms.

Travel with the caravans that cross these dangerous lands, heading east toward the kingdom of Cormyr, fabled realm of ancient forests, land of chivalry and romance. Stop over in the Dalelands, home of the crusty old wizard Elminster and the birthplace of many heroes and heroines. Then continue onward to distant Thay . . . and beyond.

In your travels, you will encounter many folk from highborn to low. Among the beautiful and deadly Seven Sisters are Storm Silverhand, the silver-haired Bard of Shadowdale, and High Lady Alustriel, the gentle and just ruler of Silverymoon. A third sister is the Simbul, fey and wild-tempered Witch-Queen of Aglarond. There are four more sisters, each beautiful and powerful in her own way.

If you meet them on the road, do not meddle with the mysterious Harpers, who work to uphold freedom and the causes of good throughout the Realms. You may, however, share a drink with the eccentric explorer Volo, and pick his brain for a wealth of information about your next destination. Beware that sinister-looking fellow in the corner of the common room. He may be a Zhentarim agent, gathering information for a takeover of the Heartlands.

Should the surface world not prove exciting enough for you, make your way beneath Mount Waterdeep to traverse the miles upon miles of tunnels and caverns known as Undermountain—but beware its deadly traps and skulking monsters. If you survive these hazards, press on to the subterranean city of Menzoberranzan, home of the deadly drow and birthplace of the renegade Drizzt Do'Urden.

When you return to the light of the surface world, you may want to explore the crumbling ruins of Myth Drannor, a storehouse of lost magic and deadly monsters in the heart of the vast Elven Court forest.

From the dangerous sewers and back alleys of sprawling cities, to glaciers, deserts, jungles, and uncharted seas (above and below the surface!), there's a whole world to explore in the lands of the FORGOTTEN REALMS.